A CONSPIRACY OF KINGS

MEGAN WHALEN TURNER

A CONSPIRACY OF KINGS

GREENWILLOW BOOKS
An Imprint of HarperCollinsPublishers

A Conspiracy of Kings
Copyright © 2010 by Megan Whalen Turner

The text of this book is set in Adobe Caslon.

Library of Congress Cataloging-in-Publication Data

Turner, Megan Whalen.
A conspiracy of kings / by Megan Whalen Turner.
p. cm.
"Greenwillow Books."
Summary: Kidnapped and sold into slavery, Sophos, an unwilling prince, tries to save his country from being destroyed by rebellion and exploited by the conniving Mede empire.
ISBN 978-0-06-187093-4 (trade bdg.)
ISBN 978-0-06-187094-1 (lib. bdg.)
[1. Kings, queens, rulers, etc.—Fiction. 2. Princes—Fiction.
3. Adventure and adventurers—Fiction.] I. Title.
PZ7.T85565Co 2010   [Fic]—dc22   2009023052

10 11 12 13 14 LP/RRDH 10 9 8 7 6 5 4 3
First Edition

 GREENWILLOW BOOKS

THIS BOOK IS GRATEFULLY DEDICATED
TO DIANA WYNNE JONES. THANK YOU
FOR THE STORIES AND FOR THE LEG UP.

A Conspiracy of Kings

T HE king of Attolia was passing through his city, on his way to the port to greet ambassadors newly arrived from distant parts of the world. The king was a newcomer and a foreigner, king only by virtue of a political marriage to the queen of Attolia and still unfamiliar to most Attolians. They massed along the Sacred Way to see him for themselves, as well as to cheer their queen, who rode beside him in the open coach. One member of the crowd, a young man with a broken nose, a lip twisted by scar tissue, and dirty clothes that combined to suggest a person of violent and criminal habits, had a particular need to get close. He was in the company of an older man, unscarred, but no less shabby, who boosted him up the side of a stone street marker that labeled the intersection of the Sacred Way and one of the larger cross streets.

"Lift your right foot up another few inches. There's a chip out of the corner. Yes, that's it. Are you secure? Can you see?"

"Yes, I am set, and I can see. Stop nagging," said the younger man. With one foot on a narrow ledge and the other pressed against the chipped indentation, he was high enough to wrap his left hand around the narrow top of the marker. From this vantage point, he could see easily over the heads of the people gathered in the streets, and with a good grip for one hand, he had the other free. They had chosen the marker the day before because it offered a view up a long straight stretch of the Sacred Way and he would have plenty of time to aim.

The crowds were growing thicker. The talk was loud, some of it the usual complaints about the cost of cooking oil and good wine, and the behavior of the young these days; some of it about the new king. One and all disparaged his Eddisian background, but a few grudging supporters mentioned his rumored love for their queen in his favor. Such romantic stories were dismissed as foolish by the more outspoken, but a few expressions softened. Latecomers eyed the position on the street marker, but the older man defended the approach to it with the unwitting assistance of a portly woman and her gaggle of small children. They blocked the access of those who might have thought they could share the high ground or force the occupier of it to relinquish his spot. The only danger came from one or two of the small children who tried to climb up. The younger man stepped on a few fingers and apologized perfunctorily. The woman gave him a dirty look but pulled her children down. As the commotion uphill signaled the approach of the royal procession, the children's father appeared, pushing his way through the crowd, wiping his hands on his dirty smock as he came. He swept up two of the smallest of the children to his shoulders, and they all watched for the arrival of the carriage bearing the king and queen.

The young man, with his free hand, dipped into his pocket and then lifted his hand to his mouth. He lowered his hand again but this time took a thin tube from the other man standing below.

The king was visible now, sitting upright in the carriage beside the queen. The carriage drew closer. The young man clinging to the street marker took his aim, waited for the right moment, and with a concentrated puff of air, fired the shot.

The pea hit the king on the cheek. He didn't react, and the small pellet dropped out of sight into his lap. He tilted his head to murmur something to his wife, the queen. His assailant waved and shouted the king's name, just like everyone else in the crowd, and when the king looked up, his eyes passed over his attacker without pause.

The royal carriage rolled by. The young man dropped from the stele.

"Did you hit him?" the older man asked.

"Yes," said the younger.

"Did he see you?"

"If he did, he didn't recognize me."

His companion looked grim. "We'd better go," he said just as a woman's voice said more loudly, "He did what?"

Both of them turned a little too quickly to see the mother of the brood of children with her hand on the littlest one's shoulder, the boy clutching her skirts. "Who did what now?" asked the father wearily. But the woman wasn't angry with her son.

"He says that one—up there on the stele—he shot something at the king and hit him in the face," she said. Her words drew unwelcome attention from those within hearing. Other heads turned toward them.

"I did not—" The young man tried to deny the accusation, but the woman was having none of his protest, and his denial was abbreviated by a stinging smack from the older man, who then seized him by the upper arm and shook him so hard his teeth rattled.

"I cannot believe you!" the man shouted. "And what your mother will say, I don't know." He swore with venom and then apologized to the brood mother. "My nephew," he explained, "he breaks his poor mother's heart." The mother nodded warily, only partly satisfied.

"I never—" said the younger man sullenly, only to be shaken again.

"You'll shut your mouth and come home with me," snarled his companion.

The youth allowed himself to be dragged off, followed by the approving nods of the witnesses, and complaining bitterly to his "uncle" that he'd done nothing at all wrong. The two men turned down the first cross street they reached and out of sight of the crowd began to walk faster, the older man still pulling the younger along by the arm.

"You know, I don't think you're allowed to treat me like this," the younger pointed out woefully. The older man laughed.

"Gods protect us," he said, "we can only hope the little monster isn't telling them right now that I handed you the peashooter."

They both glanced back. A small crowd of shadowy figures, black against the sunlit street, appeared around the corner behind them, the silhouettes of their skirts and smocks easy to identify.

"He told them," said the younger man.

"Faster," said the elder, and the two broke into a run. Pursued by shouts, they raced down the street and around another corner, and skidded to an abrupt halt, face to face with a squad of the Royal Guard.

"Back! Back!" the older man shouted, revealing, in his alarm, a Sounisian accent previously concealed. But their retreat was already cut off by the people behind them. Through that crowd came another squad of soldiers. Murmuring grew at the sight of the Guard, the two men's transgression exaggerated with each retelling. "It was a poison dart they shot at the king!" they heard a voice shout from the crowd.

There was a narrow space between two apartment houses, but it was only an alcove to a door. The older man pushed the younger in and turned to face the soldiers. The accent of Sounis now clear in his voice, he warned them, "Your king doesn't want us dead."

Hours later they sat locked in a dark cell under the palace. At last they heard a door somewhere open with a bang and a light set of footsteps approaching, followed by several more sets of footsteps, all heavier, but moving as fast. The younger man jumped to his feet, but the older, who stepped between him and the door, was first to see the face of the king of Attolia when it opened.

"We are uninjured," the magus of Sounis quickly reassured him.

"Thank the gods," said the king. "I thought to find you black and blue."

"Indeed, we thought the same," said the magus. He exchanged a look with his companion that made them both laugh, and he welcomed the king into his arms for a mutually crushing embrace.

"I cannot stay, I am between audiences," said Eugenides, king of Attolia. "All the embassies from the Continent seem to have arrived at the same time. With Eddis here as well, we are scheduled every moment." He looked at their shabby clothes in puzzlement.

"We were traveling anonymously for safety—" explained the magus.

"But surely—"

"—and then we were robbed on the road."

"Ah," said the king, "the danger in being anonymous.

Your novel approach made me think secrecy must be important, so I told my captain nothing but that you were to be conveyed quickly and quietly. I just learned that he had seen you shooting peas in my face, and I am relieved not to find the two of you hanging by your thumbs."

"Your Majesty," someone called from beyond the door, "we must go."

"Yes," said the king before turning back to the magus. "They will take you up to a room where you can get clean, and perhaps have a view." He looked around the tiny stone-walled room. "I will give credit to Teleus on safety, at least."

The young man at the back of the cell snorted at that. The king stepped around the magus to hug him fiercely. He then released him but didn't step away. Looking up, he examined the scarring on his lip that lifted it into a slight sneer, and the broken nose. "My god, you've been in the wars. Once you are clean and have had some rest, I will want to hear all about where you have been and why." He pulled the younger man's head down and kissed him solidly on his forehead, saying seriously, "Gods-all, I am glad to see you safe, Sophos."

The young man smiled back. "Sounis," he said, just as someone called from the door.

The king looked away and then back, as if uncertain that he had heard correctly. "What?"

"I am Sounis," said the young man. "My uncle is dead."

All the king's happiness was wiped away. "You're joking?" he suggested.

Bewildered, the younger king shook his head. "No, I am Sounis." He meant to make a remark about keeping a visiting king locked in a cellar, but his own happiness faltered.

"Your Majesty, please," the man in the passage called again. The king of Attolia looked to the door, and then at the magus, and then at the magus's former apprentice, the new king of Sounis.

"I'm sorry," he said, and clearly meant it. He grasped the younger man briefly by the sleeve, said "I am sorry" again, and was gone, leaving the magus of Sounis and his king standing alone, with the open door of their cell before them.

Sounis turned to the magus. "He cannot think that I cared about my uncle?"

"I think he was delighted to see you safe," said the magus, "and grieved that the next time you meet, it must be as king and king and not as friends."

"I hope that I will always be his friend," said Sounis.

"I know that he hopes so as well," the magus assured him. "But now, let us follow our escort to a bath, if you please, and some food. You will need your strength, I think, to answer many questions about where you have been and what has become of you, since they saw you last."

CHAPTER ONE

M Y father sacked another tutor. I see that doesn't surprise you at all. Terve was my eighth. The magus had been my seventh. My father and my uncle who was Sounis had sent me to Letnos with Terve to separate me from the magus after the ground-shaking set-to the three of them had had after my private correspondence was discovered. Terve was an old army veteran. He was to teach me riding and sword and military history and the hell with anything else. I didn't really mind. I liked Terve, and he didn't get in the way of my real studies. What he mainly did was drink and tell war stories. In the mornings he oversaw my sword training from a stump in the training yard with a wineskin in his lap, tending to be overgenerous in his praise, unlike all my previous tutors, shouting things like, "A natural! A natural!" in between swallows of wine.

I did some riding on my own, though not with any real discipline, and in the afternoon I studied as I pleased. By that time Terve was well into his second amphora and would lie on a couch in the study. He might suddenly shout, "You're being attacked by six men with swords!" or something similar, and I would have to come up with a plan for my defense. He would pick apart my answers and then drift off into another war story until, eventually, he fell asleep. He was there, snoring quietly, when my father arrived to check on my progress.

Terve was immediately replaced. A soldier from my father's guard was assigned to teach me sword work, and a hateful, condescending bully named Sigis Malatesta was my new tutor—from the Peninsula, as you can tell by the name, supposedly educated at the University in Ferria. He had accompanied my father to Letnos, so my father must have had some idea of replacing Terve even before he found him on the couch, though perhaps not with so much shouting.

I have no idea what my father saw in Malatesta. In the normal run of things, he doesn't give a bent pin for learning, but he'd met Malatesta at the court of Sounis, and I suspect that he thought hiring Malatesta would be a poke in the eye for the magus, whom he has never liked. Years ago he sent me to be the magus's apprentice with the explicit hope that the magus's razor tongue would be the end of my intellectual pretensions. When that didn't work out as he intended, it only made him dislike the magus more.

Of course the magus had long since left Sounis, stolen away in the night by the Thief of Eddis, though my uncle didn't know who was responsible at first. I'd heard rumors, which I didn't believe for a minute, that the magus was an Attolian spy who'd fled the city when he was about to be discovered. I was not surprised at all to learn subsequently that it had been Eugenides at work. By the time Malatesta came, I was positive the magus was busily tramping around the mountains of Eddis, collecting botanical specimens and enjoying his "captivity" as a prisoner of the queen of Eddis. I am quite sure he was not suffering any distress because I had a new tutor.

I hated Malatesta. He could barely manage the multiplication of greater numbers, and he didn't know any prime over thirteen. He'd never read the *Eponymiad*, but he tried to pretend he had. I doubt very much he'd ever set foot in a seminar at the University in Ferria. He'd studied no medicine and no natural history. The only thing he'd read was poetry. That should have made us friends, but I hated his taste in poetry, too. Where he admired the sweet and the overwrought, I liked the *Eponymiad*.

My mother knew how I felt, of course. She and my sisters sympathized with me, but there was little they could do. My mother would never act against my father's judgment, no matter how poorly she thought of Malatesta. If my father had stayed at the villa longer than a day, she might have changed his opinion, drawing him into alignment with her own as invisibly as a magnet works on a lodestone, but my father had been gone within a day of installing my new tutor.

I knew that it made my mother sad to see my distress,

so I hid it as well as I could. I also knew that with the slightest encouragement, Ina and Eurydice would have filled Malatesta's bed with bees. They are delicate girls, so small in stature, and fine-boned like my mother, that I can still lift both of them with one hand. You could be forgiven for thinking them the incarnation of every ladylike grace, but my father has had frequent cause to swear that they got the spine so notably absent in me. A bed full of bees wasn't going to get rid of Malatesta; only my father could do that. The bees would only make him more spiteful, so I tried not to encourage the girls.

The one person I did complain to, and at length, was Hyacinth, my single friend on the island of Letnos. He lived in a villa nearby and came down to visit almost every day, arriving as my mother and sisters were rising from their afternoon rest, his visits therefore coinciding with their afternoon meal. On the rare occasions that he was late, Eurydice always saved him a cake.

He was my only companion of my own age, and I should have been more grateful to have him, but it was hard to be grateful for Hyacinth. His father was a patron with a property of only medium size, holding few of the king's responsibilities, and Hyacinth was gratified to consider himself a friend of the heir to Sounis. He was always smiling and always eager to please. Everything I said he agreed with, which was trying, and his flute playing would make the deaf wince, but I think the real problem with Hyacinth was that he reminded me of myself. He read poetry. He flinched at loud noises. In addition to having no musical skills, he had no martial skills. He avoided any situation that might require a physical effort on his part. Seeing him, I found it no wonder that my father despised me.

Yet I was his companion, and he mine, and when Malatesta beat me, I went to him for sympathy. Oh, yes, I was taller than Malatesta by inches, and long since old enough to be considered a man, but my tutor was still switching me across the palms of my hands and leaving painful blisters there. And I was still sniffing back tears of rage and humiliation like a big baby. Especially so, when I was switched for insisting that *burn* did not rhyme with *horn* or that I couldn't produce any factors for 31 or 43. Malatesta used to say things that even he knew were wrong and then watch me in contempt when I let them pass, too cowed to contradict him.

While I was failing to manage my own petty problems, my uncle who was Sounis was dealing with greater ones. After the sabotage of his fleet in its own harbor, he'd jumped into war with Attolia without hesitation. The magus would have counseled him otherwise, but the magus, as you know, was whisked away before he could counsel anything. Then Sounis discovered it was Eddis who was responsible for both the destruction of his ships and the disappearance of his valuable advisor, and he started a new war without any more forethought. He was confident, I think, of success over both Eddis and Attolia right up until the world heard that the Thief of Eddis had stolen the queen of Attolia and meant to marry her.

When the stars aligned in that very unexpected way, my uncle was at a loss. Together, Attolia and Eddis were far more powerful than they were alone. He was overmatched, and everyone knew it. There were more rumors each day. The maids picked up news from who knows where and retold it to Ina and Eurydice, who carried it to Mother and me. My mother scolded them for listening to gossip, but she never insisted they stop.

One morning at breakfast Ina said, "Our uncle has agreed to marry the cousin of the queen of Eddis."

"Your uncle who is Sounis?" my mother said, gently reminding Ina of the honorific.

"Indeed," said Ina, not touching on the unspoken truth that only one of our uncles, the king of Sounis, survived. "They say her name is Agape."

I should have been glad that it might mean peace among our three countries, but my pleasure was more selfish. My uncle had given up his pursuit of Eddis. He would marry someone else and might soon produce an heir. My mother warned me not to put faith in rumors, but I was quite filled with hope.

I wrote to my father, as politely as I knew how, to say that my sword work was improved and that I was sick of poetry (sick of Malatesta's, at least). With a marriage to the queen's cousin Agape planned, there would soon be a much more appropriate heir to replace me, and could I please come back to the mainland? I prayed to the household gods to save me from one more day on Letnos. Within a day of sending the letter, like an idiot in an old wives' tale, I got what I asked for.

I was crossing the courtyard of the villa, and it was as if one of Terve's lessons had come to life. He may as well have been there, shouting, "You are suddenly attacked by fifteen men; what are you going to do?" Only they weren't a product of Terve's imagination; they were real men, cutting down the guards at the front gate and streaming into the courtyard of the villa.

Terve's first question: "Where's your weapon?" My sword of course was in my room, upstairs at the back of the main house and as useless to me as if it had been on the moon. The men were spreading out across the courtyard toward all entrances to the house, and by the time I got to my rooms to fetch my sword it would be too late to do anything with it. Terve's sword, I was almost certain, was still in my study under the couch where my father had thrown it in disgust when he'd seen its condition. Malatesta had taken control of my study and my books, allowing me in only for his insipid lessons; he didn't know that the sword was there, and I doubted that the servants would have moved it. None of the armed men racing across the courtyard was headed for the study, which was just opposite from where I stood, its door open to the courtyard.

My feet were moving in that direction before my head had finished reaching a decision. The study had a door and a window. I jumped through the open window because it was faster and fell to the stone floor on my stomach, scrabbling in the dust under the couch until my hand closed on a stiff leather strap. I dragged the sword free of its sheath with difficulty and turned, still on my knees, as a man filled the doorway. Coming from light into the dark, he was looking ahead of him, not down toward me. My lunge, as I came to my feet, took him in the chest as I drove the sword upward with the strength of my legs. Even rusted, the sword slid through him, and I found, for the first time, how easy it is to kill a man.

Astonished, I pulled the sword free and immediately plunged it into the man behind him, who had as little warning as his fellow. I hit bone that time, but the man's momentum drove him onto the point. It was harder to draw the sword out, but I pulled mightily, desperate to get it free.

Terve's second question: "What are you going to do with the weapon?" I knew what I meant to do: defend my mother and my sisters.

The villa on Letnos is typical, with the courtyard formed on three sides by buildings of a single story—my study was on one side, close to the house. My father's study was on the opposite. In between, facing into the courtyard, were the dormitories, the stables, and the kitchen, as well as the office of the steward and the officer of the guard.

The fourth side of the courtyard was the main house, with a porch on the uppermost story for the women's rooms. There was a stair in the wall that led to the roofs of the lower buildings, and a drain tile, I knew, that offered a handhold for a climb from the lower roofs to the porch. I'd taken that route before when my father was looking for me and I was avoiding him. If I hurried, I thought I might beat the men who were already in the villa, who would be making their way up the stairs inside the house. I ran across the courtyard, now empty, and climbed the steps to the roof, all according to a plan I had once laid out in response to one of Terve's seemingly useless exercises.

Why would anyone attack an unimportant villa, I had asked at the time, and if it was important enough to be attacked, why wouldn't it be defended? Just pretend, he'd said.

I climbed up and over the railing around the porch, trampling the privacy screen in the process and getting my foot stuck through it for a moment—not a part of the plan. As I rushed through the door into my mother's rooms, the maids were screaming. I had to shout over the noise they were making, but whether she understood me or not, Ina had the sense to push shut the large wooden door at the entrance to the rooms. Someone in the hall-way outside pressed the latch, and the door started to swing open, but I ran full tilt into it and slammed it closed again. There was a shout of pain from the other side, and a thump as a body struck the door. Ina grasped the latch to keep it from moving. While her small hand secured it, the metal tongue of the latch secured the door. The door shook in its frame, but it was solid, and we had as much time as the latch would give us.

Eurydice and my mother were in the room, as well as two maids. I rushed to the door that connected my mother's room to dressing spaces and the bedchambers. There were separate doors into the bedchambers from the corridor, and I feared to see the attackers coming through them, but the dressing room was empty. I dodged through the doorway to grab a grooming set from the tray there, then shut that door and jammed its latch with the handle of a brush. I turned back to Ina. As she lifted her hand, I quickly jammed that latch as well. Everything, everything, as planned with Terve on an idle afternoon months before.

Eurydice was crouched on the floor. She'd found the wedge used to hold the door when they wanted it open and was forcing it into place to help keep the door closed. Once it was secure, I looked around. The attackers could not come at us from the porch. Only my mother's reception room opened onto the balcony, an old-fashioned way to make sure that no daughter of the house escaped for an unlicensed glimpse of the men in the courtyard below.

My mother had hushed the maids, and in the relative quiet she said, "We heard the fighting from the porch. Darling, are they bandits?"

"No," I said, shaking my head. They were organized and all outfitted alike, and no bandits would attack a villa on Letnos. There was nothing to be stolen, and where would they go afterward? They couldn't get off Letnos without passing the king's ships that patrolled around it, and the patrol ships would stop anything larger than a rowboat.

The latch wasn't going to hold long. "I want you to hide," I told my mother, and hustled her and my sisters and the maids out onto the balcony. When I explained what I wanted, the maids balked. My mother rolled her eyes at them and calmly stepped over the railing. She waited while I climbed down to the roof below, and then she let herself drop into my arms. Eurydice positively threw herself over the railing, laughing when I caught her. Ina pointed sternly, and the maids lowered themselves gingerly, one of them wailing softly, even after I set her on her feet.

When all the women were safely down, I turned to find Eurydice standing at the edge of the roof.

"Back away," I said, "in case they send someone out of the house." We could still hear the hammering on my mother's door.

Eurydice had seen the bodies on the ground, and her laughter was gone. "All the guards," she said.

"There's nothing we can do for them," I said, picking up my sword from the roof. "Bend low, so no one can see you from the courtyard." As if herding ducks, I waved them with my hand to the outside edge of the flat roof, away from the main house, toward the spot where the peaked roof above the kitchens began.

When they'd dug an icehouse a few years earlier, they'd put a door to it on the outside of the house wall, to make it easier to bring the ice in. The mound over the entranceway was just a few feet below the level of the roof. It was no difficulty to jump down and slither to the ground.

"We can go up through the olive grove to the road," said my mother.

"No." I shook my head again. "There might be more lookouts in the trees," I said. It was Terve's observation from the year before. "It will be better to hide in the icehouse until they are gone." That was my solution. The entranceway beside us might have been bolted from the inside, but it wasn't, because the house wasn't defended even from thievery. There'd never been a need.

Once inside, we barred the door behind us and went down the stairs and across the straw that covered the ice. We were underneath the steward's office. Another set of stairs led up to a door that had a lock to keep servants out of the valuable ice. It was also unlocked. The key would be hanging in the steward's room beside the kitchen.

I told my mother, my sisters, and the maids to wait in the icehouse. I found the key and locked them in, then slid the key under the door to my mother. They were hidden, and they were safe. I went to rally the servants, and my ideal plan, painstakingly worked out with Terve, came to an immediate, ruinous end.

The kitchen, too, had its own doors to the outside, to provide easy access to the kitchen gardens and the fruit trees. The room was full of servants. Everyone who had avoided the mysterious attackers had gathered there. I looked for Malatesta and, when I didn't see him, jumped to the worst conclusion.

There were no guards. Eurydice had been correct about the bodies she had seen. I could hear raised voices from the porch at the top of the house, and I knew that the latch on my mother's door had given way.

I shouted over the babble in the kitchen, "We must rally here and fight our way into the main house," and the babble was replaced by dead silence.

They looked at me like sheep. Or rather, like goats—just that look a goat gives you when it has decided not to cooperate and knows you can't make it. Suddenly, I was me again, just me, the weakling who cried when his tutor whipped his fingers with a switch.

"We have to rally here and fight," I said again, and my voice cracked. Some of the servants slipped out the door toward the orchards. "Won't you fight? I've killed two already," I said to those who were left. Their eyes dropped. More of them sidled out the door. From the house there was no more crashing, but more shouting. They'd found my mother's room empty. They were fanning out again to search.

"He's here!" The cook rushed to the door to the courtyard, shouting up toward my mother's balcony. I lunged after him in horror. Someone grabbed at my arm, and I disengaged him with my blade. Even rusted, it bit deep. I swung it again, and those around me fell back, but the cook was still shouting to the intruders that their prize was waiting for them like a complete idiot, in the kitchen, surrounded by the people he'd thought would help him. I tried to back myself toward the door to the outside, but it was much too late to think strategically. A wall suddenly appeared on my left, rushing toward me. I turned, uncomprehending, and raised my sword, but it did little good against what turned out to be a table turned on end. By the time I understood what was happening, I was falling backward. No one, not even Pol, had ever taught me how to fight off a table.

· CHAPTER TWO ·

I lay on the dirt, my hands tied behind me, my feet tied, and a bag over my head. The bag was coarsely woven and I could see a little through it. The day was bright. Men were moving around. If I hadn't had something that smelled like a dishrag in my mouth, I would have cursed them. Impulses of rage swept over me, and I kicked with both feet and struggled against the ropes, but I never hit anything, and the ropes were unrelentingly tight.

The servants had disarmed me neatly by squashing me flat with the table and then standing on my sword blade until someone could pry my fingers off the handle. "Sorry," they whispered, "sorry," through the gaps in the tabletop. I screamed at them every curse I'd ever practiced when I was alone, trying to imitate the Thief of Eddis, but I doubt I sounded anything but hysterical. When the men who had attacked the villa came in, the servants melted back against the walls. Someone pulled the table off me, and a few minutes later I was tied top and bottom, but still shouting, which is when I received the wet dishcloth in my mouth, followed by the bag over my head.

With my own voice muffled, I could hear the men around me clearly. They hadn't found my mother and my sisters.

"All right," said a voice obviously in charge, "kill all the servants and fire the building."

They'd carried me away, screaming into the cloth stuffing my mouth, and tied me, stomach down, onto the back of a donkey that had gone at an agonizing trot for long enough that I'd lost track of time, thinking of my mother and my sisters and the maids patiently waiting for me in the cool dark of the ice cellar, unaware of their danger until the burning villa above crashed in upon them. We reached an unknown stopping point, where I was lifted down and left on the ground while people carried on with some business nearby.

"He's still kicking," someone commented above me. "I am surprised. I thought he was more like our Hyacinth here."

I froze and heard someone, Hyacinth, I had no doubt, gasp in horror. It was certainly his voice I heard next. "You were not to tell him!"

I thought of Malatesta, whom I had accused in my head of being a traitor to my family. He was probably dead at the villa, while Hyacinth had never even crossed my mind.

Several people above laughed. The first voice I had heard, and the one who ordered the firing of the villa, said, "There, that has stopped him kicking." The voice was closer, as if he were bending over me, and I sat up as quickly as I could, hoping that the hard part of my head might connect with his face, but either I missed, or he jumped back in time. I hit nothing and had to drop back to the ground, my stomach aching.

The men around me laughed again. "Get that thing off his head," their leader said.

Once the hood was off and the gag out of my mouth, I could see that I was near the shore, on a level spot on a hillside, looking over the water. Behind me, the hill rose higher. Below me, it steepened and dropped to the ring road that circled the island. In the distance, down the coast, I could see the curve of the headland that hid the city of Letnos.

There were more people around me than I had expected, and they seemed to be making no effort at concealment. I glanced quickly at each of them, still expecting Malatesta, but there was no sign of him. I should have looked for their leader, but I was caught staring at Hyacinth, who was nearby wringing his hands. "You helped them?"

"Not by much," said the heavyset man on my left. His was the voice I had heard giving orders. "He described the villa for us and told us where the family was most likely to be at that time of the day."

"He wasn't supposed to know," Hyacinth cheeped pathetically. Turning to me, he said, "I didn't want you to know. You didn't have to."

"I see," I said calmly. "Can I get up?"

The stocky man lifted me to my feet easily. He turned out to be somewhat shorter than I was, once I was standing. His skin was dark and rough from long days spent in the open. He was about my father's age and showed signs of a similar life of violence. He crouched to cut through the ropes around my ankles, then lifted the rope to the bonds on my wrists and hesitated. "There are too many of us to fight, young prince."

I stared. Officially I was heir to Sounis, but no one ever called me prince. I was only a placeholder until the king produced his own heir.

"Do you understand?" the man asked.

I nodded. He cut the ropes. I rubbed my wrists for a moment and flexed my hands. The skin where the ropes had burned was sore, but my hands weren't puffy or weak. I looked around me, and the man who'd spoken was right. I was in the middle of a group of men. There was no chance to run and nowhere to hide, even if I got away. The hillside above us was bare. Below was only a small camp, probably the kidnappers', a wagon beside a few shabby tents, and an empty road.

I hardly cared. I took two running steps and lunged for Hyacinth. I had my hands around his neck before anyone else could move. I wasn't heavier than he was, but I was taller and bore him to the ground, where I did my best to strangle the life out of him.

"Is it because my sister set aside pastries for you to eat when you visited? Is that why you betrayed her? Is it because my mother admired your horrible flute playing? Is that why you betrayed her? Is it because they were kind to you?" I screamed as his face turned purple.

Hyacinth writhed ineffectively under me and clutched at my fingers. He rolled his eyes in appeal toward the men looking on, but it was a long time before any of them moved. At last someone did grab me under the arms and try to pull me back, but I didn't let go of Hyacinth's neck, so he was raised, still choking, off the ground. Another man put his foot on Hyacinth's chest and pushed down until my grip broke. It was not much of a rescue. He slithered away sobbing, and once he'd gotten his breath, he cried in earnest, while my abductors looked on in contempt.

"You said he wouldn't know!" he shrieked between sobs. To me he said, "We would be friends and you would do me favors when you are king!"

"He'll do no one favors when he is king," said the stocky man, "least of all you," he added, and turned his back on poor, pathetic Hyacinth, who continued to look at me for forgiveness.

"They want to make you king. That isn't a bad thing. And no one was hurt, no one important. Your mother and your sisters weren't even home."

"They were hiding," I said.

"Oh," said Hyacinth, "outside?"

"In the house."

The amusement of the onlookers faded. The leader

swore. He looked to one of his men, who shook his head. They had seen no one leave the villa as it burned.

"I didn't know!" screamed Hyacinth. "It isn't my fault!"

I turned my back on him as the tears filled my eyes. I sank to the ground and cried into my hands, not caring if my captors looked at me with the same disgust that they cast on my worthless former friend.

The camp below was that of a slave trader. Because slaves don't often change hands nowadays, the slaver traveled from place to place, buying up slaves one at a time. My parents could remember when there was a regular slave market in most towns of any size. Now families sell off slaves only when they are desperate for the money, and their neighbors look down their noses, as if the family has been reduced to selling off children. There are new slaves, of course, people who can't pay their debts and other criminals, but the slave markets on Letnos happen just a few times a year, and slavers must travel to gather their wares.

The trader was the stocky man who was giving orders. I learned that his name was Basrus and that he had a string of fifteen or twenty slaves camped below us next to the road. The rest of the men around me were soldiers of some kind. In the next few minutes they disappeared, probably back to some villa where they would be hidden, and I was left with three men and Hyacinth, still sniffling.

"You can't get off the island," I told Basrus. "Some of the servants will have made it to the nearby land-owners. They can't all be in league with you," I said, glaring at Hyacinth. "The island governor will call out the soldiers quartered in town and the navy. You won't get past the war galleys. You can hide your men because no one knows who they are, but you can't hide me. They will look from house to house in every closet and every cellar. They'll search every cave deep enough to hide a rabbit."

"Oh, but you won't be in a cellar, my lionhearted young man, or in a cave. You are going to be out in the open. Hold his arms." He was pulling on heavy leather gloves. The other men who were with us had seized my arms and pulled them behind me.

"What are you doing?" Hyacinth asked. He was truly stupid. Even more stupid than I had thought. I stared at him amazed and never even felt the first blow, scientifically aimed, as it hit me in the face.

CHAPTER THREE

I woke slowly with everything hurting so much I didn't know at first what it was that hurt. I put my hands to my face. That was what hurt: my head, my face. My whole head felt enlarged to twice its natural size. I couldn't see more than a bright haze between swollen eyelids. Someone was sponging me off with a cloth, wiping down my neck and along my shoulders. My shoulders hurt, too, or rather my back, but it was a stinging pain, not the disabling pain in my head that made it hard to link my thoughts into any sensible order.

"Lie still, lion, while we get this dye off," said a voice over my head. "We're almost done with you. We'll have you at rest in a moment." As good as his word, he soon left off wiping and lifted me to my feet and helped me walk. We descended the ridge. I still couldn't see, but I could feel the ground dropping out from below my feet. The bright haze visible through my eyelids faded as we passed into the shade, and my feet tangled in blankets. He held a cup to my swollen lips and I drank, tasting lethium and wine.

"Down," he said, and I sagged to my knees and then to my side and lay there with my insensible thoughts linking up randomly and breaking apart again until I fell asleep and it was dreams, not thoughts, floating through my empty head.

I woke the next morning to a headache, a vast and tiresome pain that seemed outside my head as much as in it, a headache and a very sore and swollen face. I had a vague memory of Hyacinth whispering more tearful apologies into my ear, but he was gone when I opened my eyes as much as the swelling would allow and peered around me. Hyacinth might have been a dream. I lay under a striped cloth, which dropped to the ground on one side like a tent. When I sat up, the skin tightened across my back like lines of fire. I couldn't seem to twist my head far enough to see over a shoulder, but on my upper arm I could see the red line of a lash. I blinked hazily, and for a moment wondered what I could have done to so infuriate Malatesta. My tongue caught painfully on something sharp; one of my teeth was loose, connected only by a narrow bridge of flesh.

The slaver squatted beside me. "You'll be wondering, my lion, just what we are up to. You were right that we cannot easily get you off the island, but we mean to try. Your own mother, I'm sorry, may she journey safely, but even she wouldn't know you."

I lifted my hand away from its explorations of my face and up to the top of my head to find my hair all cut away and ragged.

"It's darker now," Basrus said. "No one will pick you out among my slaves. No one here but myself and my lieutenant, Gorgias, knows who you are. As far as the rest of my men and the other slaves know, you are a very troublesome slave who has killed another slave in a fight and you are on your way to the galleys."

"And if I shout to one and all that I am the heir to Sounis?" I asked as clearly as I could, past my swollen lip.

"That's the question, then, isn't it?" He held up a gag with leather straps.

It's not so terrible as it sounds. They loaded me into the back of the cart, where I lay for the first day, grieving for my mother and my sisters and cataloging my mistakes, unfairly blaming Terve for not warning me that the villa might be burned, hating Hyacinth, and the slaver, and all his men, and, most of all, with excoriating rage, myself.

We were stopped by the island's guard, and each time they looked through the slaver's receipts it was clear that all was in order. Basrus even pointed me out as his most recent purchase, and not one of the guard looked twice at a troublemaker sold off for fighting. The first time it happened, I shook my head as fiercely as the pain would allow, only to have the guards assume I was protesting a bad reputation. After that I gave it up as useless.

As I was bounced and jolted toward the town of Letnos, my uncle was lured out of the city of Sounis by news of fighting between two of the coastal barons. The two, Comeneus and his neighbor, had squabbled often enough that it was no wonder that the king rode out immediately with a century from the garrison at Sounis. He was to have been killed on the road just outside the city, and I was to be installed as a puppet in his place.

The assassination attempt was a catastrophic failure for the rebels. My uncle fought his way clear and pulled his men to order. He guessed correctly that the gates of Sounis would be closed to him, and instead of riding to the city for aid, he turned across country, eluding his would-be assassins. Heading north, with a handful of men, he made his way toward his loyal barons.

On the second day, I was well enough to walk. Gorgias, on the slaver's orders, offered to leave off the gag if I gave my word to be silent. I tried unsuccessfully to spit in his face. I also screamed like a speared rabbit when he put the gag in. Gorgias looked at me in a puzzled way when I dropped almost to my knees and then struggled back to my feet, feeling utterly unheroic. My hands were tied behind me, and I was off-balance. The gag, pushing the loose tooth into my tender gum, was infuriating.

Basrus came over and pushed me back down. He efficiently removed the gag and tilted my head back, holding me pinned in the crook of his elbow. I struggled like a piglet in a farmer's grasp. Like a farmer, Basrus expertly ran his finger inside my mouth, found the tooth, and yanked it out. I yelled again and kicked, but he held me immobile. Not ungently, he rubbed my head.

"It will be better now, lion," he said. He put the gag back in, and he was right that it was far less uncomfortable with the tooth gone. When he released me, he stepped back carefully. I had seen Pol, captain of my father's guard, treat an angry Eugenides once with the same caution, and for good reason. It was ridiculous that Basrus would treat *me* so, and humiliation made me more enraged. I would have run myself into him headfirst if Gorgias hadn't grabbed me by the arm and held me back, saving me, not Basrus. My head was too sore to use as a battering ram, and I would have hurt only myself.

When we reached Letnos, we marched past the holding pens at the harbor and out the pier to a boat. I was so tired my only feeling was one of relief that we had arrived. The swelling in my face had gone down enough that I could see more clearly, but my head still hurt. My hands were still tied, my legs were shackled as well, and I had to be helped aboard. I'd spent the day twisting between extremes, crying at the thought of my sisters and my mother and snarling in rage. I'd used my feet to kick until Basrus had them shackled, and then I'd used my elbows until my hands had been retied, and my arms cinched tight to my body.

My back ached and stung like fire in turns, and my

stomach had refused any food. Once in the boat, I was shoved to one side and locked to a thwart. It wasn't a large boat, but the other slaves settled as far from me as they could. All they knew of me was that I tended, when I was on the ground during rest periods, to lash out with both feet together. As we settled in, the slave trader looked over at me. He pinched his nose thoughtfully and said aloud to Gorgias, "A lamb, they said. No more trouble than snatching up a little lamb."

The center of town was alive with the king's soldiers, like an ants' nest that had been kicked to pieces. The king's soldiers moved with no more direction than the ants, and I watched them balefully as we pulled away from the pier.

As we left the harbor, a galley pulled up beside us and ordered the steersman into the wind. The sail flapped overhead as Basrus made his way to the bow and handed a package of papers across to the sailor on the galley, who passed them to his captain. Once again, all the receipts seemed to be in order. Basrus stood at ease, chatting with the nearest men about the weather and such, rocking comfortably with the motion of the waves, while the captain looked through the bill of sale for each of the slaves in the boat. I sat silent behind my gag. Gorgias had already demonstrated that he could, with a discreet tap from the lead weight he held, leave me incapable of anything beyond gasping for breath.

We were all accounted for, and there was nowhere

to hide anything the size of a prince on board, so the captain of the king's ship waved us on our way, and I added him to the list of people I hated. Once we left the harbor, however, he and everyone else on the list faded rapidly from my mind as my headache, and my empty sour stomach, made every tilt of the boat and every slosh of the waves a trial. I am not a sailor even in the best of circumstances, and I concentrated fiercely on not being sick. The gag in my mouth became more frightening. Gorgias wouldn't take it out unless I gave him my word to keep silent. I continued to refuse. Finally Basrus picked his way over to me and squatted down, leaning in so close that I could feel the warmth of his breath on my skin as he spoke very softly into my ear.

"My prince," he said. "Do you see anyone here to aid you?" He cast a significant look at the slaves and at his men. The only boats visible on the sea around us were far out of the range of my voice. "You're as green as a dead man, and I'm not being paid to bring a dead man to shore. You'll have the gag out and you'll keep your name to yourself, or I swear by my god I will slit the throat of every man on this boat but Gorgias." He looked into my horrified eyes and said, "I'll slit their throats and dump them into the sea to keep this secret, and I will never give it another thought. Do you believe me?"

I did.

He untied the gag and pulled it free. "Get him some water," he said to Gorgias, and returned to the stern.

I looked at the men who were hostage for my good behavior, and I stayed quiet. When we neared Hanaktos, Gorgias put the gag back in. When we reached the dock in the harbor, we were unloaded and marched to market pens more often used for goats than for men.

Within the hour of our arrival, we were being looked over by various townspeople, one of whom I recognized as the wife of Baron Hanaktos. Lady Hanaktia didn't know me. Neither did her daughter, who was with her. The swelling in my face felt much reduced, but no doubt my bruises were still disfiguring. Berrone and I had danced together just a few months earlier at a reception my mother arranged in the capital. It had been a failed attempt to reconcile me with my uncle and my father. I'd been, as usual, paralyzed. All the young women danced with me for form's sake, but Berrone did it out of pity as well, which was enough to cement the disaster. I was returned to Letnos the following day.

Ina tells me that Berrone is more beautiful than any other young woman in our acquaintance. I suppose my personal affections alter my perceptions. She is lovely. She is very kind, too, as Ina has also pointed out, though if you knew Ina, you would know she wasn't being kind when she did. Because what Ina was saying, without saying, is that Berrone is also the stupidest person we know.

During our dances at the reception months earlier,

Berrone had told me with delight the ridiculous amount of money she had given a shopkeeper for a magical device that would keep things from being lost. Berrone was always losing things, scarves, rings, purses. She showed me the device, which turned out to be an ordinary piece of string. She had tied one end of it to a ring and the other to her finger.

Still, no matter how silly she was, I was certain she would know me if she just looked closely enough. She and her mother stood not too far away, eyeing the merchandise as the slaver's man, Gorgias, pointed out and described potential purchases. Sitting on the packed dirt, with a wide empty space around me, I stared hard at Berrone. She did look at me, but my stare disconcerted her, and she glanced away again quickly. When she glanced at me again, I looked down and tried to look harmless and as appealing as possible. I modeled myself on my apologetic former friend Hyacinth, certain she would recognize me then. From under my eyebrows, I could tell that Berrone was asking about me, though I couldn't hear her words, spoken quietly to the slaver's man. No doubt he related my story, sold off for fighting and disobedience. The Lady Hanaktos shook her head briskly and turned to another proposed purchase. But Berrone looked back my way.

She was softhearted. She felt sorry for me. She was looking at me earnestly, and I was sure that the slaver's disguise would fail. Then her mother recalled her sharply and led her away. Crushed, I almost screamed my frustration into the gag in my mouth and prayed for some god to reach down from the sky and shake the stupid girl until her little pea brains rattled in her head.

There was no sign of divine intervention, but Berrone did glance at me again, even as her mother drew her away, and I took that as a reason to hope. Over the next hour I slowly moved closer to the edge of the pen. The slavers didn't notice the movement, but the slaves around me did, and as gradually as I moved, they moved as well, keeping an empty space between my feet and them. Finally, through the latticed sides of the pen, I saw the baron's daughter as she returned with her mother. They had a young slave in tow, no doubt a house slave, maybe for her brother or maybe for the kitchens. The slave climbed up onto the back of a lightweight carriage as the women climbed onto the cushions in front. Berrone looked over at me, and I clasped my hands together in appeal, glad that they were tied in front and not behind me. She smiled and then turned to sit next to her mother.

· CHAPTER FOUR ·

I hoped. I hoped all that afternoon and through dinner, because I knew about Berrone. I knew she spent a fortune buying songbirds at the market and then setting them free. No one had the heart to tell her that they were captive bred and that they probably starved—if they weren't eaten first by the predators of the town: the cats, the rats, and the hawks. She brought stray animals home from the streets, and the maids had to put them out. She'd convinced her father to outlaw the drowning of kittens because it was cruel, and for a year the port of Hanaktos was overrun with starved and mangy animals, until finally the townspeople had revolted and spent three days on a massacre that upset everyone and the baron revoked the injunction.

My best hope for rescue wasn't the king's war galleys or his soldiers. It was Baron Hanaktos's daughter. All night long I prayed earnestly to the goddesses of mercy to intercede on my behalf and stir Berrone's soft heart with pity.

The next morning Gorgias and the slaver went off together after Gorgias had first checked my chains and pulled tight the narrow thongs that held the leather gag in place. "We are off to arrange your sale," he told me, and I knew that anyone who heard would think I was soon for the galleys. Basrus, I thought, was probably taking Gorgias along to carry all the gold my sale would bring him.

We were left under supervision of the other slavers, and no sooner were they gone than Berrone appeared. She had a servant with her. She pointed me out to him and then retreated to a nearby market stall while the servant approached the pens and gestured to the slaver left in charge. He asked about me and was told I wasn't for sale. A bribe was offered. The guard declined, and the servant went to check with Berrone. Thank the gods her father's allowance to her was so large. Back and forth between the market stall and the guard the servant went, the bribe no doubt growing with each iteration, until the slaver's eyes were so wide that when he looked over at me, their whites showed all around.

Basrus was undone by his own secrecy. His guard knew no more than that I was an unruly slave destined for the galleys. He could keep half the money himself and still offer his master far more than he thought I was worth, no doubt expecting his master to be pleased. I could almost hear the resulting curses from the slaver. Best of all, I didn't think that the guard had seen Berrone. With luck, the slaver wouldn't know who bought me and couldn't track me down before I reached the safety of Hanaktos's megaron. All that mattered was that the deal was done before Basrus returned.

A few minutes later the slaves were directed out of the

pens and down to the shore to wash. My shackles were undone, and my arms untied. There was still a collar on my neck with a short rope attached, and the bribed slaver took me in hand. On the way to the shore he and I were at the end of the line. It was an easy matter to put the rope into the servant's hand and walk on without me. No one else even noticed. Perhaps he intended to keep all the money and tell his master that his troublesome slave had escaped.

The servant tugged impatiently, and I followed, struggling to undo the knots on the gag, but the leather thongs were thin, and the knots were too small to untie easily.

"Hurry," said Berrone when we reached her. "My mother wouldn't let me buy you yesterday, and when I asked my father if I could buy you last night, he said no." The last knot unraveled, and I pulled the bit of wood free just as she said, "He told me that he'd ordered you sold himself because you killed that man on our farm."

Their farm? I'd opened my mouth to speak but was as dumbstruck as if the gag had still been in place. Berrone mistook the cause for my wide-eyed stare.

"Don't be afraid," she said breathlessly. "I am sure you didn't mean to do it. And my father won't know I've bought you. That's why I waited for Basrus and Gorgias to be gone. I am going to hide you."

She knew Basrus and Gorgias by name. They worked with her father, or for him. Berrone's father was in league with my abductors, and his daughter, unknown to him, was going to hide me. What could I do but go quietly?

CHAPTER FIVE

HOURS later I was locked in a pantry under the house, surrounded by storage amphorae, in the pitch dark. We'd ridden away from the market, Berrone in the seat with the sullen servant, me balancing on the pins at the back, and taken the road out of town and up toward the baron's megaron. We didn't go through the gates. Just before the walled courtyard, we'd turned aside to follow the road slightly downhill again and around to the stable yard. There were two rows of stables facing each other, one row built against the solid walls of the megaron's foundation, one facing it, and a ramp that led up to an ancillary gate into the forecourt above us. On the far side of the ramp was an open terrace shaded by olive trees and scattered with the usual debris of farm and residence.

From the terrace, Berrone had led me into the kitchens, where she'd explained to the house steward that he was going to hide me. The steward, not surprisingly, hadn't taken to this plan at all. He'd presented all sorts of obvious difficulties, none of which Berrone had considered. I couldn't serve in the house without being seen by her father, and if I served in the kitchen, the staff would talk. Oh, no, Berrone had said. Oh, yes, the steward had insisted. I almost felt sorry for him. This obviously wasn't the first time that Berrone had presented him with a mess to clean up, and he could afford neither to offend her nor to disobey her father. I stood by, trying to look as innocuous as possible and not at all like a dangerous, man-killing slave, while the steward gave me the evil eye and tried to convince Berrone to take me back.

Finally, they locked me in one of the underground storage rooms and told me to wait. The floor was packed dirt, which might as well have been stone, it was so cold. I had no idea who, if anyone, was going to come for me. If the steward revealed my presence to the baron, I was doomed, and for all I knew, the baron's plans were common knowledge in his household. Servants, in my experience, always know everything.

Behind me a mouse crept through the dark. The packed earth was probably riddled with mouseholes. I was hungry and wondered if the mouse was getting anything to eat, so I crawled across the floor myself, feeling in front of me until I reached the storage jars I had seen in the dim light before they closed the door. I rose up onto my knees, running my hands up the sides of one jar until I reached the waxed seal at the top. I could feel the symbols in the wax that would have told me what was in the jar, if there'd been any light to see by. I felt further, to the next jar and then past it, looking for more accessible food, a bag of nuts, perhaps, or root vegetables, but everything was in clay, safe from the vermin.

I may have been meek, but I was more able than a mere mouse. I broke the wax seals and lifted the lids, then dipped my hand into a jar, hoping for the best. The first jar was pickling juice with little lumps, which turned out to be onions. The next jar held olives in salty brine that left me wishing for a drink. I looked further but found nothing but olive oil. If there was anything else stored in the bottom of the jars, I was unwilling to plunge my arm into the oil to the shoulder to find it. All I could do was go back to the onions pickled in vinegar to try to slake my thirst.

I fell asleep in the dark and woke in the dark and began to be more afraid. I couldn't guess how long I'd been in the cellar. Had Berrone forgotten me? Would she decide to make a clean breast of her mistake and hand me over to her father? Or would she just leave me to die in the dark and be carried out in a week or two, when someone came for more pickled onions?

I considered banging on the door but was worried that announcing my presence to others in the household would only get me an audience with the baron. When I heard the key turning in the lock, I scrambled to my feet and was standing when it opened to admit the light of a lamp. The steward hung it on a hook near the door and looked me over. A taller, heavier-set man looked at me over his shoulder.

"He's dangerous," warned the steward. I almost laughed. In one way I was no danger at all but in another more dangerous than he could imagine. Someone somewhere was sweating over my disappearance, I was sure.

"You let me worry about dangerous," said the other man. He leaned against the doorway with his arms crossed, muscles bunching, and I swallowed my laugh.

The steward said, "This is Ochto, overseer for the baron's field hands. You'll go with him, and if you give him trouble, you disappear, do you understand?"

I nodded.

"We'll tell the lady you ran off."

"I won't be any trouble," I promised.

"No, you won't," Ochto agreed.

"And you'll keep quiet about where you've come from. Or maybe you'll find yourself under the baron's eye and wish we had knifed you and buried you out by the olives," the steward said. Just then he saw the broken seals on the storage jars. You would have thought I'd been eating infants. He stepped around me to get a better look.

"What have you done? Nine!" he shouted. "*Nine* broken seals?" It occurred to me only then that the carefully sealed jars would have to be repacked and resealed and that those that couldn't be resealed would have to be consumed or wasted. No slave, no matter how hungry, would have helped himself to the provisions stored in the room.

"I was hungry," I explained, afraid that my disguise was slipping already. He was not sympathetic. "I'm sorry," I added humbly, but he waved me toward the overseer with a glare and went to mourn over his ravaged pots.

Warily, I stepped into the corridor, intimidated by the bunching muscles of the overseer, but Ochto only directed me to walk ahead of him toward the stairs to the upper level. With a creeping feeling between my shoulder blades, I preceded him down the dark passage and up the steps to the kitchens. Outside the kitchen he tapped me on the shoulder and pointed to a path next to the stables. The path led downhill to more outbuildings and a long, low barracks for field workers.

There was a narrow yard with a wellhead and two doors into the barracks. Ochto pointed me toward the one on the right. I ducked my head through the low doorway and found a large room lined with pallets and men dressed in the simplest and coarsest clothing.

They were all sitting on individual pallets or lying down. Ochto nudged the one closest to the door. Without comment, the man swept a small collection of items out of a niche in the wall behind him and moved to another pallet farther away, the occupant of which packed up his things and moved as well. This continued down the row until the youngest in the room, younger by a year or two than myself, shifted to a pallet that was empty. When Ochto nodded at me, I sat on my new bed. To the entire barracks, he condemned me with a single word: man-killer.

I hunched, pulled my knees up to my chin, and wrapped my arms around my legs. The room was quiet, the others flicking glances at me. I ignored them. After years in Sounis's palaces being eyed with disgust by my uncle and my own father and courtier after courtier, I assure you I am unrivaled at pretending not to notice other people's glances.

In time, quiet exchanges began among the field hands. No one met my eyes, and I didn't meet theirs, but I sent quick glances around the room. It appeared to be half the length of the entire building. To my left was a door that led to the other half of the barracks, probably with a private room for the overseer in between. At the opposite end of the sleeping quarters, there was another door that led outside. There were open spaces in the stone walls that let in the light but not too much heat.

We seemed to be waiting, but I had no idea for what until the door opened again and a husky young man brought in a large pot, which he set on the floor. Behind him several young boys carried stacks of wooden bowls and spoons, which they distributed among the men. When the overseer pointed at me, I rose and served myself some soup. By the time my bowl was full, the rest of the men had gathered behind me for their servings. I went back to my new bed and ate.

So I became a slave. Before I had been a prisoner, the

captured prince of Sounis. Now, in the eyes of Ochto, sitting on a stool by the door, slurping his own soup, I was no different than any of the men around me. My freedom was like my missing tooth, a hole where something had been that was now gone. I worried at the idea of it, just as I slid my tongue back and forth across the already healing hole in my gum. I tasted the last bloody spot and tried to remember the feel of the tooth that had been there. I had been a free man. Now I was not.

After eating, the men carried their bowls and spoons back to the boys who'd brought them. The soup pot was carried away, and everyone lay down. I did the same and was surprised to be woken bleary-eyed by the call to rise. The sun had dropped in the sky. The worst of the day's heat had passed, and the men were to go back to work. I stumbled after the others out of the barracks and along the path to the fields.

The baron's fields rolled down toward the water and stretched for some miles along the shore behind his megaron. We hiked between mature grapevines, into folds of land and up again, climbing rolling hills, until we were walking through olive groves and came to an undeveloped hillside in the process of being cultivated for more trees.

There were piles of rocks by the road, and digging tools. The slope was being terraced for new planting. Several men headed off to spots where the waist-high walls were partly built. They were masons who knew their jobs. Others were ferries, carrying the rocks to the masons. The rest of us picked up the digging tools and climbed up the hill or down to shift the dirt. Those heading downhill moved the dirt shovel by shovel into the space behind the newly built walls, creating flat terraces to hold a tree. Those uphill had a more difficult job, cutting through the roots of the dried grasses into the rocklike soil to gouge a space for a wall to fit. I grabbed a shovel and headed downhill before I could be sent upward.

In terms of my freedom, I may have been no different from the other slaves around me, but in other ways more significant to the job at hand, I was as unlike them as it was possible to be. The first time I swung the shovel into the dirt pile the newly healing skin split under the scabs on my back, and my muscles burned like fire. My hands slipped along the shaft of the digging tool. I gripped harder, strained at the load, and tipped a pathetic half shovel of loose dirt, dry as dust, into the empty space behind the stone wall.

The man beside me looked at the results of my effort and then at me. I could hardly excuse my performance by telling him of my sheltered childhood as the nephew of the king of Sounis. All I could do was scowl and wait for his contemptuous comment. To my surprise he only shrugged and moved away to work somewhere else.

I tipped another tiny shovel's worth into place. Ignoring all the others, feeling more and more humiliated by my own performance and more sullen every minute, I worked stubbornly until the sun dropped to the horizon. When I heard a shout from above, I looked uphill to see the overseer resting on his shovel. He was a worker as well, and he was calling it a day. All around me, the men moved slowly to the rock piles, where they left their tools. Together we made our way to the barracks. My back hurt so much I was afraid that if I took a misstep on the rutted path, I would drop like a sack of oats. I watched every step as if it were my last, but I made it to the sleeping quarters and to my own pallet, where I fell, without a thought of dinner, into a dreamless sleep.

I woke in the morning starved. I was also, I found, when I levered my body into a sitting position, chained to the wall by a bracelet around my hand. I was looking at the smooth iron ring, remembering Eugenides once in a similar position and wishing that I had his pluck to deal with the situation, when Ochto squatted beside me to unlock it.

"Not used to that, are you?" he asked.

I shook my head.

"Better this than a galley, though, right?" He watched me through narrowed eyes as he spoke, and continued to observe me even after I nodded my agreement. He popped the lock off as the potboy brought breakfast. My whole body protesting, I was still first in line for the food.

I dragged myself through the next days, working, resting in the afternoon, digging until the light was going from the sky. I ate and then slept dreamlessly. Slowly I grew stronger and was awake longer. During rest periods I watched the other men as they wandered in and out of the barracks. I began to wait with them when we came in from the fields for my turn to rinse myself at the wellhead instead of going directly to my pallet of blankets in anticipation of my next meal. I was still first in line to eat.

Every night the men entertained themselves under the overseer's watchful eye. They talked until by mutual consent someone's offering of poetry or song was chosen, a different man each night, in a subtle order of rotation I didn't understand. Some knew only one piece, others had a broader range, and they were careful, in an unscripted way, not to overuse anyone's limited repertoire. One evening, as I lay on my pallet, with my right hand chained to the ring in the wall, I heard a man across the room reciting Eacheus's speech from the ending of the *Eponymiad*.

I hadn't really listened before because I'd been falling asleep as they started. I was falling asleep then, but a mistake caught my ear: "laughing-eyed chorus" instead of "doe-eyed Kora."

Without lifting my head, I recited the line correctly, not considering if anyone would hear or care what I said. There was an uncomfortable silence before the speaker hesitantly started again, and in the space of the next few lines, I was asleep. In the morning, as I shoveled my meal out of my wooden bowl, I realized that everyone was staring at the man on the next pallet and that he was eyeing me. A chill settled in the muscles of my back. Then, like someone tensing before a dive into cold water, the man beside me said, "You know the *Eponymiad*?"

"Your pardon?"

"You were in-house? You know the poets?"

I shrugged. "Some," I said, not sure where this was headed. Nowhere, it seemed, as everyone went back to his food and then trailed off to the fields. They talked among themselves about me, I could tell. I wondered if I'd revealed some weakness, lost the protection of my invisibility.

That evening the skin between my shoulders crawled as I received my portion of food, and it took all my self-control not to hurry to my bed to get my back against a wall. Eugenides wouldn't hurry, I reminded myself. I wouldn't, either.

Later, when everyone was fed, there was a stirring at the far end of the room. A scrawny boy, the youngest in the barracks, who nonetheless could shift twice what I could per shovel, came crouching down beside me and hesitantly offered me his bread from the meal. "Did you hear anything of the choruses from the plays this year?" he asked.

The baron's food was sufficient, not generous, and I was hungry, but the boy's ribs showed, right up to his collarbones, and I pushed his bread back at him. "I heard all of them."

I recited the opening of the history of the Mannae. Every man, even the overseer, listened, rapt. Instead of being tired when I was finished, I felt more awake than I had since I'd been captured. Lo, the power of poetry, I suppose. So I gave them a sketch of the plot and a few bits of the important speeches. I've done recitations at wine parties and in front of tutors and at the court when duty obliged. I've never had an audience as gratifying. I could have talked all night, but after I'd finished with the Mannae, the workers sighed happily and lay down to sleep. I lay down as well but was awake in the quiet dark for a few minutes more.

So I took my place in the rotation and settled into the company of laborers. I rose with them in the morning and worked with them all day, slowly coming to recognize them by name and to know the jokes they shared, the friendships between them, and the animosities. They were good men, and their friendships were common and the animosities very small, in part because Ochto was a direct and effective overseer and not reluctant to clout on the head a man who was resting while others worked. Ochto had a cane to enforce his judgment, but it hung on two pegs near the door to the barracks and was rarely used. We worked with a sense of companionship and common cause, and I looked forward to the evenings, when I joined in the talk and listened to the recitations. I performed no more often than anyone else. I was a treasure to be parceled out slowly, and I savored the experience.

My uncle had made it to his allies in the northern part of Sounis and was raising his armies against the rebels. We heard little news at first, but that much we knew in the field house because Hanaktos had sent soldiers to join Baron Comeneus. Why he was the leader of this rebellion I couldn't begin to guess. I wouldn't have expected him to be able to lead the more fractious of my uncle's barons out of a hole in the ground if it was filling with water, especially after making a botch of the assassination attempt.

The men in the barracks seemed to care very little and assumed it would all be over soon, that the king would deal as summarily with the rebels as he had in the past. I could not imagine what good result the rebels thought could come from weakening the nation when it was already in such peril, but it was the opinion of the men I worked beside that none of it had anything to do with them. By and large, I agreed with them.

By this time I had realized that not all the men around me were slaves. Some were okloi tied to the baron's family who worked for room and board, and some were salary men, free to go at the end of their contracts. They earned a pittance, paying most of their wages back to cover the cost of their lodging, and would have been better off tied to the baron and working for no wages at all. They had no guarantee of more work or pay at the end of their contracts, though in practice, I suppose, the baron was unlikely to let them go. I knew that I hadn't yet grasped all the details of the pecking order, because one of the men much admired was a slave, and Ochto himself was a former slave set in place over free men, who worked very comfortably beneath him.

One day, after I had been in the field house for a few weeks, a new worker joined us. The new man thought he should be first in line for food. When he stepped in aggressively between me and the potboy, my first reaction was surprise. Before I could register anything but that he was both taller and heavier than I was, the man behind him tugged urgently at his arm and hissed a warning under his breath: "Man-killer."

The new worker paused to reevaluate, but I didn't. I couldn't afford to lose my reputation, and I certainly would if there were a confrontation. I scooped up a wooden bowl and collected my supper. Then I walked to my bed and sat, making a show of careless bravado by crossing my legs and slumping as if I had not a worry in the world. In other words, I gave my best imitation of Eugenides. All I could do was hope the other men didn't see through the act.

The new man collected his own dinner and sat across the barracks from me. I spooned my dinner into my mouth as quickly as I could to hide the fact that my hands were shaking. Finally, I screwed my courage to the sticking place and looked over at him to find him staring warily back. I essayed a conciliatory smile. He hastily dropped his eyes to his supper and didn't look up again. I glanced around at the other men, realizing that they, too, must be wary of me to let me eat first every night. Wary of me. Not of my father or the power of my uncle. Me.

I swallowed my laugh but couldn't stop my smile.

The new worker's name was Runeus. After the meal, as we returned to work, he muttered a complaint about giving way to a slave, but Helius, who was the undisputed second-in-command to Ochto and also a slave, looked over his shoulder with a glance that silenced him. I put everything I had into looking like someone who has killed another man. Telling you this now, I realize that two men were already dead at my hand, but somehow, I didn't think of them then. I was acting a part for the other men in the barracks.

To my continuing but carefully hidden amazement, Runeus never challenged me again. Instead, things continued much as before. Only now I knew that my place in the food line was not a happy coincidence but a marker of my place in the hierarchy of the field hands.

✦ ✦ ✦

The next rest day one of the men looked to me and then to the overseer. "We thought to go to the shore. Man-killer, here, can he come?" The men often went down to the water in their free time or walked out to visit friends in other field houses or to watch the dice games up on the terrace beside the megaron.

Ochto looked me over. I had been careful to offer no trouble, and Ochto hadn't bothered putting the bracelet and chain on my wrist at night for many days.

Ochto nodded. Delighted, I jumped to my feet and followed the other men away from the megaron. We took the road toward town and then cut in the direction of the shore on a narrow path that led us to a break in the rocks where we could climb down to the sand to swim and then lie in the sun or the shade as each was inclined to be warmer or cooler.

I was happy. As difficult as that must be for you to believe, and in spite of the grief I still carried for my mother and my sisters, I was happy. No one was angry at me, disappointed in me, burdened by me. I had nothing to do but sit in the warm sand and look at the sea.

Oreus, the man who'd provided my day at the shore, dropped to the sand beside me. "So, man-killer," he asked. "Do you have a name?"

I thought before I answered. Wisdom is not a name for a slave. Stone, Mark, Faithful, Strong are slave names. I had a nurse once who had named her son Shovel. She was a foreigner, from somewhere far north, and she told me that she liked the way it sounded. She'd taught me a few words of her own language, but the only one I could remember was Zec, and I couldn't quite retrieve the meaning, though it sat on the tip of my tongue.

"Zec," I said, as if my tongue had decided to speak for itself.

"That's a Hurrish name." Oreus looked surprised. "You are from Hur?"

"No," I said. "My mother heard it once."

"It means 'rabbit,'" Oreus said.

I smiled. Rabbit was perfect.

"Tell me, Rabbit. Is that your happy face you make? I can't tell."

I felt my upper lip and rubbed my thumb against the scar tissue. I could feel it distorting my mouth. My nose had a new bump in the middle of it as well. Maybe I looked more like a man-killer than I'd realized.

"Zecush, we should call you," said Oreus. "Bunny." He punched me lightly enough in the arm, and I almost fell over. "Come for a swim."

The other men seemed to think that a man-killer called after a rabbit kit was a good joke. From then on they sometimes called me Zec or Zecush, but more often just Bunny. That night I slept more lightly than before and dreamed for the first time since my capture. I dreamed of a library with books and scrolls in ranks on shelves, all flooded with clear light. When I opened my eyes, the shed around me was still dark. The call to rise hadn't yet come. I lay in the dim quiet of the predawn, listening to the breath of the sleeping men around me and thinking of my dream.

I was still happy. It was no rest day. I faced a day in the hot sun, shifting dirt and stones, with scant food and ignorant company, and I'd never felt so much at peace. I laughed at myself as I shifted on my pallet for a more comfortable spot and a few minutes' more rest. Let me be beaten, I thought, and then see how well I liked being a slave. Too soon the overseer knocked on the doorway with his stick, and we all rose, grumbling, for another day.

I had grown more skilled at shifting dirt. If I couldn't compete with some of the men in the field with me, I could keep up with most of them. I worked hard, I slept well at night, and I dreamed often. I grieved, but a part of me felt a lightening of a burden I had carried all my life: that I could never be worthy of them, that I would always disappoint or fail them. As an unknown slave in the fields of the baron, I knew the worst was over. I had failed them. At least I could not do so again.

My dreams were lucent and vivid, as if the peacefulness of my days had put spurs to my imagination, and I dreamed again and again of the same place, the distant library with its endless collection of books and scrolls.

In my first dream, I only wandered through the space in awe, sensing that I was impossibly far from the ordinary world of Hanaktos's field hands. I was in an enormous room, filled with light from windows high up on the walls near the white coffered ceiling. On the wall that faced north, glass-paneled doors opened onto a balcony that looked over a green valley far below. Beyond the valley was a wall of snow-covered mountains with tops so bright they hurt the eye, and behind them an even brighter blue sky that never showed a single cloud.

Inside the room, opposite the glass doors, were carved wooden ones that remained closed in all my visits. I had no idea what might lie beyond them, probably because I had no interest. Everything I desired was in the room with me. Between these doors, and on every other space of wall, were shelves for books and scrolls and packets of papers and every kind of writing you can imagine, even tablets impressed with minute scratches that I not only knew were writing but could read, by the magic of dreams.

There were painted pillars to hold up the ceiling high overhead, each one covered in its own design of interleaving foliage, people, and animals. The figures repeated on the carved trim of the shelves: a set of lions on one case, a set of foxes smiling on another. They drew my touch like lodestones, and I ran my fingers over them as I explored.

In my later dreams I wandered the shelves, selecting books and scrolls and bringing them to the tables to pore over. There were tablets of wax and clay impressed with tiny characters. There were books I knew and had already read, books the magus had told me of that I'd never seen, and even books I knew of only because their titles had been listed in ancient times. Plax's lost plays, Dellari's histories of the Peninsula's War, the poetry of Hern. They all were there.

And I had a guide as well. Still resenting Malatesta, I dreamed myself a far better tutor, who could answer my questions on every subject and never switched my hands. She was waiting for me one night. Tall even for a man and much more so for a woman, she wore a white peplos and looked just as if she had stepped from an ancient vase painting. She was like the Goddess appearing as the mentor in an epic, and I felt like a young Oenius. It was her library, I was certain, and I a welcomed guest.

I'd dreamed the night before that I had held Poers's *History of the Bructs* in my hands and read the first part of it. The magus had once summarized the book for me, from his notes. He had read it in a library in Ferria but had no copy of his own. I had been thinking lately of my uncle and what sort of king he was, and no doubt that is why the book had been on my mind.

"What do you think of Poers, Bunny?" my tutor asked me. "Was Komanare of the Bructs a bad king?"

She waved me to a chair and sat in one opposite.

I wasn't sure how to begin.

"Do you trust Poers?" she asked.

"No."

"Well, that was clear." She smiled, and I relaxed. "Tell me why?"

So I picked through Poers's arguments, looking for the places where one might suspect the author was concealing something, without knowing exactly what. It was my first talk with my imaginary tutor and the first of many times that she listened patiently, as Malatesta never had, to everything I had to say and then asked a gentle question or offered an observation. Poers makes excuses for Komanare of the Bructs. The king was forever arriving on the scene too late to do anything but patch up a mess his own people had made, always trying to get them to work with, instead of against, one another, and Poers offers one reason after another why each attempt of the king's failed to make a lasting peace. Poers insists that none of it was the king's fault, but Poers shows signs of fudging his historical facts in order to get his arguments to hold water, and I say that if a king can't make his people behave, then yes, he is a bad king.

"Well," my tutor murmured, "at least he stayed."

I woke to the morning call to rise.

In subsequent dreams, we talked about the nature of man and my uncle's nature in particular. We did not always see eye to eye. I sometimes disagreed with her but often talked myself around to her position.

She was amused by my interest in the system of natural categorization that the magus had taught me. I explained the importance of understanding how things are connected.

She only smiled at my earnestness and said, "Everything is connected, Bunny, to everything else. If a man tries to transcribe each connection, thread by thread, he will only make a copy of the world and be no closer to understanding it."

It is a new idea, this categorizing of the world, and I suppose it seems silly to some. They think a fig tree is a fig tree, and what more do they need to know? Ambiades, who was the magus's apprentice far longer than I ever was, never could see the point in it. The magus thought it important, though, and so did I.

I had missed the magus sorely in the time since we had been separated. Terve was a kindhearted old drunk, and my mother and the girls were always willing to listen to me natter, but I'd had no one who was interested in the things I wondered about. Hyacinth used to cover his ears. It was no wonder I defended the magus's work to the tutor I had replaced him with in my dreams.

News of the outside world came to us, even in the baron's outbuildings. Gossip flowed down from the megaron as freely as water, so it wasn't just my own dreams that I had to think about. By late summer we heard that my uncle had retaken most of the hinterland. When he reached Mephia, we heard about the massacre. There was debate, of course, in the barracks, about the rights of the king and the punishment for rebelling. Mephia could have turned on her baron and surrendered to my uncle, but I am not sure any fewer Mephians would have died.

I alone heard the irony as loyal retainers of Baron Hanaktos argued that the king's rule is inviolable and that it was only right that the people of a rebel baron must suffer the consequences of his disloyalty. They didn't seem to consider that the fate of the Mephians could be their own.

There was less news about the islands, or rather, conflicting news. We heard that all the navy had been sunk by Attolia or that none of the navy had been sunk, that various islands had held off attacks or that they had been sacked and burned. We heard that Eddis had swept down from the area of the Irkes Forest and was building fortifications at the base of the foothills. Better that Sounis not be able to retake that property and never threaten Eddis there again, I thought.

As the winter rains set in, the news changed. The king controlled the countryside, and the rebels were walled up in their megarons, but inside with them were the harvests they had brought from their fields. The countryside was nearly bare, and the king needed to feed his army. He chose to withdraw toward his allies farther inland and north to resupply. As the king was driven back, the conversations around me changed: a king who loses turns out not to have been a king at all, but only a usurper, a misruler it is right to overthrow. There was talk of the Eumen conspiracy and the deaths of my uncle's brothers.

The men in the barracks spoke very freely. I had never in my life heard anyone but the magus speak so frankly about the Eumen conspiracy. Talk had always been in whispers and half-finished allusions, as if people feared their words might be reported to the king and they, too, might end up condemned and executed. What I knew I had overheard in bits and snatches until I was apprenticed to the magus, who dismissed with contempt any fear of the king's anger. He told me that my uncle's older brothers were killed and that my uncle took the throne, arrested the conspirators, and in the space of a single day executed them all, leaving no one alive to accuse him of being involved.

No one cared what my workmates talked about among themselves, and they blithely argued my uncle's guilt with an openness impossible in Sounis's capital. Most believed my uncle guilty. I had never had any doubts, nor that my father was involved as well—in exchange for a promise that his son would eventually inherit the throne. My father, a royal bastard who never had any ambitions for himself, wanted his son to be king.

It was only when I proved to be a disappointment

that my father agreed that my uncle should marry and get an heir of his own. Sounis's choice was obvious, and I don't think it ever occurred to him that he might be declined. When the messenger returned from Eddis with a definite "no" for an answer, my uncle was mad with rage. I don't know if it was thwarted greed or pride, but I know that the magus played on both to get my uncle's financing for his expedition to steal Hamiathes's Gift. He was determined that the two countries would be united, and insisted that Sounis could use the gift to force an alliance and a marriage upon Eddis. We know how that turned out.

Our jobs changed for the winter season. We worked on indoor tasks more often, repairing tools, patching clothes, fetching in loads of wood for the household. Helius spent hours carefully carving spoons. There were many days we were out in the cold rain, shaping the land and directing the flow of the water as it drained off. There were dams to be repaired, and ditches dug. We came in cold and wet and huddled around braziers set in a row down the middle of the room. The eaves of the building were open at either end, and the smoke rose to the ceiling and blew out downwind. It was warmer inside than out, but never warm enough. The baron provided blankets, which we wrapped around ourselves. Some of the men pushed their pallets together and slept under shared coverings, but I was not so close to any of the men to feel comfortable joining them. There was jockeying to be closest to the braziers. Ochto allowed no one to force anyone else out. Still, there was a pecking order, and I was near the top, for my man-killer reputation or maybe for the high value my workmates placed on my poetry repertoire.

I was hungry all the time, I longed for a hot bath, and still, I wouldn't have changed my situation for the world. I loved the evenings and the storytelling, even the idle talk among the men. Better the honest and companionable chatter than all the patronoi of my uncle's court.

As a slave I thought I had a better understanding of why those in the villa had turned on me but found I was not entirely correct. Some of the slaves around me would have been happy to fight for their baron. Others weren't so sure. Their willingness to fight was dependent on the certainty of winning, and they wouldn't take on a losing battle for their lord.

"I'm his slave, not his liegeman," said Pundis. "He bought me at market when I couldn't pay my gambling debts. He can sell me just the same. My body is for sale, not my loyalty. I owe him nothing."

"But you belong to your baron," I said. "Surely that means there is something more between the two of you. If you were crippled tomorrow in an accident in his fields, would your baron throw you out in the street to starve? I think not. Not unless he wants to be shamed in front of the patronoi."

I knew that there was at least one blind slave in the kitchens and any number of older slaves around the household who didn't do enough work to justify their keep, but they were kept nonetheless. Hanaktos may have rebelled against his king, but he was a man who honored his obligations to his people.

"Of course there are good masters and bad ones," I said. "There are some that would chuck their slaves out to starve at the end of their lives, and I say, don't fight for them. But even as a slave you are part of your baron's household. It is his responsibility to support you." I lifted a fold of the warm wool blanket I was wrapped in, provided by the baron we worked for. "And yours to support him," I said.

Luca, at the end of my row, laughed harshly, and we turned as one to look at him. "You talk," he said. "It's talk, and that's the all of it."

I shrugged, and Luca laughed again. "You keep saying 'your baron,' Man-killer. Isn't he yours as well? Are you going to rush up the hill to save him, or do you just expect us to?" The other men saw me struck back and laughed. My face reddened. I had no desire at all to defend their baron from any passing murderers, and they could tell. I asked myself whom I *would* fight for, with the people I loved most already dead.

"I'd save Berrone," I muttered, thinking that she'd been kind to me, that she held my debt, even if she was too stupid to know it.

"Oh," said Luca, taking my words in an unintended fashion. "I'd save Berrone, too," and they all laughed. The conversation continued on in a different direction, and I fell silent.

I thought of the servants in the villa at Letnos. Free and slave, they had turned on me. They could have chosen to fight, and they hadn't, probably because they judged it a losing battle, and I couldn't blame them for that. They had seen me in desultory practice with a sword or reading poetry. They'd seen me whimpering after my tutor switched my hands. It was no wonder they thought they would be asking for their own deaths by following me. So they had made their choices and died of it anyway.

I don't know if we would have won the fight in the villa if they had stood with me. I know that it was my fault that they didn't try. My entire life I had been no better than Hyacinth, who chose to betray me and then stood wringing his hands at the consequences. All my life I had been aggrieved to be the prince of Sounis, wailing, "Why me? Why me?" and looking for some way to deny my responsibilities.

Of course the servants had chosen not to follow me; I'd failed them already by refusing to be a man they could believe in. I was, in that sense, as responsible for their deaths as I was for my mother's and sisters'. I was sorry that I hadn't done better for them and glad that I would not fail anyone else.

CHAPTER SIX

IN one of my dreams, my tutor told me a story, and I would like to tell it to you. I don't know why I was dreaming of it, but it has come to my mind often in recent days. It is the story of Morpos's choice.

There once was a young man named Morpos who lived in a small village at the edge of a great forest and was known to all his neighbors as a fine pipe player. The nearby forest was filled with bandits, and hidden in the middle of it was a temple belonging to Atrape, goddess of wise decisions. The temple was guarded by a wolf, and stories told of an opisthodomos filled with treasures. Any one of those treasures—a bag of gold, a necklace of rubies, an enchanted shield or sword—the goddess would give to any who got past the wolf at the door.

Few people took up the offer. Not only was there the wolf to consider, but also the bandits who would catch those who survived a visit to the temple and strip them of anything of value. And those who didn't have gifts of value were stripped of their lives. One wise supplicant had survived to ask the goddess for the gift of prophecy and been given it, only to be captured immediately thereafter. He shouted, "I am going to die, I am going to die," and he did.

Another man asked for a magical sword. He left the temple and became king of the bandits for a time, until he was stabbed in his sleep. The sword rusted away soon after.

One night, as he was sleeping, the young man in our story dreamed of the wolf. In his dream, the wolf revealed that he had once been a king who had offended the gods and been transformed into a beast. He had been sent to guard the temple but was forbidden to attack anyone who came in peace. All that was necessary to enter the temple was to bow to the wolf and offer your throat.

The young man had no desire to go to the temple and gave little thought to his dream. His own wish was to travel far from the forest, to see the world and play his pipes. In the night the wolf came to him again. And again. Finally, late one winter afternoon, the young man was walking at the edge of the forest when rain began to fall. He moved under the trees for shelter but continued to get wet. He moved deeper into the woods, and the rain came down more and more heavily. Ahead he saw a small hut made from branches left by a woodcutter. He ducked through the low opening on one side and came face to face with the largest wolf he had ever seen in his life. It was as high as his chest, with teeth like awls in a row, and there was no hope of escape. Remembering his dream, he offered the wolf his throat. Perhaps if the animal was not hungry, the two might share the shelter awhile.

He was much astonished when he heard the wolf say, "Your grandfather's brother was welcome here once."

Lifting his head, the young man looked around and found himself in a temple with marble floors and pillars and a roof high overhead, not the crossing branches of the hut he had seen from the outside.

"He asked for a sword," said the wolf over his shoulder as he padded away toward the fire in front of the altar.

The young man looked out the open doors of the temple at the rain.

"The bandits will expect you to have gold, and will kill you if you don't," the wolf said. "Though, if you have offended the goddess by leaving without her gift, your problems with the bandits will be inconsequential."

Sighing, the young man moved to the fire. He could at least be warm and dry. He found a tray of food waiting and made himself at home. The wolf was surprisingly good company, telling stories of the people who had come to the temple in the past. Some had taken the gold, hoping to sneak past the bandits. Some had taken weapons and then spent the rest of their lives fighting. The young man played his pipes for the wolf and eventually lay down to sleep as the rain fell outside. In the morning the goddess appeared to ask him what gift from the temple he would choose.

"Does anyone who takes the gold get to keep it?" he asked. "Does everyone who takes the sword end up a bandit?"

The goddess smiled. "Everyone thinks he will be the exception."

Morpos asked if he could have another day to think about it.

"Tomorrow at dawn," said the goddess, "you must choose."

The young man talked things over with the wolf all day and slept well that night. In the morning, when the goddess came and asked if he had made a decision, he said he had.

"Goddess, I must choose a gift from your temple."

"There is no must," said the goddess. "I offer you a gift of your choice, and you may choose to decline."

Morpos knew it was a foolish man who declined the gifts of the gods.

Morpos said, "Then I will take the wolf, if you please."

The goddess smiled. She said, "You may take him with my goodwill, but once he leaves the temple he will not be under my power or yours. He may eat you."

"He may, but he may not. I cannot like my other choices, and indeed, I believe he will not."

The goddess freed the wolf, and he did not eat Morpos. They walked together out of the forest, the wolf warning the bandits away with a wolfish grin and Morpos playing his pipes.

In my dreams, I tasked my tutor. These stories always seem to me to have more holes in them than story. Why did the temple look like a hut on the outside? Did the goddess mean to trick Morpos? Wasn't the temple supposed to be in the middle of a forest? Surely the young man would have noticed if he'd gone that far. Why was the goddess giving away gifts anyway? And why would someone who took a sword or a spear necessarily become a bandit? Obviously it was so some lesson could be taught, but I found it frustrating.

I said, "Why didn't Morpos ask the goddess to turn him into a mouse or a wren so he could escape the bandits that way?"

"Maybe he was afraid she wouldn't turn him back."

The clear light of the library was slanting in through the glass-paneled doorway to my right, falling on the table between my tutor and me and on dust motes hung in the air. The tiny flecks drew my eye, and I watched as they dipped and swirled in invisible currents.

"They are beautiful in the light, are they not?" my tutor asked. They were, catching the sun and shining like tiny stars themselves.

"You know, there are just as many outside the sun's

rays that are invisible," she said. Then, in the way of dreams, she lifted her hand into the air and moved a single dust mote into the light. "And you?" she asked. She lifted her hand again, just beyond the edge of the light, and I knew she held another mote and could move it as easily into the way of the sun, and I said, "No, thank you. I am content where I am."

A few days later I was beaten. It was entirely my own fault. I forgot that my standing in the barracks was not universal in reach.

There were twenty-two of us in the barracks, ranging from fourteen through fifty or so in years. I had as much freedom as any of the men. With permission, we walked down to the shore in our free time if the day was sunny or lounged in the courtyard. On very rare occasions the men of the megaron might go into town for a festival, but that was only once or twice a year, and it had not happened in my time there. Those with friends in the megaron itself could wander up the slope, across the stable yard to the terrace, and from there into the scullery and the kitchens. None of the field hands went farther than that.

I had been up to the kitchens a number of times with a man named Dirnes and Oreus, the one who'd named me Bunny. At the end of the day after my dream of the dust motes, as the last light was just gone, we were walking up past the stables, intending to cross the yard to the entryway into the lower levels of the megaron. Dirnes was friends with one of the lesser cooks, a baker, and he had hopes of coming by a soft roll or two.

As we rounded the corner of the stables, Dirnes rammed into someone coming the other way. It was a direct collision; neither had the time to turn aside, and the other man was knocked backward. Clutching at Dirnes, he fell, taking Dirnes with him to the ground and swearing a blue streak. Dirnes popped up, apologies on his lips, but the other man, a soldier and a drunken one, was having none of it. Still sprawled on the ground, he struck Dirnes, who was bending over him, hard in the mouth.

Instead of falling back, Dirnes stayed for another blow and went on trying to help the man up. Angry, I pulled Dirnes aside and seized the soldier by the shoulders. Using both hands, I heaved him to his feet. Standing, we were eye to eye, and his belligerence was impaired by the close look into my face.

"Better now?" I asked, and he nodded warily.

I turned him toward his friend and pushed him, not too gently, on his way. He gave me an evil look over his shoulder but didn't come back, heading on unsteadily toward the entrance of the megaron instead. Dirnes and Oreus, I realized, had left me and gone back down the path toward the field house.

When I caught up to them, I found to my consternation that Dirnes was angry, and angry with me.

"What did you think you were doing?" he snarled.

"He was drunk. There was no point in letting him hit you."

"Just hope nothing more comes of it," Oreus advised Dirnes, nudging him on toward the barracks. Unsure of my ground, I held my peace.

In the morning, just after the call to rise, as we all were climbing stiffly to our feet and stretching our muscles to face the day's work, there was a disturbance at one of the shed doors. It was the soldier of the night before and another man, his officer, I supposed. They came to complain of an unruly slave. Any number of eyes flicked toward Dirnes, who was still sitting on his pallet. But I rose first, drawing the eye of the soldier.

"Him!" he said. Dirnes had knocked him down, and no doubt the soldier would have settled for exercising his revenge there. He may not even have realized, until I stood, that I was also a slave, but he knew that I was the one who had embarrassed him.

With no other choice in the face of a complaint from a free man, Ochto walked me out to the punishment post and tied my hands to the ring there. When he was finished, my knees no longer held me. I don't know who untied me, but they carried me back to my pallet and left me there while they went off to work.

At the midday break I could get myself to my feet. No one got between me and the first place in line. I had to eat on my knees, the bowl on the ground. Then I lay down again, praying that Ochto wouldn't expect me to work in the fields after the break.

He didn't, and I slept on and off through the end of the day. It was interesting. My back was certainly sore, more damage done there than Basrus had done when he was disguising me as an unruly slave, but it was damage to the skin, nothing much deeper. The pain, no matter how sharp, was not as distressing as the aftermath of Basrus's beating, perhaps because it wasn't my head that hurt, or because I was not so shattered by other events as I had been then.

I felt no particular distress, but a little surprise.

When we were adventuring after Hamiathes's Gift, I had watched the magus beat Eugenides. We'd thought he was no more than a common thief from Sounis's gutters, and had listened to him whine and complain for days. When food was missing, it was easy to blame him. The magus used a riding crop on his back, and holy sacrificial lambs, Gen had come up off the ground like he'd been catapulted. It was as if he was a different person, some stranger who'd manifested in Gen's body. He'd dumped Pol flat onto his back—something I never thought I'd see—and gone for the magus. If Pol hadn't been up again so quickly, the magus was ready to run and dignity be damned. Even with Pol between him and Gen, the magus had been wary.

I thought later that this was the real Gen revealed, the person who'd been hiding behind a screen of complaints and needling humor. But I spent whole days with Eugenides after our adventures, and that Eugenides was exactly the Gen I had traveled with. Maybe I don't know which Gen is real. But I know there was nothing feigned about his emotions after he had been beaten.

Where, I wondered, was *my* wounded pride? Where was my outrage? My self-respect? Nowhere, it seemed. My back hurt. I lay there on my pallet, hoping it would improve soon and wondering, in a distant, unreproachful sort of way, if I was any kind of man at all, and decided that I probably wasn't.

I got up the next day. Very sore but well able to move a shovel. Though reduced to half a shovel again at a try, I was no more pathetic than I had been when I first arrived in Hanaktos's fields, and Ochto didn't seem inclined to push me. I worked alone. Dirnes wasn't speaking to me. He cast me bitter looks in the barracks and turned a disdainful shoulder on me if he caught me looking in his direction.

There was nothing I could do about it, so I worked. Ochto was watching me carefully, and I didn't want to give him the idea that I might be contemplating anything in line with my man-killer reputation. The sweat in my stripes stung, and I was looking forward to rinsing it away with fresh well water once we were back at the barracks. I certainly didn't want to find myself chained again to the ring in the wall by my pallet.

Alas, when we reached the barracks, I discovered an unanticipated difficulty. Ochto had pulled my shirt off before using the cane on my back. In the morning, moving very carefully, I'd managed to get it on. Now I didn't think I could get it off. Not only was it much too painful to lift my arms over my head, but the stupid thing had gotten stuck to me in places. I was at a standstill, staring wistfully at the well, and noticed that several of the other men were looking daggers at Dirnes.

Reluctantly, he came to help, but he was still angry, and his ministrations were not gentle. He pulled on my shirt, and I swore at him. He was more careful then, but his scowl was no less black. I cared little for that once he was tipping the bucket at my neck. It felt divine. He patted me dry with my own shirt, then handed it to me and walked away without a word. I shrugged cautiously and went to lie down for an afternoon rest.

That night he appeared, to my utter amazement, with an iced cake. He could only have gotten it from his friend the cook, and the cook could only have provided it at some significant risk. Yet Dirnes was still clearly angry with me, and I couldn't think why he was asking for favors on my behalf.

"Dirnes," I said, "I don't want your cake."

I did, actually. I wanted it a lot.

The men in the barracks were watching us.

"I didn't ask you to do me any favors!" Dirnes said, very nearly shouting, not just angry, upset. His distress touched me when his anger hadn't, and I suddenly understood what I had failed to see before: that Dirnes was a slave, like me. He had nothing, or anyway, very, very little. I had saved him a beating from the soldier and taken a beating from Ochto that might have been his. He couldn't pay me back. An iced cake, a trivial thing, had no doubt cost him all his credit and more with the cook, and he was still obliged to me, would be obliged until he could somehow sacrifice to do a favor in return, with no end for that obligation in sight. This was a principle of indenture of which I had been unaware. Slaves don't do favors for other slaves.

"Dirnes, I am sorry," I said, reaching out to grab his hand and squeezing it hard. "It was nothing, really." I lifted my arm to show him how much more easily it moved. "By rest day it will be healed. Ochto won't even have left marks."

Dirnes stared at me as if I'd said I was going to grow a pair of wings and fly up to visit the gods. I was uncomfortably aware that everyone else was staring at me, too. Ochto in particular. Hastily I broke the iced cake in half.

"Here, share with me," I said.

My previous life just seemed to slip away. My dreams of the library grew more rare and less vivid. I was more cautious passing soldiers. I knew my place. I enjoyed an occasional tidbit from the kitchen, shared in friendship with Dirnes, and hardly thought about the dinners at the Sounis megaron that lasted until dawn. My uncle was losing more ground, but I was less and less interested in the news of the outside world. Dirnes's pursuit of the cook's goodwill was more important to day-to-day life. Our progress in terracing the baron's landscape and digging the ditches to carry the run-off of the heavy winter rains was what mattered, not battles that took place miles away. When my uncle's army was defeated at Thylos, it hardly seemed to have anything to do with me.

As the rains lessened and the days grew warmer again, I was promoted to wall building and found I had a gift for it. Something about the careful choosing and positioning of stones, something about the way something so durable grew out of an accumulation of small decisions, filled me with satisfaction.

On a day hotter than usual for so early in the year, we had been working on the landward side of a low hill, cut off from the sea breeze. Dirnes had asked for permission to go down to the shore for a quick swim before returning to the barracks to eat. It wasn't unusual for the men to take a quick break in the middle of the day, and Ochto had agreed, so four of us had hurried down to the shore. We'd stayed overlong and were hurrying back, busily undoing all the good of our swim, but unwilling to risk missing our meal entirely. There were plenty of men ready to eat whatever was left in the pot if Ochto thought we were away too long. We were on the road when we heard horsemen behind us and moved off to avoid the dust they would kick into the air. I looked up as they passed and saw my father.

CHAPTER SEVEN

H E was mounted on a bay horse, surrounded by ten or fifteen of his men. I stood stock-still and watched them go by. My father never looked anywhere but ahead.

"Bunny?" Dirnes asked.

I shook myself. "Nothing," I said. "A former master of mine."

"Good one?" he asked.

I shrugged.

Hanaktos was an enemy of the king. Was my father perhaps changing sides? That was a laughable idea; my father is the opposite of changeable. It was far more likely that my uncle had sent my father under a flag of truce to woo Hanaktos back to his side.

I was thoughtful as we continued back to the field house. Should I have called out to my father? I was a failure as a man, a prince, and a son, and I doubted very much that he would care that I was still alive.

Ochto was waiting for us, and there was little I could do but eat my meal and sit on my pallet with my back against the plastered wall while the other men lay down to rest. Was I of any use to my father at all? Would it make any difference to anyone but me if I stayed right where I was?

"There is no wolf to eat you, Bunny," my tutor reminded me. "Stay where you are, and no man will know and no god will be displeased." She pointed to a space in the air where I could see nothing. She pursed her lips and exhaled, and a tiny mote appeared, moved by her breath into the broad beam of light. "What do you want, Zecush?" she asked.

My chin dropped to my chest, and I woke, lifting my head abruptly and slamming it into the wall behind me. Eyes watering, I realized that I had been asleep. My tutor had not in fact appeared in the field house of Baron Hanaktos.

The others were still at rest. The room was full of indirect light, though the sun came in none of its doorways and there were no dust motes shining in any sunbeams. It was warm, and I was sweating. I thought of another swim with longing, but I wasn't a free man, to swim when I pleased. I swam, as I rested and as I ate, when I had permission. I was a slave, owned by the baron, waiting for the call to rise and go with the others to work in the fields. When it came, I pulled myself to my feet and followed Ochto out the door.

✦ ✦ ✦

Out among the olives, as I began to fit stones into place in the wall I was building, I thought, as if it were the first time, about what I wanted. All of my life people had chosen for me. My father or the king of Sounis, his magus, or the king's other advisors. All my life they had made choices for me, and I had resented it. Now the choice was mine, and once it was made, I would have no right to blame anyone else for the consequences. Loss of that privilege, to blame others, unexpectedly stung.

I didn't want a choice; I wanted to stay right where I was and build walls and share poetry with an avid audience and enjoy a swim with friends, but I didn't want it to be my *choice*.

Goaded by self-disgust, I worked faster, picking the largest rocks and throwing them into place and then watching in rage when they landed awry. Ochto sent Runeus to give me a hand, but Runeus collided with my glare and backed away. Shrugging helplessly at Ochto, he went to work elsewhere. Only when I caught the tip of one finger between two rocks and stood cursing and swearing like, well, just like a field hand, did I stop. I wiped tears of frustration out of my eyes and faced the truth.

I had been happy. And I could stay if I wanted to. I could spend my life contemplating olives and reciting old plays to a friendly audience and building excellent walls that would outlast my lifetime. I could save the occasional coin that came to me by way of the baron's feast day generosities and in time buy a book or two, a blank scroll, ink. In thirty years I might be the poet Leuka. He wasn't a field hand, but he had been a slave, and his poetry has survived him by four hundred years. No one would know but me and the gods, and I was sure the gods didn't care. All I had to do was hold my peace, and I knew that I couldn't do it.

What would I choose if I could have anything? Well, I wouldn't be useless. I would be the statesman my father wanted and the prince my country needed. But that wasn't what I was offered. I was still the same poor excuse for a prince that I had always been. Quite likely I would fail to be of any use at all—to my father or anyone. When the rebelling barons were put down, I would see my uncle marry and produce an heir far superior to me, and I would be despised as useless and unwelcome even in my own home. That was what I was choosing.

I wonder if people always choose what will make them unhappy.

In the evening we walked back to the barracks. We ate our late meal as the light began to fade from the sky. Up in the megaron, guests would be gathering to dine. As the other men were settling down, tired from a day of hard work, I picked through the small collection of shells and rocks that I had found while at the shore and selected my favorites. Then I wrapped them in a rag I was using as a pocket and tucked them into the waist of my pants.

Curious, the other men grew still and watched. Standing, I turned to Ochto and said, "I'm going."

Ochto started to give a puzzled assent, then realized I wasn't stepping out to relieve myself before bed.

"You can't get far, Zecush," he said.

"I'm not going far."

He looked up toward the megaron and over at Dirnes. He must have heard of my comment on the road earlier in the day. "We don't get to choose our masters."

"I do," I said.

"And why would I let you go?"

I swallowed. "We all have to make choices, Ochto. I'm sorry."

He stared at me. With a word, or just the wave of his hand, he could stop me. The men in the barracks would jump up and seize me. The chain for the bracelet that was still on my wrist was right by his hand. His cane of office hung by the door.

He also knew that I could have walked away without saying anything, as if on my way to the latrine, and he wouldn't have had any hint that I was gone until it was far too late.

He shook his head slowly. "You were never a slave," he said.

"Berrone bought me for gold," I said honestly, but Ochto shook his head again.

"Gold doesn't make a slave, and it doesn't always buy one. You stop work every time a woodcock sings. I've watched you move the mother scorpion out of the way when you should be setting stones in a wall and waste half a morning watching a grasshopper. You have no sense. What will you do out there in the world, Bunny?"

"Whatever the gods and the king ask of me," I said.

"Ah," said Ochto. "He is our baron, but he never was yours, was he?"

"Indeed, he is not," I said. "You still have to choose."

"I know nothing of the business of gods and kings," said Ochto, and he looked away. I waited for him to turn back, then realized that he had made his decision.

There had been no sound in the barracks. I turned to nod farewell to the men who had been my companions and found them also looking away. Swallowing a rock in my throat, I turned back to the door.

"Should we come?" Luca's voice rose sardonically. He sat at the far end of the room, with one knee pulled up and caught in the circle of his arms. He spoke, but he still didn't look in my direction.

My own eyes dropped toward the floor. "Believe me, that if I were you, Luca," I said, "I would stay right here."

In the twilight I headed up the path to the stables and from there to the kitchens. They were a bustle of activity, and I had no trouble slipping in unnoticed. I sidled up to one of the houseboys and followed him until an opportune moment when he was alone in the corridor between the kitchens and the main rooms of the megaron.

"Lend me your shirt for a minute," I said.

"Why?" He recognized me. I was familiar enough that he wasn't frightened, just puzzled.

"Because if you don't, I'm going to hit you really hard and take it anyway."

He looked around for help, but we were alone.

"Better make up your mind quick," I said, and lifted my fist. He loosened his laces and pulled the shirt over his head.

Wearing only his undershirt, he said, "I'll tell."

I pulled the overshirt out of his hand. "You do that," I said as I hurried back toward the kitchen. He ran off in the opposite direction, and I stopped. I'd headed toward the kitchen only so that he would head the other way. It would take him longer to find someone to listen to his story, and by the time he came back I would be gone. I reversed direction and headed farther into the megaron. I pulled the shirt on as I went, and pushed up the sleeves of my rough work shirt underneath it. The overshirt was tight, but it covered enough of the dirty cloth underneath that I could pass for a few moments unnoticed as I found a stairway and hurried up to the residence above.

I'd been in the Hanaktos megaron several times. Berrone's room was where I expected it to be, and the door was open, making it easy to confirm that I was in the right place. I knocked on the frame, and when I heard her voice, I rushed inside.

"Mistress," I cried out, dropping to my knees in the sitting room, where she was, thank the gods, instead of visiting some household pet somewhere. "Like a goddess, you have aided me, and I beg your aid again."

I knelt there with my hands clasped in front of me, praying, not to her but to the old god of deception, Eugenides, that she wouldn't recognize me. She didn't. Not at all. I'd been worried that she would see the prince of Sounis. It hadn't occurred to me that I wouldn't strike some chord. That she would look at me without any glint of recognition.

Hastily, I explained that I had been a poor lost soul when she had rescued me from certain death in the galleys.

"Oh," she said, "you're that slave that I bought."

"Please help me," I said. "You are my only hope in a dark, dark world."

I told her a tale of woe and horror that could have come straight from the stage. I was the son of a minor landowner. At the untimely death of my father, his partner, an evil okloi, had made off with all the money in the business. My sister and I had been sold into slavery to pay debts.

"They took her away from me, though I tried to stop them. I was sold to an overseer of a farm on Letnos. Your father, of blessed renown, mistress, was the farm owner. He was a good master, and I was not unhappy, but you must believe that I ached and grieved for my sister." I thought of Eurydice then, though I hadn't meant to, and suddenly the tears I faked for my imaginary sister were all too real. "But she was not lost, mistress. In a chance that could only have been decreed by the gods, she was sold to the owner of a villa nearby. He was a brutal man, mistress, and his overseer worse. Not like the honorable man who runs your father's farm."

I looked up to see if I was laying it on too thick, but Berrone was watching with fascinated horror. Her servant woman, however, was skeptical. She was eyeing me from the doorway.

"He attacked her, mistress. What could I do but defend her? And so"—I hung my head—"you see me now, a man-killer, despised and despairing."

"What can I do?" Berrone asked breathlessly.

Success, I thought. "I have seen, just today, a man coming to dinner with your father. He was a friend of my father's. He will vouch for me, and I know he will help me recover the money that was stolen. My sister and I can be free again. I can pay a blood debt to the owner of the man I killed."

"He doesn't deserve it," cried Berrone. "The beast."

"I do not care," I cried. "I will pay anything to free my sister. Mistress, can you help me?"

The steward summoned by Berrone stared at the mess of broken crockery on the carpeted floor.

Berrone hadn't understood the first time I explained my plan, so I had explained it again more slowly. Hiding behind the curtain to her bedroom, I could only hope she would remember her part.

"Who was it?" the steward asked.

"I don't know which one, but you'll know him when you see him. He has wine down his shirt."

"He spilled some on his shirt, you say? I understand now, mistress, and I will deal with him." The steward went off to chase down the houseboy, whose story of being assaulted by a scarred slave would be dismissed as a lie concocted to explain the absence of his shirt with its incriminating stain.

"What now?" asked Berrone, turning to me as I stepped out from behind the curtain.

I looked at her, sitting on an upholstered stool with her knees together and her ankles apart like a little girl, her hands clutching her skirts, and my conscience was suddenly painfully wrung. I was returning a bitter payment for her kindnesses, even if they were stupid kindnesses.

"Are—are you sure you want to do this?" I stammered.

"Oh, *yes*," said Berrone.

Over Berrone's head, I saw her maid, and from her expression, I knew that she hadn't been fooled by my theatrics. Pinned by her gaze, I froze.

She stood, arms crossed and unmoving. At last even

Berrone realized that some decision still hung in the balance, and she swung around on her stool and clutched her maid around the waist.

"Oh, Sylvie, don't be a spoilsport. Don't, please?" And I still waited, because there was no point in lying to Sylvie. The maid looked at Berrone, and her face softened. She nodded.

Freed from my momentary paralysis, I stifled my remorse and began to explain the next step. A new shirt to go under my houseboy overshirt. Then I would go down to dinner. The houseboy would be in his dormitory, probably nursing his bruises, and not nearby, ready to denounce me. I would wait on the men as they dined and seize my chance to speak to "my father's friend."

The maid fetched a clean shirt for me, and under cover of helping me with it, she said, "You are no slave; that much of your story is true."

"I will get her in terrible trouble if anyone finds out she helped me," I confessed.

"Hush, there is no trouble I cannot bring her out of, and if I tell her to keep silent, she will. It will be her secret and keep her warm for weeks." She looked me in the eye. "You will remember what you owe her."

I promised I would.

Suddenly the door was opened, and on the threshold was an angry young man I recognized after a moment of blank incomprehension as Berrone's brother. I dropped to my knees and hastily started picking up the pieces of the shattered amphora still on the floor.

"Berrone!" he shouted. "You've gotten Timos in trouble, and now he can't dress me for dinner."

"I'm sorry," said Berrone. She was flustered and looked to me. If her brother noticed, we all were doomed, but he was too interested in his own problem.

"That doesn't help me, does it? My long knife needs to be polished and honed and its sheath oiled." He looked sly and pleased with himself. "We are to wear them to dinner."

I swallowed, my mouth dry. I had meant to be reunited with my father. I had meant to whisper in his ear and then slip away to the stables to meet him when he left. My father was the baron's guest, and though I knew that Hanaktos was a traitor, it had not occurred to me that he could fail to honor the most basic law of hospitality. Still, if Berrone's brothers had been told to wear their knives to dinner, I had to believe that my father might not leave the dining hall alive.

"I—I can hone and oil it for you, master," I heard myself say.

"Can you? Have you done it before?"

"Yes, master."

"Come along, then," he said. He strode away without another word to his sister, and I rose to follow him.

· CHAPTER EIGHT ·

I had expected the men to be in a private dining room on couches, my father alone with the baron and his murderous sons, but the household was eating at the long tables in the great room. My father was there, with the men who had accompanied him. Most of them I recognized; the rest I knew by their uniforms. They were scattered in ones and twos down the length of the tables, with the baron's men on either side. None were at the head table, not even my father, an insult so stunning I was surprised he had tolerated it. He was flanked by two beefy guardsmen and looked smaller than I had ever seen him.

The head table held only Baron Hanaktos and male members of his household. His eldest son sat beside him, but the other sons were at the lower tables. The baron's insult would work against him. As a mere houseboy I couldn't have approached the head table, but I could easily make my way to my father.

With an amphora under my arm, I moved from man to man along the table, pouring out the wine. My father saw me drawing nearer, and each time I came to his eye, he looked away with no sign of recognition. I admired his self-control until I bent close and said, just loud enough to be heard over the roar in the room, "Baron Hanaktos means to kill you tonight."

My father jumped as if I'd stuck him with a white-hot awl. He had watched me filling wine cups all the way down the length of the table without any idea who I was, and only by my voice did he know me. He was swinging around to look up into my face.

"Hold still," I hissed in his ear, and he froze, either because of what I'd said or because he had succeeded in turning enough to see me over his shoulder.

"The household is wearing knives," I said. "I will tell each of your men to be ready to fight when I drop my amphora."

I wasn't sure he was listening. His face was growing darker and darker. I'd seen him in a rage often enough to know that the next words out of his mouth were going to be easily audible over the roar of the room. Hastily I tipped the wine cup onto the table, hoping that anyone looking just then might have thought the spill preceded my father's anger instead of following it.

"Sorry! Sorry!" I said loudly, and leaned in close enough as I wiped up the spill to snarl, "Hold your tongue!" under my breath.

That was something I'd never imagined doing, even in my freest flights of fancy, and my father was stunned silent. He sat motionless while I first used the cloth I had over my arm to wipe up the spill, then refilled the wine cup and pushed it into his hand. He took it mechanically, still staring at me.

"Be ready when I drop the amphora," I said, and started to move on. His iron-hard grasp closed on my wrist, and I almost despaired, but he only emptied his cup in a single gulp and put it on the table to be refilled, his face blank. As I leaned to fill the cup, I felt a weight drop into the pocket stitched to my tunic.

Stepping back, I reached with my free hand and hunted for what I'd felt. I knew it as soon as I touched it, his lion's head ring, to show his men in case they didn't recognize me, either.

Hastily I moved to the next man. I didn't dare look toward the head table, where the baron sat. I doubted that he had heard anything of Timos's story—there was no reason to mention something as trivial as a house-boy's fabricated story to the head of the household—but I still didn't want to catch the baron's eye. I moved on to the next man, and the next. There were no ladies present. It wasn't going to be an event for ladies.

I bent to whisper into the ear of each of my father's men as I poured the wine, and showed them his ring, holding it in my fist and opening my fingers briefly to allow them to see it. When I'd worked my way around the table, I left the dining room. My father's small group of men had no chance against an entire megaron. They needed to escape, and quickly. I left my amphora in a niche and ran down the flight of shallow steps outside the great room to the pronaos of the house, where the doors out to the forecourt were standing open. No one took any notice of me as I cut across to the narrow gate at the top of the ramp that led down to the stables.

The baron liked his horses, and the stables were extensive. There was a separate shed reserved for guests' animals, and I went there first to find a stable boy. "The baron's guests leave early. Bring the horses up."

The stable boy was already nodding in compliance and getting to his feet when someone behind me spoke.

"Since when did you become a houseboy, slave?"

I turned slowly. It was the soldier who had beaten Dirnes and cost me the skin off my back.

He smiled unkindly. Unsure how to react, the stable boy looked from one of us to the other. I was at a standstill. I couldn't bluff my way past the soldier, and I couldn't bully him as I had Timos. I could attack him, but I wouldn't win, and while we were fighting, the stable boy would run screaming for help.

The soldier knew it, and his smile broadened. "You'll come with me to see the captain," he said, and nodded toward the open doorway of the stable. Swearing under my breath, I walked as he indicated. As I passed outside, a dark movement at the door frame caught my eye. I stopped abruptly and said over my shoulder to the stable boy, "He'll find out about you soon enough."

The soldier also stopped, as I'd hoped he would, and

turned back to the stable boy, who was protesting his innocence but backing away nonetheless. The soldier grabbed him by the collar and pulled him along through the doorway, where Ochto, his face obscured by a piece of cloth, hit the soldier from behind and dropped him like a sack of dirt. Dirnes, coming from the other side, was naked to the waist and had his shirt in his hands. He wrapped the boy's head with it. There was a muffled cry, and then Ochto dropped the stable boy as well.

"Did they see us?" Dirnes asked fearfully.

Ochto shook his head.

"Get his feet," he said.

He and Dirnes carried the soldier into the feed room. I lifted the lightweight stable boy on my own, even as I asked Ochto what in the name of all that was sacred he thought he was doing.

"Helping you," said Dirnes.

"Why?"

They put the soldier down, and Ochto straightened to look me in the eye. "Because I know nothing about kings and princes, but I know men."

"Are you *mad*?" I asked.

Ochto shrugged. "In a few minutes I'll have to go up to the kitchens to tell the steward that you are missing. I'll tell him that when you didn't come in for the night, I suspected you had run off and sent Dirnes to see if you'd been incapacitated at the abattoir. I'll say I followed him, and when we found nothing, we came back together. I doubt the steward will pursue it."

Indeed, he would not. I had forgotten that in order to report me missing, the steward would first have to tell the baron that he'd been keeping secrets for his daughter. "Tell him"—I licked my lips—"tell him, least said, soonest mended."

"You'll want to find another stable boy quickly," Ochto advised. Dirnes pulled his shirt back on and nodded to me; then the two of them headed back down to the barracks.

"Come with me!" I said after them.

They paused, even as I reconsidered. I might not live out the night, and no one knew of their part in recent events. "If you like," I added lamely.

Dirnes waved farewell.

"You know where to find us," said Ochto, and they disappeared into the dark.

So, I found another hand in the stables and told him that the horses were wanted, and then I made my way back up the forecourt of the megaron and from there to the great room.

I'd collected my amphora, and I began pouring wine again. When I reached my father, I told him of the horses and then continued working my way along the table. I'd made it only halfway when I looked up from a cup I was filling and saw Timos standing in a doorway opposite. He stepped out of sight, but he'd seen me, I was certain. There was nothing I could do except continue on to the next of my father's men, skipping everyone between, and hoping none of the slighted drinkers called me back.

I spoke to three more of my father's soldiers, but they were the last because Timos was waiting for me at the end of the table. He'd gone to get help and was flanked by several husky housemen. I dropped the amphora, hoping to touch off the fighting, but to my consternation, one of the housemen caught it. He then passed it to Timos, who held it tight. Strong hands gripped me and began to heave me across the floor. I drew my breath to shout, but someone covered my mouth. I tried to bite the hand that was stifling me, but its owner just ground it harder against my mouth, forcing my lips against my teeth. I dug in my heels and surged against the men, sending all of us crashing into Timos. The men holding my arms pulled me back again.

It takes more time to tell of it than to live through it. The whole great room was frozen in surprise, but I knew that at any moment the baron would recognize me or would signal his men to attack, while my father's men hesitated, waiting for their signal, and Timos was still clutching the amphora to his chest like his lost reputation. I threw myself forward again, trying to hit him with my shoulder. Finally, he lifted the amphora high to keep it safe, and I kicked him hard where it would hurt the most. The amphora dropped.

It smashed on the tiles, and the room exploded. Benches tumbled over, and men shouted. My father's voice rose over the rest as he shouted for his men to press for the forecourt. The hands holding me weakened, and I struggled free. My father was soon surrounded by his men and began forcing his way to the doors. There were smaller fights all over the room, but the element of surprise was no longer in the baron's favor, and enough men knew that the horses were waiting. They had a goal to reach instead of standing their ground to fight to the death surrounded by enemies.

A man came at me with a knife, and I punched him in the face with the accumulated force of a thousand thousand shovels full of dirt. His eyes rolled up as he slowly tipped backward. Poor Timos was still crouched on the floor, and I stepped over him to grab the shoulders of another man and throw him aside. Ahead of me was someone I recognized, Hanaktos's son Kimix. I called his name, and when he looked up in surprise, I punched him, too.

By this time the fighting had spilled through the doors of the great room and down the steps into the entryway of the megaron. I hurried to catch up, dodging between knives and delivering a blow or two when I could, but mostly just grabbing my opponents and tossing them into each other in order to get past.

Outside of those at the dinner, no one seemed to have known of the baron's inhospitable plans. The guards in the forecourt certainly didn't know whom to fire upon. In all the confusion, there was no organized attempt to stop us. My father and I were side by side as we raced down the steps toward the waiting horses. I snatched a set of reins from a startled stable hand and scrambled into a saddle. The gates of the court were still standing open. I turned my horse toward them as the baron himself appeared on the porch above me. Our eyes met, and in the flickering light he knew exactly who I was. He launched himself from the top of the stairs and nearly knocked me from the saddle. Dropping to the ground as the horse reared, he ruthlessly used the long knife he carried to stab the animal in the belly. The horse screamed, tottered on its back legs, and slammed to the ground. I rolled away, struggled to my feet, and raced for the gates, Hanaktos not far behind me. The gates were too far away, and there was no sanctuary behind them anyway, so I turned to face the enraged baron as he raised his knife in a brief moment of triumph.

My father rode him down. His horse's shoulder sent the baron flying, and my father's hand was in mine before I was aware of reaching for him, and then he was pulling me up behind him. Arrows and crossbow bolts clattered on the stones around us as we raced for the gates, and then we were safe in the darkness beyond.

Trusting the horses to keep to the road, we rushed downhill. At the bottom of the hill, the road divided, one part going on into the town and the other circling outside it. We stopped there, to listen for pursuit and gather our bearings. The darkness that had hidden us from enemy fire was treacherous to us as well. The horse was staggering under our weight, and my father leaned forward to thump its shoulder in appreciation. The other riders stopped beside us, their horses stamping and jostling. Several men bent to catch up the reins of riderless animals, their owners lost to the quarrels and arrows shot from the megaron or perhaps lost in the megaron before my father's men reached the courtyard. By ear as much as by eye, I counted. Only ten of the fifteen men my father had brought were with us.

"Conyx is dead," said a voice in the dark.

"Troyus as well."

No one had seen the others fall. If they were wounded, they would be cared for. If they were wealthy, they might eventually be ransomed or bargained for in other ways if events went against Hanaktos. If events went for Hanaktos, they might someday be in the very barracks I had left, working for Ochto, building stone walls in my place.

Unexpectedly my father swiveled in the saddle, bringing one arm over my head and seizing me in a bear hug. His arms locked around me, and mine around him, although on my part it might have been less affection and more a result of being dragged off-balance and in great danger of falling off the horse. The beleaguered animal sidestepped uncomfortably. I tightened my hold on my father a little further, swung my leg free, and, as he reluctantly released me, dropped to the ground. My father caught me by the hand as I slipped down and held it while he looked into my face, making out what he could in the darkness.

"I will kill the man who did this," he swore. "With my own hands I will kill him."

I laughed. My father might kill Baron Hanaktos, but I had no doubts that the cunning slaver was long gone.

CHAPTER NINE

WE rode into the middle of the armed camp just before dawn. On foot, feeling my way through familiar fields and groves of trees, I had led my father's men in a game of cat and mouse across Hanaktos's land. Unable to find us on the main road, our pursuers soon retreated to the megaron. When we'd covered enough distance to hide the sound of our hoofbeats, I had mounted one of the spare horses, and we had ridden inland, first picking our way slowly in the dark and then moving faster when the moon rose.

As we dismounted, I found myself seized by my father's men. Grateful for their escape, they nearly squeezed the life out of me and thumped me on the back until I staggered. My father tore me free and pulled me toward the open doorway of a well-lit tent. In silhouette, I saw a man I would recognize in any light and threw myself at him in delight, shouting, "Magus, you are returned!"

"I returned?" he said. "It is you who are—"

When he stopped, I knew the light from the tent had fallen on my face.

"Dear gods all above and around us," the magus said,

staring at me. Measuring myself against him, I realized we now saw eye to eye. I had not seen him since I was exiled to Letnos, and he'd been forbidden to write to me. All I had heard of him had been rumors, first that he was an Attolian traitor, then that he was an Eddisian one, which I had dismissed as ridiculous. I had never doubted him, and suspected from the beginning that Eugenides might have had a hand in his disappearance. I hadn't realized how much I had counted on the magus to solve all of Sounis's problems until I realized we stood shoulder to shoulder and he was not in fact larger than life.

He grabbed me and held me tight. I had to pull myself away before I began to blubber like a baby. Fortunately he deferred to my dignity and let me go. He turned to my father. "Thank the heavens you have rescued him."

"Backward to the facts, as usual," my father said as he swept the magus and me into the tent ahead of him. "He has rescued us and brought us safely out of Hanaktos's trap."

"It *was* a trap."

My father said testily, "I told you that we had little choice but to try. Hanaktos holds the bargaining power. Melenze is Ferria's dog, and their fee for aiding us will be the Melenze–Sounis pass, which they are filling as we speak."

From which I gathered that Melenze was assembling its army on our northern border and offering to come to save us from Attolia. No doubt they wanted the port of Haptia back as well, to be the final link in their trade route from the center of the Continent to the Middle Sea.

"And what cost doing business with Hanaktos?" snapped the magus. "Even if he hadn't spitted you? Our entire country the lapdog of the Medes?"

"Always yapping about the Medes. What have they to do with Hanaktos?" responded my father. "I have said already, the Medes are too far away to rule over us with any attention. Let them have their tribute, and they will leave us to ourselves."

"I have told you, the Medes will wipe us out of exis-tence!" insisted the magus. "As they have every other nation with which they have 'allied.'"

Clearly Father and the magus had had no rapproche-ment in my absence.

"Hanaktos held my wife and my daughters and my son," my father said. "Tell me, then, how shall I not deal with him?"

"H-he didn't have me," I stuttered. "I was under his nose, but he didn't know it." My mind raced. Perhaps help had arrived after Basrus carried me off. Perhaps the fire had been put out before it was too late. "My mother and sisters are not dead?"

"They are hostage," said my father heavily, "held by rebels who have some connection with Hanaktos, who claimed that he wants no more part in this rebellion, only the settling of it. He offered a mediation and restoration of Sounis."

"He is in league with the Medes," said the magus.

"You have no proof," my father countered while I was still reeling at the idea that Eurydice and Ina and my mother were somewhere living and not dead in the destruction of the villa on Letnos. It was a moment before I paid more attention to the exchange of fire between my father and the magus. They were deep into what was obviously a familiar rut.

"Surely this is my uncle's decision," I pointed out. Their argument cut off more sharply than I anticipated.

My father said, "Your uncle is dead."

The magus said, "You are Sounis."

CHAPTER TEN

I should have stayed in Hanaktos and built walls. "More than a month ago," the magus said when I asked him how long it had been since the death of my uncle. "Sounis had a fever before a day of hard riding and died that night."

The magus and my father had told no one except a few officers. To the men in the army they had said the king was elsewhere, raising more forces.

"Your Majesty"—the magus addressed me, and I flinched—"we are near to being overwhelmed by Eddis and Attolia. They only wait for us to be at our weakest. We have lost the navy and most of the islands. Eddis has fortified the ground at the base of the Irkes pass. The Mede emperor and the prince of Melenze are also waiting. There is a chance that if Melenze knew your uncle who was Sounis had died, they would not wait to make an alliance with us; they would attack."

"Attolia and Melenze will tear us apart between them," said my father, and got a glare for it from the magus.

"We need to make an alliance with Melenze before the news gets out," said the magus while I stared at him like a pilchard.

"We need to make an alliance with the Medes before war breaks out between Melenze and Attolia with us in the middle," my father said more forcefully.

"The Medes," the magus countered, trying to keep his temper, "started this rebellion, direct this rebellion, and nearly saw you dead tonight!" He pinched his nose and drew a deep breath. He said to my father, "Hanaktos will be on your heels."

"Hanaktos, thanks to my son, doesn't know where we are." He told the magus of our trip through the dark.

"Thanks to His Majesty," the magus said, and my father seemed startled at the correction but not displeased. On the contrary, he suddenly looked much like Ina when she has all her embroidery threads arranged to her satisfaction. He looked so pleased that I checked over my shoulder to see if there might be someone else behind me who had drawn his attention.

"Your Majesty," said the magus deferentially, trying to restart the conversation. "I am sorry to put you in this position, but I believe Hanaktos might still attack."

"He has no idea where we are!" my father argued.

"The Mede will have told him!" said the magus.

"The Mede again!" my father said, throwing up his hands.

"The Mede what?" said a voice behind me. "What will I have told whom?"

I spun around to see a man standing in the open doorway of the tent. Only the lack of reaction from my father and the magus stopped me from jumping at his throat. He was clearly a Mede.

"Aah," he said in theatrical delight. "The rumors running around the camp are true: Your lost lamb has been found."

Then he looked at the magus and said pointedly, "Won't you please present me to your king?," confirming that he'd been listening outside the tent and had heard everything that had been said within. Which is a reason you should not discuss important business in a tent or at least should keep your voices down if you do, as my father and the magus emphatically had not. The Mede was pleased at the magus's discomfort, and his saturnine smile showed it.

The magus stiffly said, "Your Majesty, permit me to present the ambassador Akretenesh from His most Excellent and Sovereign Majesty Ghaznuvidas, emperor of the Mede."

Good thing that I hadn't strangled him, I thought.

"I am most honored, Your Majesty," said Akretenesh, with a deep bow.

"You are welcome, Your Excellency," I said, tilting my head, probably a little too far. "I am of course gratified, though very surprised, to receive you in such"—I couldn't think of a diplomatic word and settled for—"unusual circumstances."

"Allow me to say, and to speak for my master when I do, how pleased we are to be introduced to you in any circumstances. We are delighted that you are found safe and returned to your anxious parent."

He turned to my father then. "And your wife and daughters are as well, I trust?"

"No," said my father. "It was a trap." He told him of Hanaktos's treachery.

The Mede was horrified, stopping just short of saying that it was the sort of thing one could expect from barbarians like us. He asked how my father intended to free my mother and sisters, and my father had no answer except, "They do not matter. Only Sounis is important."

I glared at him, but he would not meet my eye.

"Indeed," the Mede murmured, forfeiting any tolerance I might have had for him. He turned to me and said earnestly, "Your Majesty, you can count on our support. We have the ships to patrol your coast and to retake your islands from Attolia. We have the armies to aid you here on land. With our help, you can be secure on your throne."

I said, "Our thanks, Excellency. I believe we would benefit more from your gold . . . as Attolia did."

Akretenesh's expression didn't change, but it was a hit. We both knew that the Mede emperor had provided gold to Attolia, thinking he was buying control over her country from a foolish queen. If he had been successful, Akretenesh wouldn't have been in a tent in the dark with me, offering his emperor's support. Instead,

Attolia would be a subject state, invading us with those very same Mede armies at her back.

"Permit me to say that your youth is refreshing, Your Majesty, but perhaps it should be tempered by experience. Will you have a regent?"

"Nonsense," said my father.

"Surely he is not confirmed king? Not yet elected by your barons?"

It's true that the kings in Sounis are confirmed in a meeting of all the barons, but I was the appointed heir. My father explained that in such cases, the Barons' Meet was a formality.

He extolled my many virtues in the fight at Hanaktos and the escape afterward. A year earlier I would have been gratified. Contrariwise, all I felt was resentment at being talked of as if I were a tent pole. Behind my father, the magus was signaling. He hadn't liked my comment about the Attolian gold, and he didn't want me pricking the ambassador.

"He is a fine king already!" my father said in conclusion.

Eyeing the magus, I demurred. "His Excellency may be right, Father," I said. The magus nodded, and my father stared at me.

"Perhaps the right regent," hinted the magus.

My father opened his mouth to call me a fool and froze. As the magus had pointed out earlier, I was his king. His ambitions had elevated me beyond his dictatorial control. He turned on the magus instead. "This is your doing," he snarled. "You have corrupted him with your incessant nattering. Next he will say that we go to Melenze."

"I do," I said. "I do say we should go to Melenze. You will take the army north immediately."

That was the bitter end of my brief moment in the sunshine of my father's affection. It was also the beginning of a shouting match between the magus and my father that could be heard on the other side of the camp, never mind the other side of the tent walls.

My father accused the magus of manipulating me and of being a power-hungry monster. The magus called my father beef witted and lamented the combination of his dim wits and his short temper. All this in front of the Mede ambassador. My father has always been prone to temper, and the magus acid-tongued, but they were like schoolboys. I hardly knew the magus. I feared I had made a terrible mistake following his lead, and Akretenesh didn't help, spreading oil on the waters only to set fire to it.

I didn't know what to do. I stood there indecisive, until suddenly the magus fell silent and seemed to be staring intently at the ground. So strange was his behavior that even my father paused in his diatribe. The magus looked up, and his face was almost purple. He took a single explosive breath, the color drained out of his face, and he fell at my feet.

"Magus!" I squealed, and dropped to my knees beside him. I shouted at my father to call the camp physician and cradled the magus's head. His color was better, but he was insensible. I ignored the Mede ambassador's hastily excusing himself and listened for a heartbeat. I sighed in relief when I heard it and then waited impatiently for the physician.

The magus stirred in my arms and whispered brokenly, "I am fine. My tent, take me to my tent."

My father returned with the physician, both looking concerned. I helped lift the magus and carry him to his tent. We laid him on a bed there, and I stood wringing my hands while the physician listened to his heart and tried to get him to speak. I told my father that he should prepare for Hanaktos's attack. My father wanted to disagree, but he looked to the magus, lying nearly insensible on the bed, and acquiesced. I told him that if Hanaktos did not attack, we should move north anyway, as soon as possible. He clamped his jaw and, when I didn't back down, bowed without speaking and left. The magus's hand lifted, and he reached for me.

I went to him and bent to hear him as he whispered again. "Speak to you," he said hoarsely. "Private."

"Yes," I said, "yes," and chased away the physician and his assistants, who seemed to have nothing useful to do anyway.

When we were alone, I bent over the magus again. He

opened his eyes and sat up so quickly I nearly knocked heads with him.

"You fraud!" I said.

He held up his hands for silence. "Indeed," he said quietly, "I could think of no other way out of the tent. Your Majesty, we must get you out of the camp immediately."

"We will be prepared for Hanaktos's attack," I assured him.

"There is more, I am afraid. I fear that you will be conveniently dead in the attack, and I can think of no way to prevent this except to flee." He watched my face closely as he said, "Akretenesh has too many supporters here."

He was warning me that I was going to be assassinated by my father's men.

I thought he couldn't be serious. Things couldn't be that bad, but he was already up from his bed, stuffing clothes into a set of saddlebags.

"Why is the Mede ambassador in the camp at all?" I asked.

"Your father. He cannot stand the idea that Melenze wants Haptia back and thinks that the Medes are a better ally. I am sorry. My every effort to change his mind has entrenched him deeper. I should have stayed in the mountains of Eddis."

I shook my head. No one could have convinced my father to cede land back to the Melenzi. "Akretenesh only suggested a regent in order to set you and my father against each other."

"Indeed. It was a fine distraction from the immediacy of Hanaktos's attack. We must get you safely away."

"But they need me as a pawn," I said. "Why would they want me dead?"

The magus snatched a few things from a writing desk. I'd forgotten his lopsided smile. "A *pawn*," he emphasized. "You are not one. They cannot afford to have you independent of their control, with your father's army at your back."

"I saw your signals," I protested.

The magus shook his head. "Akretenesh saw as well."

"Ah," I said, "er."

"Indeed. Not only have we convinced him that you are more cunning than they realized, but we've also made it clear that if you were a puppet, it would be me pulling your strings. A mistake all around, and my fault. I apologize, My King."

I shuddered at the address as if someone were walking over my future gravesite. "What about my father?" I asked.

"I believe that he will go north as he was told. Especially after Hanaktos attacks. We can decide on a safe place to rejoin him later," the magus said.

"No," I said. "My father will take the army north on his own. You and I go to Attolia."

The magus didn't hesitate, didn't even look at me. "As

you wish" was all he said as he went back to packing, leaving me to wonder if I was the only one who felt the world spinning.

I had never meant to go to Melenze. I had known from the moment I'd learned of my uncle's death that I would go to Attolia. Eugenides was the king of Attolia and my friend. If his wife was the wolf at my throat, surely I could still trust him. I wanted the army in the north, not to make an alliance with Melenze but to prevent more deaths while I secured peace.

The magus, when the bags were packed, cautiously approached the side of the tent. Standing on the fabric to pull it tight, he lifted his knife to carefully slit the canvas. He paused, and in the distance I heard shouting as Hanaktos's men attacked our pickets. The magus paid no attention. He had run his fingers across the fabric of the tent and was sniffing them. He looked up at me, startled, and seized me by the shirtfront. Dispensing with subtlety, he slashed open the side of the tent and dragged me through it as the walls caught fire. Soaked from the outside in lamp oil, they were engulfed in flame in an instant. Stumbling in the dark, we staggered away from the heat and kept going, trying to distance ourselves from whoever had struck the light. Whoever it was must have made haste to get away as well. No one pursued us. It's possible that no one even saw us, as men raced toward the tent, shouting.

In the confusion of attack, and fire, and darkness, we slipped away. The magus was right that we would have burned in the tent, and who could have said it was anything but a tragic accident with a lamp?

By daylight we were not so far away that we could be sure we had outdistanced pursuit. We crawled into a screen of spindly bushes, sheltered from view from above by large rocks, where I changed into the clothes the magus had brought. They were his but fit me well. We quietly waited out the day. I broke the silence only to ask about my mother and sisters.

"We received a written message from them," said the magus.

"My mother neither reads nor writes," I said, immediately suspicious of a hoax and frightened that my relief had been unfounded.

"It was from Ina," the magus reassured me. "She provided information only she could know."

"You are certain?"

The magus's quiet laugh relieved my anxiety. "She mentioned that your tutor, Malatesta, had survived the attack on the villa by jumping into the latrine pit."

"That's Ina," I said. "Thank the gods."

"She crept into the steward's room when you didn't return. She heard the order to fire the villa and convinced your mother to move out of the icehouse. They hid themselves in a playhouse she and Eurydice had made in the bushes nearby and remained there until the smoke from the fire drew the neighbors. Unfortunately, they accepted the hospitality of a neighbor, we don't know which one, who turned them over to your rebellious barons."

I knew which one, and told the magus about Hyacinth.

"Ah," said the magus. "She made an allusion to flowers that I didn't understand. She also revealed that they were in Brimedius. I do not think the rebels meant to inform us, but the information was coded in the text."

I snickered. Ina indeed.

When darkness fell, we continued, still cautious, though we both thought that Hanaktos's men would expect us to be heading north toward Melenze and would look for us there. We traveled at night for the next few days but eventually reached roads that were sufficiently well trafficked that we could walk unremarked by anyone. We made it to Selik and paid a ridiculous amount for horses. I was worried that we might not have enough money left for food, but that night the magus reassured me. I had just gone through an entire loaf of bread and half a chicken, which we had purchased already cooked in a food stall near the horse-trading market. I'd suggested eating it before we left the market. I'd also suggested eating it on the road. I was not so comfortable with my new authority that I could say, "We eat the chicken now!" but the magus had seen that I was considering it. Shaking his head, he had said, "Your Majesty, with your very kind permission, we will find a place to sleep for the night off the road, and we will eat the chicken then."

Once we were at the campsite, and the chicken was gone, I had asked about money. "My purse is full enough," said the magus, "to keep you supplied with roast chickens."

"So, so, so," I said. "We know who the power behind the throne is," and the magus laughed.

"You eat more than Gen did after prison," he said.

"I have more sympathy with him all the time. Are you going to finish that drumstick?" I asked.

"I am. Stop staring at it."

We had to sell the horses in the tiny town just past Evisa and didn't get a good price for them, but where we were going they would be of no use. The magus and I both thought it was unwise to use the main pass, and we went back to the one we had used years ago when we went adventuring after Hamiathes's Gift. Both of us were thinking of that trip, when we had ridden out of Sounis with the conquest of Eddis in mind. So much had changed since then.

We approached the pass cautiously but found no one guarding it. Either the rebels didn't know of it, or they were still searching for us on the roads to Melenze. We spent the night in the empty farmhouse that had once belonged to the magus's family, and in the morning we began the climb.

It was only a little less daunting than it had been on the first trip. Our way was cut through solid stone by the trickle of a stream at the bottom of a gorge, and there were many places where we climbed straight up with only shallow handholds carved into the rock for aid. I was stronger than I had been, and the handholds seemed closer together than they had been before, but still, it was hard going, and I was tired out by the end of the first day.

In the evening, at a tiny cookfire, looking at the climb that waited for us in the morning, the magus said thoughtfully, "That lying little monster complained about everything: the food, the horses, the blankets, the company. He even found fault with the stories I told by the fire, but I cannot recall that he ever once complained about the climbing."

"So many things are obvious in retrospect, aren't they?" I said.

The magus looked at me seriously, and then he smiled. "Indeed," he said.

We crossed through Eddis without pausing. The magus said that a royal visit had been planned with Attolia and that the megaron at Eddis would be empty. I knew it was Attolia I needed to make peace with. Eddis had mercenaries who might help me win back my state. Attolia had the gold.

Everything, it seemed, depended on gold. The magus and I had fallen easily back into our old habits. He lectured constantly, and I asked questions to my heart's delight. Where he had once been my master and I his apprentice, I had become king and he my sole advisor. Where we had once focused on natural history and philosophy, we now concentrated on administration, taxation, and the prosecution of war.

He had begun his lessons by quoting the duke of Melfi: "To make war you need three things: one, money; two, money; and three, money." He went on to tell me the things I should have known already, that I would have known if I had been a more promising heir to the throne and not exclusively interested in poetry.

A bronze cannon costs ten solids to the ton. Eddis's iron cannons cost less but are too heavy to move. Even a bronze cannon, at six thousand pounds, takes twelve horses or fifty men to shift. The horses cost a subit a head and have to eat. The men expect wages, and they also eat. The horses have harnesses and iron shoes that need to be replaced at three octari apiece, while the men must have weapons and uniforms, and all of them paid for out of the treasury. I learned that my uncle who was Sounis had run through his ready gold and was in debt to the number of twenty-five thousand solids to moneylenders on the Peninsula. He had promised the Hephestia Diamond as security. He had already sold the Soli Diamond and a number of lesser stones from the treasury to purchase the ships to replace those that Eugenides had blown up. He had then tried to squeeze still more money out of his barons, and that, the magus thought, had been the sun that ripened the rebellion. The patronoi were sick of paying the costs of the king's wars.

When Eugenides married the queen of Attolia and made peace between Eddis and Attolia, the Mede ambassador had offered my uncle a treaty of protection from his now far more dangerous neighbors. Sounis had taken Mede money and hired men to assassinate Eugenides, but he had stopped short of accepting an alliance, refusing to cede any power to the Mede. He still insisted that he could defeat both his enemies, but his barons no longer agreed. They wanted the security of the alliance with the Mede, and my father wanted it as well. Though my father and uncle had argued, his loyalty was unfailing. Not so the barons', evidently.

By the time we reached Attolia, I understood better the wonders that had been achieved in Eddis with so small a treasury, and I was even more impressed with Attolia for squeezing so much gold out of the Mede emperor when he thought he was buying her sovereignty. Attolia still had that gold, and if she let me use it, the magus warned me, it would be a loan, not a gift, and there would be costs attached. The magus was very clear about the dangers of my decision, but he never questioned it.

"Have you and my father discussed something like this?"

"Never," said the magus. "It isn't a decision either of us could make. Only you, My King."

The magus, unless we could be overheard, addressed me formally. As if being addressed as King was something else I needed to be prepared for before I reached Attolia.

CHAPTER ELEVEN

"WHERE is it?" the burly man shouted, with his hand still in my left boot, as he searched it for some valuable that hadn't fallen out when he'd turned it upside down.

"Where's what?" asked the magus, mightily confused. The robbers had already stolen away our purses, and neither the magus nor I had any guess what more they could want.

We both had been asleep. There had been no sign of Hanaktos's men, and we'd taken no precautions except to check that the road behind and ahead of us was empty before we retreated into the woods to camp each night. We'd been taken by surprise when we were tossed from our blankets like seed scattered on the ground and found ourselves on our backs with daggers at our throats. The robbers had searched our bags, throwing our spare clothes every which way, checking the seams, and pulling the bags themselves to pieces as the horses we had purchased only the day before stood by whickering anxiously at all the fuss. The magus and I watched bemused.

Their leader had tipped the contents of the magus's

purse into his hand and thrown the little leather pocket contemptuously to the ground.

"Whatever it is that you are carrying so carefully, with an eye on every man you meet. We've watched you these last two days. What are you carrying? Gold? Silver? Where is it?"

I almost waved a hand and said, "Here. Me." But I didn't. The man was too frustrated, and I was very afraid that when he found his careful hunt had yielded nothing, he would spit us both. I looked over at the magus. He looked back, bone dry of ideas.

"It was gemstones," I said, "matched garnets the size of your thumb, but they're gone already. We handed them off."

"Handed them off?"

"At the inn, last night. The, uh, man was there. He was the merchant we were bringing the gems for." I racked my brains to remember some specific man from the roomful we'd eaten with the night before.

"The man in the booth," suggested the magus.

"Near the door?" snarled the man.

"Ye—es," said the magus, as if reluctant, trying hard not to sound like someone scrambling for a safe lie. His hand waved in a vague gesture.

The bandit looked thoughtful. "The second booth? Blond, with rings in his ears?"

"That's him," I piped. "He was to take the garnets on to the baron."

"What baron?"

Suddenly I couldn't remember the name of a single Attolian baron and couldn't guess, even if I'd been able to come up with one, who might be a plausible recipient of a matched set of large garnets. What a time to have my mind go all to pear. Only by a god's will did I remember a crossroads we had passed the day before. "He was taking the road for Pirrhea," I said. Gen had stolen us chickens in Pirrhea, which was why the sign at the crossroads had caught my eye.

Without another word, the robbers left us, taking our spare clothes and our horses with them and heading through the woods toward the road, back to the crossroads and Pirrhea. We watched them without saying anything until they were long gone. Even then we didn't speak, only stuffed our feet into our boots, which they hadn't taken, and legged it ourselves in the opposite direction, as fast as we could go. We cut back toward the road to reach it some ways ahead of where we had been traveling. When we did, we ran, not sure if someone had followed. We jogged steadily until we were in sight of the next town. By then the sky was light, and the sun was near rising. The gates in front of us were open, and the merchants would soon be doing business.

"Garnets," said the magus.

"The size of your thumb," I assured him.

Both of us silently hoped the blond man was on his way anywhere but on the road to Pirrhea.

CHAPTER TWELVE

WE were in the city of Attolia three days later, after catching a ride in the back of a wagon from a farmer delivering olive oil to the capital. We were starving. The magus had spent our last lone coin, found stuck in the seam of his purse, on bread. In the city we tried to bluster our way into an inn but were turned away on the first two tries when the landlord, spooked by our lack of traveling bags, asked to see our coin before he showed us a room. Finally we found a shabbier hostel, where the magus's easy confidence carried the day. We got a room and some food and considered our strategy. The magus was afraid to approach the palace. There was every chance that the Mede agents whom we had escaped so far would be lurking, waiting to catch us as we approached.

"It's what I would do," said the magus, "were I the Mede. They know by now that you are not with your father."

"We could send a message," I said. "If we promised payment on delivery, we could send it by messenger, but would any message sent by a common carrier and delivered to the gates be carried to the king?"

What a quandary!

We tried approaching Baron Susa, but we were turned away, even from his back door. We thought we might contact a merchant who would pass our message to a patronoi, who might deliver it to the palace, but that failed as well. I picked up a job unloading a cart and earned us enough coins to buy food, but not enough to make a bribe of any significance, and without a bribe we could not seem to contact anyone of any importance in the city. The public day in the royal courts wasn't to be held for weeks. While there were people the magus could contact outside the city, that would mean more traveling. We didn't have the time.

The magus was growing more concerned each day that Mede spies would locate us, two Sounisians in the city, behaving oddly. We were sure to draw attention, and after our experience in the woods, neither of us was too sure we would see the Mede agents before they saw us. Equally worrisome, the landlord of the filthy, flea-ridden inn where we were staying was becoming suspicious.

The magus went out the door first. When it was my turn, I nearly landed on top of him. He dodged and I rolled, and we ended up facing each other, sitting on the hard stones of the road with our legs splayed out in front of us.

"Thank your gods, I don't call the city guard,"

shouted the landlord, and slammed the courtyard door. He opened it a minute later to throw the magus's overshirt out after us.

Rubbing my bruised elbow ruefully, I asked the magus, "If he called the guard, do you think we could tell them who we are?"

The magus shook his head. "Attolia is pressing every prisoner they arrest onto their ships in order to fortify the islands she has taken from Sounis. We're far more likely to end up on a galley, revealing our true identities to the passing sharks."

I got up first and helped the magus to his feet. Sighing, he picked up his overshirt and threw it over his shoulder. We walked up the street.

It was later that day, when we were selling off our clothes in exchange for grubbier ones and the cash to buy food, that we heard a rumor in the marketplace that the king and queen would be riding to the harbor to greet arriving ambassadors. We put together the peashooter and snagged the dried peas out of a market stall. The magus wanted to spit the pea, but I demonstrated my knack for accuracy, and he agreed that I should be the one. I did think of the changes to my face, but I was sure that Eugenides, if he looked, would know me, and I was more distressed than I can say when he passed by without any sign of recognition.

The magus and I had some very uncomfortable moments when we were arrested by the guard. Our only hope was to convince one of them to send a message to the king, but the squad leader gave us no opportunity to speak. When the magus tried, a guardsman had him pinned by the throat before he could get more than a word out. So intimidating was he that we kept silent all the way to the palace and down into the cells. Only when there was a closed door between us and the very angry guards did the magus shout that Attolis would want to know we were in his prison. I was already imagining myself chained to an oar.

We spent our time while we were waiting discussing just what we could say that might warrant the attention of the king. We agreed that telling the prison guards flat out that I was the king of Sounis probably wouldn't work. The magus thought he could say that he had information valuable to Relius, whom he knew by name, and that might get us an interview with him. Not that an interview with Attolia's master of spies would be wholly without risk, but face to face the magus thought he could convince the man of our identities.

Then Gen appeared at the door, and we didn't need to convince anyone of anything after all. Instead we followed the guards he left us to a set of rooms that were a welcome change from our infested inn of the previous week.

"Ridiculous to think what indignities I would suffer in silence, if I knew that I was to be rewarded with an oversize bucket of hot water," the magus said as he settled into the bath the servants had filled for him. He leaned against the higher side, leaving his arms and legs dangling over the lower edges and looking something like a pale spider, but more like an overturned terrapin. I'd already had my bath, at his insistence, and was getting into clean clothes with the help of a dresser and trying to eat the food that had been brought at the same time. The careful attention of the manservant was rather amusing to me after all the time I'd spent in the same set of pants and loose shirt.

The clothes were rather startling in their finery. "Do you think Gen picked them?" I asked, posing in my new overcoat. The decorative fabric panels hastily tacked to the front and back made an already handsome piece of clothing into an ostentatious one.

The magus eyed me from the bath.

"I would believe it. All that embroidery suits you."

"Makes me look less like riffraff, you mean?"

"Yes," he agreed with mocking gravity. "That's it exactly."

A barber came to trim us and shave us, taking off the last of my darker hair and leaving it tidy, if short. When he was done, Hilarion arrived and introduced himself as one of the king's attendants.

He asked if we would be able to join the king and queen for an audience. I should have paid more attention, but I was still eating what I could from a plate of fruit and trying not to drip anything on my coat. I didn't realize until we had followed Hilarion through the narrow corridors to the main staircase that we were heading toward the megaron of the palace, the largest of the throne rooms. When we reached the doorway, we could hear the quiet rustling of the crowd beyond, and when I looked past Hilarion, I could see only a narrow aisle open in the center of the room. I had forgotten the arrival of the ambassadors from the Continent.

Standing just inside the doorway, no more than a few feet away from me, was a party of Medes, distinctive in their brightly colored and more loosely cut clothing. I was surprised that Attolia, who had so recently and insultingly sent home a Mede army, would be entertaining an ambassador from the empire.

I was suddenly glad that our clothes were meant for ceremony. Even so, if I could have, I would have signaled Hilarion and waited until a less public moment to talk with Attolia and the new Attolis, but it was too late. We were swept into the room, announced, lauded, eyeballed by the crowd, and moved to the foot of the raised dais almost without our own volition.

Attolia was just as I remembered from our briefest of meetings, when the magus and I had been apprehended after attempting to steal Hamiathes's Gift. She looked as regal and every bit as intimidating as she had before. She greeted me, while Eugenides reclined on his throne, his elbow on the arm of his chair and his thumb tucked under his cheekbone to prop up his head. With his fingers cupped against his forehead he eyed me from under the arch they made, as a man does when he is looking at something very far away.

The magus and I had talked for many long hours about this marriage of Eugenides and the queen of Attolia. The magus insisted it was Eugenides's choice and his desire as well, but it was impossible to know whose influence would prevail and if Gen would grow more like his wife, or his wife more like her king.

Down in the prison cells, he had seemed everything that I remembered. So much so that I hadn't even noticed the hook in place of his hand. In the throne room, the differences were hard to miss. I'd been told that he wore a false hand on formal occasions, but it seemed that his habits had changed. His right arm lay across the arm of the throne, and at the end was a pointed hook.

The last time I had seen Gen he had been whole, if slightly damaged, after our escape from captivity in Attolia. I hadn't realized the strength of my habit of picturing him in my thoughts as he had been when we first met: skinny and prison pale, incongruous in the clean clothes the magus provided. I did remember just enough of his taste in clothing from the weeks I had stayed in Eddis that I was not completely taken aback by his grandeur. Gods know, he does play up with his beaded jacket and his lace trim. I almost laughed aloud when I saw that the design of his boots remained unchanged, though even they had gold dusted in their tooled leather patterns.

It wasn't a moment for laughter. Not with Attolia coolly admitting her surprise at the unforeseen arrival of a foreign ruler, especially one with whom she was currently at war.

At war with my uncle, I said, and not, I hoped, with me.

Attolia nodded. I will tell you honestly, I wish it had been you I addressed. I would have felt better just to have seen you in the crowd, but I didn't. I had the sense that Attolia might not feel any more bound by the rules of hospitality than Baron Hanaktos, and her expression gave me no clue to her thoughts. I feared that I could find myself on my way back to the underground cell at any moment.

Attolia asked what brought me to her court. Poor prince or not, I hadn't sat through a thousand boring ceremonies without learning something about diplomatic language. I dug through my memories for the right formulaic phrases, and then with as much dignity as I could muster, I explained that I had just escaped from my own country, a country in the greatest peril, lost either to the Mede or to Melenze or both. I pointed out that none of these outcomes would profit the state of Attolia. I had come to my friends to ask for the men and the gold to win my country back.

Attolia watched me with close consideration as I

spoke. When I finished, there was a moment of polite silence. As she opened her mouth to speak, Gen, who had been silent throughout, sat up and laid his hand across hers. I could hear the Attolians sucking in their breaths. Attolia slipped her hand away, but she sat back in her chair and nodded a deferral to her king.

Then, as you well know, Eugenides looked me in the eye as if I were a complete stranger and said, "The simplest way to end a war is to admit you have lost it."

The silence after that was not polite.

Little could convince me more that I was fit to be king than that moment when I acted like one and didn't tell Attolis something very rude that he could do with his own throne and mumbled instead a few more ritualized phrases about momentous decisions, and the time they take, and then walked myself and the magus out of the room before I had a real fit of apoplexy in front of the assembled courts and ambassadors of Eddis, Attolia, and the Continent with a few condescending Mede visitors looking on.

I came upstairs to these rooms, where I told the magus and the guards to wait in the anteroom, as I did not want his company or anyone else's. That seems to have meant very little, though, because no sooner did I close the door than it opened again. You came in. You took one look at me. And you laughed.

· CHAPTER THIRTEEN ·

THE Queen of Eddis protested. "I did not laugh," she said.

"You did," Sounis said. "You are laughing still. And why didn't those guards turn you away?"

Eddis studied him. His face was much changed by Basrus's fists. He was also taller and heavier than when they had last met. His shoulders had grown broad from his working in Hanaktos's fields, and she could easily imagine him dropping a man with a single blow. She did not think he realized how fierce his appearance had become; though his smile had changed, his easy blushes remained. She did not know how to put into words the relief it was to see him safe, and so the feelings escaped as another laugh. Still smiling, she defended the Attolians. "They are guards," she said. "They could not deny a queen."

Sounis returned her smile and conceded. "No, and neither can I. You asked to hear the story of events that brought me here, and I have given it to you, as I am sure anyone would give you anything you asked. I am only sorry that all my face can offer you is amusement," he added.

Eddis reached to touch her own crooked nose. "If I laughed," she said, "it is only at the idea that we make a matched pair now, you and I." She asked him, more seriously, "Your uncle who was Sounis learned of our letters. That was the cause of your exile to Letnos?"

"An unfinished letter was stolen from my desk and delivered to him," explained Sounis. "He had my rooms searched and intercepted your next letter. He and my father and the magus spent the evening in a shouting match, and I was sent away the next morning."

"So you did not receive the letter? You have not read it?"

"No."

"You made a proposal in your previous letter. Perhaps it was only hypothetical?"

"It was not."

Eddis gently chided, "All that time in the fields of Hanaktos, you thought of many things and many people, but never, it seems, of the queen of Eddis."

The color rose in Sounis's cheeks, but he did not look away. He had thought of her every day. "When I was working in the fields, I knew how unfounded my hopes were," he said. "I was a poor excuse for an heir of Sounis when I made the proposal and then became even less than that."

"How less?" asked Eddis.

Sounis looked down at her hand, lying in his, and covered it for a moment. Still holding it lightly, he stood and stepped back until her hand slipped away from his grasp. Then he crossed to the far side of the room. Without looking back, he said, "That look on Gen's face. Does he think I am a fool? That I came to Attolia instead of Melenze because I was naive? Did he think I was asking him to give me soldiers and gold to fight a war as a personal favor? I came here on my knees to offer him Sounis, and he looks at me as if I were my uncle and grabs it out of my hands."

Eddis asked, "The magus did not talk about this on the road?"

Sounis shook his head. "He tried to warn me, and I refused to listen." He shook his head again, this time in bewilderment. "Eugenides offered his life once to save me. Why should I doubt that he is my friend?"

"He is the king of Attolia," said Eddis.

"And no particle of your Thief remains?"

Eddis searched for words. "He swore an oath to be Thief on his grandfather's death. But the oath is a mystery of the Thieves, and no one alive but Eugenides knows what it requires."

"So now I must deliver my country into the hands of enemies? The magus no doubt thinks I am a fool."

"I cannot believe that," said Eddis. "Nor will I believe you could have a better friend than Eugenides."

"I should throw something, perhaps," said Sounis, "but I do not think it would relieve my feelings."

"I have not found it to do so," said Eddis.

"Gen evidently does."

"Gen is Gen," said Eddis.

"Gen is a *bastard*," said the king of Sounis.

Eddis looked sad, and Sounis was sorry he had spoken so harshly. He returned to sit by her side.

He said, "Sounis is lost. I know what comes of the Mede occupation. In a generation, or perhaps two, Sounis and Attolia and Eddis will be gone. Only Medes will serve in the government, only Medes will hold public office, only Medes will own land or hold wealth. They will knock down the old temples and control the guilds and the trades, and the Sounisians will be left okloi, or worse, beggars in their own cities.

"I could sell half my country to Melenze to get its protection, but that would only delay the Medes, not turn them back. Also, there's little hope that Melenze would be satisfied with half of Sounis. They would eat up the rest of it in the next few years, and I would be in no position to stop them. I am in a war with Attolia I cannot win, with a civil war at home that I have fled.

"But Sounis is not the only country at risk. This war drains Attolia's resources and endangers her as well. I thought . . . I *thought* that Gen would be satisfied with an oath of loyalty to him and a negotiated surrender on my part. Sounis would give up the islands we had lost, and in exchange, I would still be king. Sounis would be free, only allied as a tributary of Attolia, much as Melenze is allied with Ferria. And instead I find that

Attolis demands a complete surrender, to depose me from my throne and disenfranchise my patronoi."

"He did not say that," said Eddis.

"You were there? You heard him?" Sounis asked. "He said I should admit my defeat. You heard his voice and saw his face. What else could he mean?"

"Would you give up being Sounis?" Eddis asked, too casually. "Would you allow your country to become just another part of Attolia?"

Sounis's eyes narrowed. "No," he said. He stood, and his restless energy carried him across the room again. "I will go to Melenze. And hope to delay the Medes long enough to find some other solution to their imperial expansion. Of course, that assumes the king and queen of Attolia intend to honor the laws of hospitality and allow me to travel safely to the border."

Eddis nodded. Sounis dropped into a chair on the far side of the room and stared at Eddis. "He sent you."

Eddis's slow, broad smile appeared. Sounis crossed his arms and bolstered himself against it.

"Why?"

"Because he wants no more than you thought to give him: your allegiance and the islands he already controls."

"That is not what he indicated in the throne room."

"He needed you to know that he meant to take Sounis whether you offered it or not. He would have taken it from your uncle."

"I can see that," said Sounis. "Did he think I didn't know it? The king of Attolia is a bastard, but an *honest* one? I *came* here to offer him my allegiance. I came because I trusted him. So why does he make me think I should not?"

Eddis sighed. "Maybe, Sophos, because he is an idiot." She shook her head. "He sent me to ask if you will negotiate a surrender. I cannot speak for him otherwise, but Sophos, I know he is your friend."

"So he sends you to ask me to forgive him?"

Eddis was silent. Eugenides did not expect to be forgiven.

Sounis sat down and lay back in his chair. He put his arm across his forehead and snapped, "Oh, of course, I will forgive him. What choice do I have?" His own words seemed to give him pause, and after a moment's thought, he sighed heavily. "I will forgive him," he said more calmly, "because I have heard him scream when someone pulled a sword out of him that could have just as easily gone into me. And because I believe I know him, all evidence to the contrary, and that if he is Attolis, he is also my friend Gen. But he could have trusted me to begin with, instead of acting like an idiot and treating me like one."

"No one would argue," said Eddis, revealing some of her own exasperation with the king of Attolia.

"I'm not a fool," said Sounis.

"No."

"I cannot win a war with Attolia and at the same time put down a rebellion."

"I do not see how."

"Sounis could not yield to Attolia, but I believe I can yield to Eugenides as the king of Attolia and still be Sounis and still hold my country. We can unite against a far greater danger."

"Yes."

"I do not actually need you to tell me that."

Biting back her smile, Eddis shook her head. "No."

Sounis smiled, too, though it was a sorrowful smile. He stood. "I suppose I should tell the magus."

Eddis stood as well. As he passed on his way to the door, she stopped him with one hand on his sleeve.

"How less?" she asked him, serious again.

It was obvious to Sounis. "A slave in the fields of Hanaktos, and now, not much better. I am a king with no country. Would you have that?"

Eddis seemed to consider. "Yes."

Regret and pleasure were in equal measure when Sounis said reluctantly, "I am not sure that is wise. I would have to question my own feelings, because I do not think I love you so wildly that I would drag you into such a poor match."

"It might have been preferable," Eddis admitted drily, "if you had thrown off your chains of bondage solely for love of me. It would certainly have been more flattering." Standing so near to him, she was looking up into his face and watching it closely. "I am willing to accept, however, that we are real people, not characters in a play. We do not, all of us, need to be throwing inkwells. If we are comfortable with one another, is that not sufficient?"

"Were I a king in more than just name, it would be all, all I dreamed of," said Sounis, and it was Eddis who blushed.

"You wish to wait, then, until you are confirmed as Sounis?"

"If . . ."

"When," said Eddis firmly.

"Yes," said Sounis, "then."

CHAPTER FOURTEEN

A s Eddis left, she gathered in her wake most of the crowd that Sounis found squeezed into the anteroom outside his door when he opened it. People flowed out of the room like a tide, leaving only two of the Attolian guard, and the magus, standing alone, as unaware of the empty room as he had been of the full one.

He looked old, Sounis thought, and it seemed a shame that such a man couldn't have a better king to serve. "I'm sorry," Sounis said. "You tried to warn me that he is the king of Attolia now, and I should have listened."

To his surprise, the magus walked forward and dropped to his knees.

"Don't," said Sounis, but the magus took each of the king's hands and kissed them before holding them to his eyes. Embarrassed, Sounis pulled the magus to his feet, but the magus was unperturbed. He smiled as he stood, and looking Sounis in the face, he said simply, "My King, I am at your disposal."

The conversation between Sounis and his future overlord was carefully arranged and far from private. Sounis was conveyed through the palace by an amorphous crowd that expanded and shrank as he progressed; guards, escorts, majordomos, and hangers-on surrounded him as he went up stairs and along corridors until he arrived at the private apartment of the king of Attolia and was announced. His first thought, upon entering, was that his own guest apartment in the palace was the more luxurious. His walls were covered in patterned cloth and trimmed with molded plasterwork. The king's walls were plain plaster above and plain paneling below, with benches on three sides to provide seating. Though the cushions were worked with embroidered figures, the chamber's appearance was reminiscent of nothing so much as a patronoi's waiting room for okloi petitioners.

The door to the next room was open, and Sounis was surprised to see that it was the bedchamber. He had thought that any room of measurable importance necessarily had an antechamber, and often more than one. In the megaron of Sounis, his uncle had lived in a room behind a room behind a room, each one lined with silk wall coverings or fine murals and far removed from the people he governed. Sounis thought Gen, cheek by jowl with his guardroom, must be rather more closely entwined in the lives of those around him. On reflection, he suspected Gen was more closely entwined than any of the polished young men standing around the guardroom suspected.

The men in uniform were obviously the king's guards. The others were like Hilarion, Sounis assumed, more of the king's companions. They were attractive in the way only the very well heeled can be. Trained in all the arts of riding, shooting, fighting, dancing, and clever court dialogue, their kind had intimidated him for years, and Sophos, now Sounis, quailed at the idea of surrounding himself with such companions. He wondered how Gen got along with them.

Eugenides waited for him in the bedchamber, sitting on an upholstered bench. He indicated the seat beside him. Sounis stood for a moment looking down at him before taking the seat. He was looking for some sign of the friend he had traveled with through Eddis and across Attolia in pursuit of a mythical relic and saw none. The king of Attolia's expression showed no sense of irony or humor, just a blank courtesy. Sounis sat beside him and looked straight ahead.

Everyone else in the room, including the magus, remained standing. Neither the queen of Eddis nor the queen of Attolia attended.

The king of Attolia nodded agreeably but made no personal comment. He asked if Sounis would give his oath of loyalty.

"If Attolis can make it worth the sacrifice," Sounis answered.

"And if not?" Attolis inquired politely.

Sounis crossed his legs, as if at ease, and offered

his intention to go to Melenze and use their resources to fight Attolia and to delay the encroaching Medes. "Better to be king of some part of Sounis than of none of it."

"The oath of loyalty would pertain to all of Sounis, not part," Attolis said.

"You would have my loyalty, but no right to interfere in the internal management of my state."

"That is acceptable," said Attolis.

"Then we are in agreement," said Sounis.

After a dry and formal parting, Sounis was led back to his own rooms, the magus beside him. Sounis was thinking over his decision. A hallway, filled with various members of the court, was no place to discuss such private thoughts. "The king's rooms are very plain," he observed instead.

Attolis's attendant, walking just ahead, turned to speak over his shoulder. "They are not the royal apartments. His Majesty chose these rooms in preference and has arranged for the queen to remain in the royal apartments, as it suits them both." He managed to convey that they had rooms every bit as nice as any in Sounis and also that it wasn't anyone's business but theirs where their king slept.

Sounis straightened up, and when the attendant turned away, he made a face at the magus. Gen was welcome to his attendants. "They looked familiar, didn't you think? Just like—"

"Yes," the magus replied.

The attendant's ears were all but standing out from his head as he strained to hear what the king's rooms looked like, but Sounis left the rest of his sentence unsaid. The magus had also seen the resemblance in the plain walls and plain paneling, and in the king's desk with its careful arrangement of papers and pens, to the library of the queen of Eddis, where Eugenides had lived as her Thief.

When they were back in Sounis's own bedchamber and the attendant was gone, Sounis spoke more freely.

"I thought he would be more like the Gen I know once we were in private."

"You were never in private," said the magus.

"Still," said Sounis.

"My King," said the magus hesitantly, and Sounis waved him to speak. "I believe we must go forward with the understanding that Attolis's responsibility as king will outweigh his affections as a man. But that does not mean that I doubt his friendship. Or that I believe his friendship is unimportant. On the contrary, no treaty, no matter how cleverly worded, will hold without it."

Sounis threw up his hands. "Tell *him* that," he said.

In the ways of accommodation between nations, many viewpoints were exchanged in the process of moving from an agreement in principle to one locked in words.

Sounis had no supporting barons with him, and so he and the magus wore themselves hoarse in one meeting after another. They talked long into the night, so that Sounis could make informed decisions and the magus could carry Sounis's words back to more meetings the next day. Sounis was ferried from appointment to appointment by one or another of the king of Attolia's companions. They took it in turn to be available at all times, waiting in his anteroom with a brace of honorary guards, ready to lead him up and down the endless corridors of Attolia's palace.

In his meetings, Sounis was careful to keep to words he had discussed in advance with the magus, well aware that each one was a link in a chain that would bind him and his country to Attolia. He was determined that his agreements would engender no unforeseen consequences and that the ties between Attolia and Sounis would not be all at the expense of Sounis.

In the evenings, after a day of meetings, he sometimes walked in the queen's garden, with the king and queen of Attolia and a crowd of others or, more rarely, with the queen of Eddis. She had not yet returned to her own home and had announced that she would remain until negotiations were complete.

The queen's garden lay behind the palace. Large and walled for privacy, it was a miniature world of alleys and outdoor rooms. There were fountains and reflecting pools with benches beside them and expansive lawns around them, and there were smaller benches discreetly tucked into alcoves between high hedges.

Attolia remained as intimidating as ever, cool and beautiful, with never a word that was unkind or one that was kind, either. She was a wellspring of information that had, as far as Sounis ever found, no end. She spoke freely about the organization of her army, and her creation of a separate branch of it specifically for her artillery. She offered ready information on how she moved her cannons, how she supplied her ships, and how she circumvented the destructive traditions of the patronoi by making the best use of her okloi, offering promotions and land grants for twenty-year veterans and receiving in return their uncorrupted loyalty. It was information too important not to have, and Sounis steeled himself to continue asking questions as often as she would answer.

Eugenides remained as distant as his queen. His mask of formality seemed unassailable, and Sounis continued to search without success for some sign of his friend in the king's remote expression.

For many reasons, Sounis preferred his quieter walks with Eddis. These were more lightly companioned, with her ladies and one of the king's attendants following some distance behind. At first the discussions were much the same as those with Attolia. Eddis was a welcome anchor in his unsure navigation of the political seas, and he turned to her for advice to supplement the magus's. On occasion the magus walked with them, though as the days passed, he excused himself more often than not, leaving Sounis and Eddis alone in each other's company.

It seemed to Sounis that if he was not in a meeting discussing an interest rate or a trade of goods or if he was not walking in the garden, he was reluctantly standing in the light of a window while being fitted for clothes. He wouldn't have minded the never-ending measurements if he could have eaten during the process, but the tailors insisted that raising his arms would spoil their work. If the measurements were irksome, the clothes themselves, when they began to arrive, appeared disturbingly expensive.

After the third suit of the day, he called for the magus. Leaning down from where he was posed on a felted wooden block, he said quietly into the magus's ear, "Do I need this much lace? And how are we paying for it?"

The tailors paused in their work as if under a magician's spell, their pins poised, their lips pursed. The king's attendant on duty that day was Ion, standing patiently in a corner. He cleared his throat politely and said, "His Majesty's wardrobe is a gift from My King."

Sighing, the tailors returned to their work. "Attolis is very generous," they murmured.

"Indeed," said Sounis, thinking that the attention to

frippery was the only sign of the old Eugenides he had seen. When the tailors were finished and had stripped away the carefully marked patches of fabric, he stretched and stepped down from the wooden stand.

"Your Majesty?" said the tailor apologetically.

Sounis had been heading back to the clothes that had been borrowed for him to wear until the tailoring was done. "You said that suit was the last?"

The tailor bowed. "We still have the uniforms to fit."

Sounis sighed as he stepped back up, suspecting that the king of Attolia was torturing him.

"Would I be wrong," Sounis asked one evening as he walked with Eddis, "to think that I talk to you, you talk to Gen, and Gen talks to Attolia, who talks to the magus, who talks to me?"

Eddis laughed. "Not always. Sometimes, as in this case, someone approaches my Eddisian ambassador Ornon, here in Attolia, and he talks to me, I talk to you, you talk to Attolia, Attolia talks to Gen, and he talks to me."

"I see you appear in that progression twice."

"Oh, more than that, because after Gen talks to me, the process reverses. He goes back to Attolia, who talks to you, who go to the magus, who repeats the information to me, who gives it to Ornon, who takes it to whoever started this particular political ball rolling in the first place." She ended breathless, but smiling.

They had been discussing the Neutral Islands, the

scattered island states that were spread off the shores of Sounis, Eddis, and Attolia. Most of the islands in the archipelago changed hands intermittently between Sounis and Attolia, but some had established their independence from either power and maintained it by keeping a scrupulous neutrality.

With the exception of a few lying very near Sounis's shore, all islands but the Neutral ones were in Attolia's hands. When Sounis's barons had risen in rebellion against him, the navy of Sounis had disappeared into division and disarray. The nucleus of Sounis's navy was owned by the crown, but all the other ships were owned and outfitted by individual barons, who called them back to their home ports, isolating them from one another and from any central command, making them easy pickings for Attolia's fleet and pirates. What was left of Sounis's navy was trapped in the harbor of the capital city. Unable to break Attolia's blockades, Sounis's islands had surrendered one by one.

Sounis had assumed that he would cede them permanently to Attolia, but Eddis was suggesting that he argue for possession of Lerna and Hanippus. Lerna was the largest of the Ring Archipelago; Hanippus was almost as big, though isolated from the direct sea lanes.

Eddis had explained that the Neutral Islands would not be at ease surrounded entirely by islands under Attolian control. "Attolia does not want drawn-out hostilities off her shore. If she gives up Lerna and

Hanippus, it is a means to assure the Neutral Islands of her peaceful intentions," she said.

"So Hannipus and Lerna controlled by Sounis, which is in turn bound to Attolia, will make them more comfortable?"

"Yes."

"Very well," said Sounis, bemused but willing. "I will direct the magus to raise the issue and discuss it myself with Attolia. I am surrendering myself to Attolis, but all my conversations seem to be with his queen."

Eddis nodded. "Gen leaves the reins in Attolia's hands. Which is not what either I or Attolia recommended, but wisely he ignored us both."

"Wisely?"

Smiling, Eddis said, "He hasn't the temperament. He gets angry. She only ever gets angry at him."

Sounis, having seen the Thief of Eddis lose his temper, could see her point. "But it is not what you advised?"

"No," Eddis replied. She said thoughtfully, "She and I both thought his presence must inevitably weaken Attolia and if he didn't become a strong king, the court would soon be unstable. He proved me wrong. Either because he can see what we can't or just because he demands the world conform to his own desires. I am never sure which it is that he does. In this case, he managed to so terrify his barons that they have assumed a semblance of conformity without undermining Attolia's power after all. No one will cross her."

"Understandable," said Sounis.

Seeing his shudder, Eddis said, "Give her time. She is slow to trust."

"What need is there for her to trust me?" Sounis asked, surprised. "Am I not the one exposing my neck to the wolf?"

"Oh, I hope you haven't said that to her," Eddis said, laughing.

"Indeed, I am not that brave," Sounis admitted.

Eddis did not say what she was thinking: that Sophos held Gen's heart in his hand, that he was one of very few people who could destroy the king of Attolia, and that Attolia knew it.

"I did say, though, that I wasn't surrendering to her and I wasn't swearing any oaths to her, either."

"And?" Eddis prompted. "Was she angry?"

"She seemed to be pleased," said Sounis, "for what that is worth. I find it impossible to know what she is thinking."

"She probably was pleased, then. She has her reasons, I am sure."

"You trust her?"

"I'm not swearing any oaths to her," said Eddis.

Sounis laughed. "I should hope not."

Eddis changed the subject then, asking, "Do you sleep? You look tired."

"Not well," Sounis answered. "I mostly lie in bed tracing the patterns in plasterwork." Every night he picked apart his decision to surrender his sovereignty to Attolis and then remade it before morning.

Eddis said, "You should think of something else or you will end up like poor Polystrictes, asleep in the middle of the day."

Sounis smiled. He had never heard of Polystrictes.

"How can you not know Polystrictes?" Eddis asked.

"Poor tutoring," said Sounis, glancing over his shoulder at the magus far behind them, walking with one of Eddis's attendants on one arm and one of Attolia's on the other. "Tell me?"

They had reached a long, narrow alley between two hedges that reached over their heads. Leaving the magus and the attendants to be lost from sight, they turned up it, the shells on the path crunching underfoot. "He did a favor for the god Ocrassus, and Ocrassus repaid him with a goat."

"Not very considerate of the god."

"It was a particularly fine goat, a nanny with a silky coat, and best of all, she answered to her name, Eleutheria. As long as you called her by name, she would come when she was called and stay when she was told and give fine milk. And Polystrictes was very pleased."

"And?"

"The next day Ocrassus brought him another goat. Named Eleuthemia. She was also very fine and answered to her name."

"And another goat after that?" Sounis asked.

"Yes, Nigella, and Noxe, and Omerga, and Omerxa, which you understand was easy to confuse with Omerga, and—"

"And so on," said Sounis.

"And so on," said Eddis. "Hundreds of goats, a new one every day, and poor Polystrictes was forever running around, calling, 'Nigella! Nogasta! Come down from the roof!' 'Poppy! Promiseteus! Pausanius! Stop eating the lettuce at once!' 'Zenia, Zeta, and Zara, come to be milked!' While the goats ran wild and ate through all the flowers in the courtyard and the vegetables in the garden and a great deal of the family's laundry besides. The god brought a new goat every day, and poor Polystrictes couldn't say no. One does not refuse the gifts of the god without a certain amount of peril. So Polystrictes stayed up all night, every night, reciting their names over so he wouldn't forget them. Finally Ocrassus came and found him, surrounded by goats, all of them chewing through the shrubbery and some even chewing the sleeves on Polystrictes's tunic as he sat at the edge of his fountain fast asleep."

"And then what happened?" Sounis asked. Eddis had stopped when she realized they had reached the outer limits of the garden. Above them, Attolia's guard passed on the palace's outer walls. She looked over a shoulder at the tracks they had made in the long shell-covered path behind them, but Sounis, not yet ready to go back, turned to follow the wall around the garden instead.

"Ocrassus gave him a dog," Eddis replied. "It was the first dog, and Polystrictes thought it was a wolf and ran to hide. The god had to search for him to ask, 'Polystrictes, why are you in the well?' Polystrictes said, 'It's a wolf.' And Ocrassus said, 'It's a dog.'

"'Wolf.'

"'Dog.'

"'Wolf.'

"'Polystrictes,' said Ocrassus, looking down the well, 'which one of us is a god?' And Polystrictes had to bite his tongue and climb out. The god showed him how the dog would follow his commands and keep his goats out of the laundry. So Polystrictes didn't have to remember all those names anymore. He had to remember only one, the dog's."

"Alas," said Sounis. "My problem is barons, not goats, and I have no dog."

"True, but staying up all night, reciting over your difficulties, won't help you any more than it did Polystrictes." Eddis turned him around, and they started back toward the palace. "We will be missed," she said. "And you will not want people who think we are deep in a discussion of the rights of the Neutral Islands to learn that we were instead talking about goats."

"I cannot crush a rebellion with so few men," Sounis protested.

They had met at last to discuss the army that he would lead back to Sounis. In addition to the kings of Attolia and Sounis and the queens of Attolia and Eddis, there were advisors and ministers and officers of the army. Sounis wanted to say more but was afraid to embarrass himself in front of the men he would be ordering into a war. It seemed a pitifully small number of troops that the king of Attolia was offering, much smaller than Sounis had expected. He looked at the magus to see if he, too, was surprised, but the magus was looking at his hands. Sounis looked at Attolia, and she only stared back. No doubt she had overcome her own rebels with ten men and a penknife.

Eugenides said, "These are the Eddisians who have been exerting a peaceful influence throughout Attolia since I became Attolis. They are Eddis's best mercenaries, and we will pay Eddis the gold for them. These are the best of our Attolian forces as well. We cannot send any artillery, and you couldn't use it anyway. It would only slow you down. We are taking it on faith that the Medes will not arrive on our doorstep while you have them with you, and that Baron Erondites won't rise up inside our dooryard before you return them. We will need them back," he added.

Eddis watched without speaking. She could see that Sounis was alarmed, but there was little she could say that would help. The numbers were small, and the challenge he faced was enormous.

"It is just as likely that the Medes will arrive on *my* doorstep," said Sounis. "What then?"

Attolia explained. "In either case, we have an invasion that the Great Powers of the Continent cannot fail to notice, and we all have to do the best we can. It is most likely that the Medes would land on our shores, rather than sailing around us to land on yours. Moreover, any attack on their part would reveal their plans to conquer Sounis, not ally with it, and strengthen your position as king—if you have convinced your barons that you are king. You cannot risk being seen as the head of an Attolian invasion. We do not have the troops to send in any case, but as a matter of strategy, overwhelming force will make you less king, not more."

Later Eugenides did not invite Sounis to his rooms so much as summon him there. They were to have a private discussion, or at least a conversation as private as anything could be in the overpopulated palace. Feeling as sullen as a schoolboy, Sounis followed an attendant to the appointment only to find, when he reached the guardroom of the king's apartments, that the door to the bedchamber was closed. With rising irritation, Sounis waited. The fancy guards looked elsewhere, but the attendants watched him with what he thought was concealed amusement. He set his teeth and stared back at each of them in turn. They all found something else to look at, except Ion, who smiled and bowed and asked if the king of Sounis would like some refreshment. Sounis was hungry, but he declined when he saw that the door to Eugenides's bedchamber was opening.

Two men strode through the open door and across the guardroom. One was Galen, the personal physician of the queen of Eddis. The other, Sounis didn't recognize but assumed from his green sash that he served the same function for Eugenides. Both walked with the stiff-legged gait of the bitterly offended, and Sounis warily refrained from greeting Galen, though he had met him several times in Eddis.

"Your Majesty?" Hilarion spoke from the doorway, ushering Sounis into the room, where Eugenides waited. The king of Attolia was again seated on the upholstered bench. He nodded to Sounis to take a seat that had been pulled up nearby. His unapproachable expression was just the same, and Sounis decided not to ask what had upset Galen. So long as Gen maintained his impersonal role, Sounis meant to do the same.

Eugenides's attendants moved in and out of his bedchamber while he and Sounis talked, but Gen ignored them as if they didn't exist. Taking his cue, Sounis did the same. Hoping for some reassurance that he would be able to subdue his rebel barons, Sounis was disappointed. He and Eugenides talked about the Mede and their history, and the balance of power on the Peninsula. The conversation was stilted and awkward.

Only as the interview was ending did Eugenides say directly, "You must be king. You cannot be anyone's puppet if we are to have a chance against the Mede."

"I'll do what I can," said Sounis stiffly.

He rose to leave and was halfway to the door when Eugenides asked, "Does the wardrobe suit?"

Sounis turned back. Eugenides was looking into his wine cup, and Sounis wasn't sure how to answer. Had he failed to thank the king appropriately? Was he supposed to admire the gifts more? He knew that Eugenides paid a great deal of attention to such things, but to Sounis they were just clothes. "The pockets are sewn on the inside," he said. He couldn't imagine why someone would want to keep something in a pocket he couldn't easily reach, and these were particularly useless, too deep and too narrow to get his hand into.

Eugenides shrugged one shoulder. "I sometimes find them useful," he said into his wine cup.

"Well," said Sounis, "perhaps I will, too. Thank you."

"Be blessed in your endeavors," said Eugenides, using the universal Eddisian phrase for *please* and *thank you* and *you're welcome*.

"And you," said Sounis, aping his formality.

When the king of Sounis was gone, Eugenides's attendants, waiting in the guardroom, heard the wine cup smash.

Philologos stood, saying wearily, "I'll clean it up," and went to fetch a cloth.

It was a gloomy Sounis that made his way from the private apartments of the king of Attolia to his own suite. He followed his borrowed attendant, paying little attention to his surroundings, until Ion suddenly slowed and Sounis nearly ran into the back of him. In an apparent coincidence, no doubt meticulously prearranged by the Mede ambassador, Melheret and his retinue were just climbing the stairs as Sounis arrived at the head of them. It would be impolite not to draw back and leave the landing free for those ascending.

"Your Majesty," said the ambassador, pausing to bow where he stood with one foot on a higher step and his hands bunching the fabric of his flowing trousers, lifting them as a woman lifts the hem of a dress. If it was an oddly delicate greeting, it was also blatantly self-assured. The Mede ambassador had no concerns about being taken at a disadvantage and made that much clear.

"Ambassador Melheret." Sounis returned the address, bowing politely back.

Melheret continued up the remaining steps to the landing, brushed the wrinkles from his clothes, and bowed again. He was as tall as Sounis, but more slender, with gray in his beard and in the hair at his temples. His narrow face was weathered by time in the sun, and he had probably been a soldier before he became an ambassador. He gave the appearance of good health and radiated a confidence that Sounis envied.

"A god-sent opportunity that we meet, Your Majesty," Melheret said. "I was just returning to my rooms, in anticipation of a bottle of remchik, which my secretary informs me has arrived. Perhaps you would care to join me?"

Sounis looked to Ion, who bowed to indicate his willingness to wait for as long as the king of Sounis desired. Sounis cursed inwardly, certain this meeting had been arranged for a moment when he was without the magus to act as a mediator. There was no polite way to refuse.

The Mede's apartments were as luxurious as Sounis's, but the Mede seemed to have been unimpressed by them. In the reception room, where Sounis waited for his host to reappear, cloth tapestries hung from hooks that had been hammered into the plaster walls with no care taken for the decorations already painted there, and Sounis wondered if it was an attempt to obscure spy holes. If so, he doubted it would be successful.

The Attolian furniture was pushed into the corners, and several replacement pieces of Medean design, small enough to have been shipped with the ambassador, had been put in their place. Mede statuettes of gods or goddesses or, Sounis supposed, fertility figures were scattered around the room, clashing with the rest of the Attolian background. The combined effect made Sounis wince.

The Mede ambassador returned carrying a ceramic bottle and two beautiful wine cups. They were glass, a deep blue in color, decorated on the outsides with bas-relief dancers carved in white. Sounis, taking his cup, admired it, running a finger across the raised figures.

"They are lovely, are they not?" said the Mede. "They come from a workshop in our capital. The artist has made a glass service for the emperor himself."

Holding the cup up to the light from a nearby lamp, Sounis could see that the glass had two layers, white on the outside and blue on the inside. The effect was achieved by carving away the white layer, leaving only the images of white dancers on the blue background. He had never seen anything like it.

"Our artisans have worked for centuries to perfect their art," said Melheret, as if no Sounisian artisans had ever done the same. "Some believe art is the greatest product of an enduring civilization."

Following a wave of the Mede's hand, Sounis chose a seat and sat in it gingerly. It was low to the ground, and the slanted seat tipped him against the curving back, making him wish he had pulled one of the more traditional chairs away from the wall. It wouldn't be easy to get up in a hurry—say, if armed men leaped from behind the wall hangings.

"You need not fear being attacked, Your Majesty."

Sounis suppressed a flinch before realizing that the Mede was not reading his thoughts about the furniture.

"Our nation is one of peace and great prosperity. We are not so poor of resources that we steal from our neighbors. Try the remchik?" Melheret had filled his glass.

Sounis took a drink, as he had seen the Mede do, tossing the contents of the glass cup into his mouth all at once. The liquid Melheret had poured was clear, so he knew it wasn't wine, but he was still taken aback by the powerful alcohol. It went up his nose and seared his throat all the way down to the pit of his stomach. He tried to hold his breath but only succeeded in turning a cough into a whistle. When he inhaled, his breath burned as much as the alcohol had.

"Do you like it?" asked the Mede.

"It's . . . delicious," Sounis said politely. His eyes were watering.

"Have another."

"How, then, do you explain your affiliations with my rebel barons?" Sounis thought of mentioning the attempt on his life as he had fled Sounis, but he assumed that the Mede would only deny any responsibility. If Melheret asked if he had seen Akretenesh with a match in his hand, Sounis would have to say no.

"We have no 'affiliations,' as you say," said Melheret. "Our overtures to your barons, and to your father, have been no more than an honest attempt to establish communication with a new government, and what can be expected of any wise nation. Did we not send an ambassador to your father, thinking that he spoke for your uncle who was Sounis? No one would deny your right to return to your throne. And we, my brother ambassador Akretenesh and I, would be honored to act as neutral mediators. You do not need Attolia's help to accomplish this."

"And Attolia? Does she need to fear attack?"

"Again, no," said the Mede, pouring once more.

Sounis was beginning to like the burning feeling in his middle, and after the second drink, he'd sensed a flavor in his mouth like mint and like fennel at the same time, something cool that contrasted with the heat. Still, he didn't think it wise to have another taste, and he ignored the contents of the cup.

The Mede sat again and looked into Sounis's eyes. "I will be frank with you. We are not well disposed toward Attolia. There are conventions among nations, relationships built on mutual good faith. She abused those relationships, lying about her intentions, inviting us to land our troops to aid in her defense, and then turning on them. More than that, she has cast us as aggressors, lying to you and to others in order to destroy our nation's peaceful relations here on this small peninsula."

The flavor that came after the burning flavor of the remchik wasn't mint, Sounis decided on reflection, and realized that he'd absentmindedly sipped from his cup while Melheret was talking.

"Drink," said the Mede. "Remchik is not for sipping, we say in my home. Its flavor comes in the swallow." The older man spoke with an almost fatherly authority.

Sounis obediently drank, but he declined another serving, holding the cup too close to allow Melheret to fill it without obvious effort.

Melheret said, "It is my task, given me by my emperor, to repair the battered ties between us and Attolia and encourage her to join a community of civilized nations."

"Not prepare for an invasion?" asked Sounis. "I thought your emperor was gathering his armies and building the ships that would carry them to our 'small' peninsula. Did he not send Attolia a message to say so?"

Melheret's head tilted, and his brow furrowed, as if Sounis's words had been garbled or as if he'd said the carpet on the floor had come to life. "Excuse me?"

Sounis rubbed his face and pinched his numb lips, afraid that his words *had* been garbled. "Your emperor plans to invade with a huge army and has sent word of it to Attolia."

Melheret shook his head. "Why, if he meant to invade, would he have warned Attolia of his plans?" Melheret put a companionable hand on Sounis's knee and shook it. "Think, Your Majesty. She lies. That is the obvious explanation for every story she tells. Yes, my emperor sent home her spies; would any ruler not do the same? She was embarrassed at being caught in such perfidy and lies to cover her shame. Is this any ally for Sounis? See what she offers you in exchange for your humiliating surrender. A paltry few mercenaries, a handful of gold. My emperor is a far, far better ally if your barons continue to rebel, as indeed, they may not. They, too, perhaps were unaware that you yet lived and were their king. You do not need to invade your own home to secure it. It is my belief that your barons will return to you with open arms."

"And if they don't?" asked a skeptical Sounis.

"Then from my emperor you will receive gold and the armies to secure your throne. *He* will not demand oaths of loyalty."

"Won't he? What did he demand of Suninex?"

Again Melheret looked puzzled. "Do you mean Sheninesh? Sheninesh is our ally of many years and shares in our prosperity. They choose to accept our governance because they see it as a benefit, not as a yoke. You may have read accounts that say otherwise, but if they cannot even tell you the name of a country, how accurate can they be?"

Sounis remembered an old argument. "Eddis," he said.

"Eddis? What about Eddis?"

"It isn't pronounced that way."

Melheret guided him back to the topic. "You count on the honesty and the support of your friend Eugenides, but it is she, not he, who rules Attolia. And is he in fact your friend? He does not seem so."

"He is king," Sounis said, holding on truculently to his friendship with Eugenides, spurred by the Mede's skepticism to more conviction than he really felt.

"He is a thief, his wife, a murderess. I ask again, are these allies for Sounis?"

Sounis nodded agreeably and watched the room spin. He thought of a number of things that he could say, but decided that the wisest course would be to say nothing at all. "What is the flavor in the remchik?" he asked.

"It is made with sreet oil."

"It's very good. If you will excuse me." He stood, nodded again to Melheret, and left. Ion waited for him outside Melheret's rooms and silently led him away.

At his own door, Sounis said to the attendant, "I am sorry to keep you away from your king."

"As you have noticed," said Ion, "he will not have missed me. We are merely for ornamentation, like the king's coats, his boots, and his embroidered sashes."

Sounis said, "Gen's very fond of his boots," and then, when Ion smiled painfully, wished he hadn't.

"Not even that, then," Ion murmured as he opened the door to Sounis's suite of rooms. "Verix is waiting for you and will attend you until morning."

While Sounis accepted Verix's help in getting undressed and crawled into bed to sleep off the remchik, the king of Attolia was visiting the queen in the royal apartments.

"He has had his meeting with the Mede," he said moodily.

She answered, "You know I do not see the wisdom of pushing him into Melheret's arms."

"If I am taking his country, I'll take it. I'm not going to charm it away."

"You're being a fool," said Attolia. She was sitting on a low-backed chair as Aglaia removed the pins from her carefully braided hair. There was more she would have said, but she held her tongue. Not because Aglaia was there but because she doubted words would have had any effect.

"No one would argue with that," said Eddis to the magus. She had invited him to her apartments while Sounis met with the king of Attolia. On the far side of the palace from the queen of Attolia, the magus had unwittingly echoed her opinion of Eugenides.

Eddis said, "If I bite my tongue anymore with the two of them, it will come off."

"How embarrassing," murmured the magus, and Eddis snorted indelicately.

"I've missed you since you left," she said. "I am very glad you survived the return to Sounis. I don't suppose Sophos's uncle welcomed you with open arms."

"He did not," said the magus. "But I have always been useful to him. He assumed, as I did, that Sophos had died in the kidnapping attempt and that my loyalties would no longer be unfortunately divided." He thought of the dead king, who had sweated his life away, leaving no one to regret his end. "I admit that my faith in his invitation was not perfect, but I am glad I accepted it. He was an astonishingly angry man, but he had many admirable qualities." He glanced up at Eddis and said, "He could be quite charming."

"Agape might have made something of him," said Eddis. "I could not. Have you met Relius?"

"Oh, Relius and I know each other well."

"I meant face to face," said Eddis, and it was the magus's turn to smile. Relius had been the queen of Attolia's master of spies, and he and the magus had crossed paths in the past.

"You confuse me with Sounis's baron Antimonus," said the magus. "It was he who was the official spy master. Relius and I were not adversaries."

"Oh," said Eddis, and followed it with "hmm."

"I have indeed been introduced to the former secretary of the archives," said the magus repressively.

"What do you think?" asked Eddis.

"Damaged," said the magus. "Attolia will not be able to use him again."

"I think he is more valuable now as a friend to them both than as spy master, but I agree that the Medes won that round."

"Let us hope they win no more," said the magus, setting down his glass and rising. "I must return to my king."

"One last thing," said Eddis. "Eugenides asks you

to bring Sophos to training in the morning. Gen has invited Melheret to spar."

"Why didn't Attolis ask Sounis himself?" asked the magus, then lifted his eyes to the heavens. "Never mind, I know why. Yes, I will bring my king in the morning."

Sounis was fully dressed but not fully awake. The magus had roused him at dawn and explained the king's invitation, but he was still rubbing his eyes, trying to rid himself of the vestiges of sleep and the remchik when he heard noises out in the reception room. He expected Verix and another attendant but found the king of Attolia and his entire retinue when he opened his chamber door.

Attolis engaged him with a wave and turned away. Sounis followed, the magus behind him, like obedient ducklings to the passageway outside the apartments. As he moved up beside Eugenides, Sounis said, "Chilly this morning."

"Is it?" asked the king, and Sounis dropped the attempt at conversation.

The men walked in silence to the practice field, where they found a crowd of Attolians and Eddisians idly waiting. The captain of the Royal Guard crossed the open court to meet them. He was a prickly man, and Sounis sensed a nonspecific disapproval, for Eugenides, the training, the morning, the sun in the sky, Sounis wasn't sure what. Gen nodded at him and, by the simple expedient of pointing at one man after another, arranged partners for warm-ups and sparring.

The Mede made them wait. When Melheret arrived, he warmed up on his own, and when he was willing, he wandered across the open field to where Gen was practicing with a member of his guard. Wearing only his trousers and thin tunic, he appeared fit and comfortable with his sword.

When the king of Attolia and the Mede began to spar, both proceeded cautiously. Then the Mede started to press, and Eugenides responded, just barely keeping up. The Mede grew more confident and pressed harder. Suddenly Gen surged in with a rapid set of strokes that appeared momentarily overwhelming, but he was rebuffed. He fell back, and the sparring went on. Each time Gen escalated, the Mede was just that much better, that much faster, and Gen was again on the defensive.

Sounis stood beside the magus on the edge of the watching crowd and tried not to wince. Melheret was making only a minimal effort to keep a diplomatic face on the exchange, and it was clear that Gen was both angry and embarrassed.

This was not the easygoing, sarcastic friend he remembered, nor the emotionally distant king. This was a Gen oddly impotent in anger, and it was uncomfortable to watch him trying and failing to outlast the Mede. Sounis looked away. The Eddisians around him were watching with impassive intensity; the Attolians, with amused glances.

Midway through the match, Eugenides began using his hook to deflect thrusts from his opponent.

"Do you mind?" he asked.

"Not at all," said the Mede, but held out a hand and accepted a blunted dagger from someone in the crowd as his own second weapon. Gen continued to be overmatched.

Finally, when it was clear that Eugenides was never going to do the gracious thing and admit defeat, Melheret stepped back. "Your Majesty, I must beg you to excuse me," he said. "I am afraid other duties call." He bowed with mocking deference.

Gen thanked him, standing stiffly as Melheret left the practice field. Then he threw his practice sword on the ground so hard it bounced. Cursing, he picked it up, and after obviously considering hacking at the pavement with it, he pitched it across the open court. As he seemed still unsatisfied, Sounis offered his own practice sword, curious to see what would happen. It was a borrowed one, and he minded not at all when it went sailing between two of the Attolian guardsmen standing nearby.

Gen turned to the man standing on his other side, but that man, Sounis knew, was Eddis's minister of war and Gen's father. Not inclined to indulge tantrums, the minister stood unhelpfully with his arms crossed and his practice sword held tight in the fist tucked under the crook of his elbow.

Eugenides tipped his head back to look at the sky. He said, "That was more difficult than I anticipated."

Teleus, the captain of the Royal Guard, returned with both Eugenides's and Sounis's swords. He presented the one punctiliously to his king as if it were an edged weapon, holding it out on his fingers, bowing over it. "If Your Majesty would like to retire to the dining hall?"

Gen wiped his hand down his arm as if wiping something invisible away, and took the practice sword from him, deliberately grabbing it across its edgeless blade and tucking it under his handless arm. "Yes, thank you, Teleus. Breakfast. Join me?" he said to Sounis over his shoulder.

Sounis took his blunt sword more politely from Teleus, then looked at the magus, who shrugged. They followed Attolis through the courtyard archway and into the narrow alleys between guard barracks to a dining hall. Inside the hall they passed by the long tables but did not stop, continuing down a dark hallway beside the kitchens to an empty storeroom that should have been equally dark but was lit by lamps hanging from metal pegs hammered into cracks in the stone walls.

Bewildered, Sounis stood and watched as the Eddisians paired up and began to spar. He listened as they analyzed every aspect of the Mede's style and began to piece together the best means to defeat him. Thanks to Eugenides's careful efforts to draw out the Mede, they had seen all they needed.

Sounis turned to the magus. "Did you know?"

"That he was relentless?" The magus finished his question. "Yes. That he had this in mind, no. I did not realize that he disliked the ambassador so much."

"Melheret has a reputation as one of the best swords-men in the Mede court," a soldier informed them, having overheard. "They say he trained the former ambassador, Nahuseresh."

"Ah," said the magus, understanding at once. "I see that he means to be prepared if he meets him again."

"Surely that's unlikely," said Sounis.

"I don't think *unlikely* means to him what it does to the rest of us," said the magus.

The Attolians were smiling openly by this time. Whatever they thought of their king, they enjoyed a good joke at a newcomer's expense, whereas the Eddisians seemed no less intent than they had been on the training field, though they did joke with one another as they sparred.

"No, his foot was farther back," said a voice nearby.

"Higher in the backswing," said another man.

"Why would you put your elbow out like that?"

"Airing your arm hair?"

"Boagus could take out whole swaths of Medes

that way," said someone across the room, and everyone laughed.

"Pray gods then that the Medes don't have anyone that smells as bad as me," said the smiling man who must have been Boagus.

Sounis, watching, was crushed by a sudden longing for Pol, who would have been at home with these men.

"Do you spar, Your Majesty?"

Still unused to being so addressed, Sounis jumped.

"Oh, yes, thank you," he said to the small, wiry man who had invited him to match swords.

"Will you practice against the Mede?" the man asked, as he settled into a fighting stance.

Sounis demurred. "No, thank you," he said. "I am not expert enough, I am afraid, to learn from it."

"Very well," said the man. He was a head shorter than Sounis, and Sounis thought himself prepared for attack until the man's sword suddenly caught him just above the elbow. He fell back in surprise and smiled politely, acknowledging the hit, but the other man didn't smile back. Sounis resisted the impulse to look to the magus for rescue and raised his sword again.

The wiry little man was a monster in human guise, Sounis decided, sent by the gods to humiliate him. It was only luck that the other men in the room were focused on Eugenides and his partners or they would have been snickering behind their hands. Sounis was covered with sweat and deep in confusion by the time

Eugenides finally called a halt. He'd been praying for the king of Attolia to wind up his exercise and was cursing him for his selfish delay. When Eugenides called, "Enough!," Sounis lowered his sword immediately and caught a stinging smack on his upper arm. The little man was giving him such a look that instead of being angry at the late hit, Sounis found himself apologizing for dropping his weapon too soon.

"Hmph," said the Eddisian, and walked away.

Sounis slunk out of the room, avoiding a sympathetic glance from the magus. Passing the food in the dining hall, he snagged a roll and hurried on to catch up with Eugenides, wondering, even as he did so, why he bothered.

Sounis drew closer once they both were outside, but slowed when he saw his sparring partner was closing in on Eugenides as well. The man said something to the king that made him turn in Sounis's direction. Sounis knew he would only look silly if he backed away and forced himself to continue his approach, arriving in time to hear the small Eddisian say, "That one should go back to the basics," before he stalked away like a particularly officious little rooster.

Flushed, and knowing it, Sounis fell into step with the king of Attolia and glared at the ground. "You might have mentioned this charade you had planned beforehand," he said stiffly, his irritation overcoming his reserve.

"Couldn't," Gen said coolly. "I needed you on the edge, looking slightly sick."

Sounis knew that his mind sometimes worked like a pig stuck in mud, but at other times conclusions seemed to strike like lightning, one bolt after another. He realized that Eugenides was growing more remote, not less, and almost in the same instant that he would never see any sign of his old friend if all he did was wait patiently for it. If the king of Attolia was more than just his ally, there was one sure way to find out. He stuffed the bread into his mouth and dropped his practice sword. He slid one foot around Eugenides's ankle, and using both hands, as well as his greater mass, he sent him flying.

It was immensely satisfying. Eugenides crashed into his attendants, who went stumbling in turn, a mass of windmilling arms and falling bodies as they tried to catch the king, who was making no effort to save himself. He'd dropped his own practice sword and had his arms tucked in where his hook would do no accidental damage. He slipped through their clutching hands like a fish.

Sounis stood very still, his hands well away from his body, surrounded, as he'd anticipated, by weapons that were very real and all pointed toward him. Eugenides levered himself up on his elbows, appearing stunned. After a moment he lay back down again and began to laugh. He was uncooperative as his crouching attendants tried to lift him. They managed to pull him to a seated position, but he waved them away. With a nod, he dismissed the swords back to their sheaths. "Just what makes you think you can get away with that?" he asked the young man standing over him with a butter-won't-melt-in-my-mouth expression incongruous on his scarred face.

"I am Sounis," his friend answered, and offered a hand to help him up.

Arms around each other, the kings of Sounis and Attolia walked back toward the palace. The magus, following some distance behind, watched with pleasure and the happy anticipation of carrying the news to Eddis.

"That was a compliment, you know," said Eugenides.

"What was?"

"What Procivitus said. He wouldn't have suggested you go back to basics if he didn't think you were worth training."

"I didn't realize."

"I know you didn't, you idiot. There's no time for the basics, really, but if you'd like, he'd be happy to train with you while you're here."

Sounis hesitated. "I think it might kill me."

Attolis laughed. "I'll tell him that you will wait for him in the morning."

When they'd gone a little farther, Attolis slipped out

from under Sounis's arm. "It might be beneficial to sow a little ambiguity. Really, there is very little hope that I will be able to play this trick on Melheret twice, but will you go on from here alone?"

They parted ways, and the magus and Sounis, led by Attolis's attendant Hilarion, made their way back to their rooms.

Chapter Fifteen

"S OPHOS, you sleep with a knife under your pillow? I'm hurt."

"I'm sorry," said Sounis, blinking, afraid that he had made contact with his wild swing.

"I was joking. Wake up the rest of the way, would you?"

"Gen, it's the middle of the night."

"I know," said the king of Attolia.

Sounis tried to rub the sleep out of his eyes. He was sitting up in his bed. The sky was still entirely dark, and he couldn't have been asleep for long. He suspected that he had just dropped off. The bare knife was still in his hand, he realized, and he rooted under his pillow for the sheath.

"Don't you trust my palace security?"

"Yes, of course," Sounis said, trying to think of some other reason besides mistrust to sleep with a knife. He heard Eugenides laugh.

"My queen and I sleep with a matched set under our pillows, as well as handguns in pockets on the bedposts. Don't be embarrassed."

"Gen, what are you doing in my bedroom in the middle of the night?" Sounis asked.

"Going out of my mind," said Eugenides promptly. "At least I am on the verge of going out of my mind." Sounis could just make him out in the darkness as he dropped into the chair across the room. "If I don't get away from the pernicious attentions of my attendants, the rivalry between my palace physician and Eddis's, and the need to refrain from pushing certain members of my court down stairs, I am going to be a very bad king indeed. Come out with me, Sophos."

"The magus," said Sounis, thinking that his minister probably wouldn't approve.

"He won't even know you're gone, I promise."

Sounis followed Gen through Attolia's palace as he had once followed him through the much grimmer stronghold of her fortress on the Seperchia River. This time they were not escaping prisoners, but Sounis had to remind himself of that because there was more than a hint of escaping in the proceedings.

Gen avoided every posted guard. He arrived at intersections of hallways just as they moved away, slipping behind them with no more than a few feet to spare. He led the way down servants' passages and narrow staircases that were hidden behind knobless doors that matched the paneling so flawlessly that even knowing they were there, Sounis wasn't sure if he could find them again. He was hopelessly lost.

They reached a small courtyard just inside the outer wall of the palace, with a gate and an inevitable guard, and Sounis balked at last. The guard stood in the very center of the archway, facing out. There was a low doorway opening to his right that would lead to a guardroom holding at least one more man, but Eugenides blithely set out across the open ground. Sounis set his heels and stopped. Eugenides could not possibly make his way past the guard unseen. It was ludicrous even to think of it. Sounis held his breath, knowing that at any moment the guard would catch a glimpse from the corner of his eye, or that god-sent nudge would come that causes a man to turn when someone is sneaking up behind him.

The guard would turn, Sounis thought. At any moment. And he did.

"Your Majesty."

"Aris," said the king of Attolia, and flipped a coin into the air. It dropped into the guard's open palm and disappeared into his purse. The guard resumed his position, and the king passed by.

After digging through his own purse, Sounis put a coin more clumsily into the same hand and followed Attolis out of the palace.

"You bastard," said Sounis wearily. "I don't know why I don't stab you here in this alley so I can be the annux over Sounis and Attolia." They were twisting through the narrowest of passages, with Eugenides still in the lead, turning on what seemed to be a whim from one walkway to the next.

"Well, the stabbing would be unkind," said Eugenides, "but you can have the annux part with my goodwill."

"Not Attolia's."

"True," said the king. "Better not stab me."

"Gen," Sounis said, and halted. Attolis, who had already lightly descended a crooked stair, turned back at the bottom and looked up at him.

"Yes?"

Sounis didn't know what to say.

"She cut off my hand?" Gen asked.

It was exactly what Sounis was thinking, but he said, "Did you know? When she imprisoned us after you stole Hamiathes's Gift. Did you love her then?"

Eugenides laughed and seemed so at ease that Sounis found himself laughing with him. "No," said Gen. "I wrote down exactly what I thought for my cousin who is Eddis. I meant to send it to the magus and he might have passed it on to you, but for some reason I never did." He looked around as if the reason for this lapse might be found in the graffiti on the nearby wall. "It may be lost by now. At any rate, the answer is no, I did not know."

"When then?" asked Sounis, coming slowly down the stairs. He remembered meeting Eddis and the first time she had smiled. "Or do you not know?"

"I know exactly. I was hiding in a takima bush in the

Queen's Garden, watching the older son of the Baron Erondites tell Attolia that he loved her. He was trying to propose a marriage and she thought he was talking about a poem he was writing. I was laughing like a very quiet fiend, trying not to make the branches around me shake, and then, between one heartbeat and the next, and to my complete surprise, *it wasn't funny anymore.*" He rubbed his chest, as if at a remembered pain. "I wanted to kill him. Once she was gone, I very nearly jumped out of the bush onto his head. Poor Dite."

Poor Eugenides, thought Sounis, to fall in love with a woman he had already made into an enemy. "You exiled him?" He had heard of the destruction of the house of Erondites.

"Happily, not before we resolved our differences," said Eugenides. He added more seriously, "I would have exiled him even if we hadn't."

"I understand," said Sounis, and he did. "Where are we going?"

"To a nice tavern where they have no idea who I am, so pull that cloak a little tighter over your fine clothes. I don't want them asking awkward questions. I just want a chance to have a moment without my dear companions or, gods forbid, any physicians."

"They seemed a little unfriendly with each other," said Sounis.

The king of Attolia sighed. "They purport to be worried about my health."

They had left the narrow alleys and were walking along the broader Sacred Way, and Eugenides kept his voice low. Sounis suspected that everyone in the palace worried about Eugenides's health.

"I am nothing but a bone of contention," said the patient bitterly.

Sounis was unsympathetic. "That seems unlike Galen," he said.

"Well, you try insinuating that he's a mountain bumpkin with the medical knowledge of the village butcher and see how he takes it," said Eugenides. "My oh-so-timid palace physician turns out to be quite ferocious when he thinks someone is trespassing on his medical ground."

"That also seems unlike Galen," said Sounis.

"My fault entirely," Eugenides admitted. "I asked to see Galen while he was here with Eddis and touched off a bout of professional jealousy."

Sounis snickered.

"Your time will come, puppy. You just wait," said Eugenides. He turned again into a narrow side street. "There it is," he said, "under the lantern."

The tavern had a sign of painted grapes just barely illuminated by the dim lamp. Sounis went down stone steps and ducked through a low door underneath the sign. The taproom was no better lit, and he stepped carefully around scattered tables to a booth against a wall where he and Eugenides could sit opposite each other and still each have a view of the door.

By unspoken agreement they paused in their conversation until they were sitting with the high walls of the booth on either side.

"And your attendants?" Sounis asked.

"Every one another Ambiades," said Gen, referring to the traitor who had betrayed them both when they followed the magus in pursuit of Hamiathes's Gift. "I'd had some hope for Philologos," Gen admitted, "but Sejanus won that hand neatly."

Sounis had been thinking of Ambiades. "He would have been a better man under different circumstances."

Gen looked at him. "True enough," he said. "But does a good man let his circumstances determine his character?"

Sounis couldn't argue with that. "Perhaps you can bring out better in them?"

Eugenides shook his head. "I pulled the carpet out from under them very thoroughly. They will not cross me, but they won't love me, either. I am not Eddis. People do not hand *me* their hearts."

Sounis wondered. He would have given Eugenides his heart on a toothpick, if asked. He remembered Ion's obvious wince at being rated somewhat less significant to Gen than his boots.

The barmaid came to the table, and Gen ordered wine.

When she was gone, Sounis asked if Attolis paid his

way out of his own palace often, but he needled to no effect.

"Oh, that's not a bribe to get out the gate. It's compensation for the rating he'll get from the captain of my guard. Teleus hates it when I go out, and he's going to be sullen in the morning, but I've given him enough ground. The circus this morning was largely at his insistence. My father and Procivitus would have served my purposes well enough, but Teleus insisted his guard be involved. He does not like them to be ashamed of me." Eugenides shrugged. "So. Melheret will already know I was making a fool of him, and I won't be able to trick him again, but Teleus must be appeased."

"Oh, poor king," said Sounis.

The barmaid brought the wine and cups. When she was gone, Eugenides dunked a finger in his wine and flicked it at Sounis.

CHAPTER SIXTEEN

THE long summer twilight was in the sky outside,
but the lamps were lit in the small dining room,
casting a warm glow over the diners reclined on their
couches. The king's attendants moved quietly through
the room with platters of food and amphorae to refill
wine cups.

"Why not refuse the ambassador, send him home?"
Sounis asked.

He watched Attolia out of the corner of his eye. She
was still cool, like a breath of winter in the warm evening air, but in the last few days he had begun to sense
a subtle humor in her chilly words.

When Gen had complained earlier that evening that
Petrus, the palace physician, should stop fussing over
him like a worried old woman, Attolia had asked, archly,
"And me as well?"

"When you stop fussing," Gen had said, slipping to
his knees beside her couch, "I will sleep with *two* knives
under my pillow."

Attolia had looked down at him and said sharply,
"Don't be ridiculous."

Only when Eugenides laughed had Sounis realized

her implication: If she ever turned against Eugenides, a second knife wouldn't save him. He almost swallowed the olive in his mouth unchewed.

As he stared, Attolia had brushed Eugenides's cheek almost shyly before sending him with a wave back to his own couch.

"One cannot toss ambassadors back like bad fish," said Eugenides. "You treat them with care, or you'll find you've committed an act of war."

"If we have one of their ambassadors, the Medes, in turn, have one of ours," said Attolia.

Sounis knew from the magus that Attolia's spy network had been devastatingly compromised. He understood why they were willing to accept the risk of having a Mede ambassador sowing dissent in their palace if it meant they had some representative of their own in the Mede Empire.

"We would like to know where the Mede emperor is gathering his army, his navy," Attolia said. "The Great Powers of the Continent, and those on the Peninsula, don't believe he is raising one. They insist that it is saber rattling. Which," she conceded, "it might be. The emperor is dying, and dying men rarely start wars with their last breaths. But I believe that his heir has already seized power, and a conquest is a reliable means to cement his authority."

"Only if he can trust his generals not to turn on him once they come home as heroes," said Sounis.

"In this case, his general is his brother Nahuseresh," said Eugenides. "Civil unrest from that quarter is more than we could hope for."

Eddis said, "The Continent wants proof of an attack before they take any risks to counter it. They don't want to offend the Mede Empire and so precipitate the war we all are trying to avoid. Though they would of course be willing to stage troops here," she added drily.

Sounis winced. Small countries like Sounis, Eddis, and Attolia were as vulnerable to the "aid" of the Continent as to the conquest of the Medes. In his lifetime Sounis had seen small city-states on the Peninsula absorbed by their larger neighbors in the guise of "safekeeping."

Sounis sensed that it would be impolite to ask outright if Eddis had any spies across the Middle Sea. Her spies more probably were deployed closer to home, in Attolia. Or in Sounis, he supposed. He resolved to ask the magus for more information about his own sources of information.

"The ambassadors of several states have conveyed their sovereigns' offers to improve megarons on our coast and to move their soldiers, under their own command, into the fortified positions," said Eugenides. "As opposed to loaning us the money to fortify our own borders."

"What we have received most," said Attolia, "is lectures warning us not to be provoking, that we risk losing the support of the sovereigns on the Peninsula and the Continent."

"If the Medes are going to attack, what point is there in not being provoking?" asked Sounis.

Attolia replied. "So long as the emperor publicly denies any animosity and continues to send an ambassador to my court and yours, the Continent can continue to do nothing."

"But why?" asked Sounis. "Why the wishful thinking?"

Eugenides shrugged his lack of an answer. "They may be too busy with instability closer to home."

"So we walk on eggshells?" said Sounis. "Hoping that if the Mede does attack, the Continent and the greater Peninsula will come to our aid in time rather than allow the emperor a foothold on this side of the Middle Sea?"

"Indeed," said Attolia. "And we pray that no one on this little peninsula of ours will offer them the foothold for free, which your rebels may be doing as we speak. You and your magus in your overcautious treaty writing are wasting time you don't have. You need to find your most significant adversary, and you need to destroy him, annihilate him root and branch. If you can capture him alive and have him publicly ganched, so much the better."

Sounis looked away.

Eugenides looked into his wine cup. Eddis met Attolia's gaze, but offered her no support.

Her chin up, Attolia said, "You think I am overly

harsh. You inherited your throne free and clear. And you"—she turned on her husband—"took one ready-made. Sounis has little in common with either of you."

"He *is* an appointed heir," said Gen, speaking into his folded arms, as he reclined back on his couch with the toes of his boots tapping.

Attolia shook her head. "They will deny that in a heartbeat, making sparks from his father's illegitimacy if they choose."

Gen said blandly, "It isn't Sophos who is illegitimate."

"He has the magus," said Eddis, turning the conversation back to the point.

"The magus is not much beloved in Sounis these days," Attolia responded.

"There is my father," said Sounis.

Attolia looked at him. "And are you certain he will support you when he learns that you have sworn loyalty to Attolis?"

Sounis said nothing, staring down at his wine.

Later they rose together and made their way toward one of the larger throne rooms where there would be music and dancing. The kings of Attolia and Sounis fell a little way back.

"Is she right?" Sounis asked bluntly.

Attolis shrugged. "She is right that I took the throne she secured. Eddis has her barons in the palm of her hand, and they would follow her cheerfully through the gates of the underworld, but Attolia is not wrong that my cousin inherited her throne on the strength of my father's right arm. He swore that she, and no one else, would be crowned. Only Attolia has faced a revolt in her own house."

"Then you think I should take her advice?"

"I know that if you don't look for an alternative, Sophos, you certainly won't find one."

The next day, as Sounis crossed a spacious flower-filled courtyard, Ion asked him if he would like to take a seat on a bench in the cool colonnade that overlooked the garden.

"Perhaps Your Majesty would like to rest a moment?" Ion suggested. Sounis was on his way to another appointment with his tailors, and not looking forward to it. He'd thought they were finished with their work, but Eugenides had ordered an armored breastplate— out of sheer perversity, Sounis was certain. The tailors wanted to be sure the fabric of the embroidered coat he would wear under the armor wouldn't bunch or chafe. Sounis had little patience left for the tailors, and he said yes, he would like to delay just a moment to look at the flowers.

He was grateful for all that had taken place in Attolia. He could have been in a dungeon, or still at work in Hanaktos's fields, or dead, for that matter. He wasn't. He was sitting with an appearance of ease in the shade, but he was growing desperate to return to Sounis. He had been weeks in Attolia without news of his mother or sisters. His father had reached the border with Melenze; he knew that much but could only guess at the activity of his rebel barons. The queen's warning about the passage of time had been unnecessary. Sounis's every worry pricked him like the tailors' pins. He sat for a moment to pick through them and to consider the queen of Attolia's troubling advice.

Ion had wandered down the colonnade to give the king of Sounis his privacy. Or so Sounis had assumed. When he caught a glimpse of bright fabric moving between the garden beds opposite, he leaned forward and tracked its progress. The woman was moving toward the corner where Ion was waiting. When Ion stepped from the colonnade down into the garden, he disappeared from sight, but Sounis's ears were good, and he heard the murmur of greeting.

Sounis sat back with a smile. He was jealous. Were it not for the inconvenient meeting he was presently avoiding, he would have been walking with Eddis in the far more spacious and private gardens behind the palace. His smile faded the instant he saw the ambassador for the Mede Empire approaching from the opposite direction.

"Please, Your Majesty," said the Mede politely, "do not rise. I have no desire to interrupt your contemplations."

"Won't you join me?" said Sounis diplomatically, his heart sinking.

"If you can spare a moment of your time?" Wrapping his robes around his knees, Melheret settled beside him on the stone bench.

"Certainly," said Sounis. Impossible to say no when he was already sparing the time on his own self-indulgence.

"The king of Attolia keeps you close," said the Mede, by way of an explanation for his unusual approach.

"He is a good friend," said Sounis.

"Or perhaps just a jealous one," said Melheret gently. "His invitations take precedence and leave little room for you to confer with others . . . others who may have information of great use to you."

Sounis wondered if he was supposed to be surprised. Of course the constant meetings with the Attolians prevented even more awkward meetings with the ambassadors of the Peninsula and the Continent. Sounis had sent the magus to deal with those ambassadors, with careful instructions to make no commitments. The Mede he had meticulously avoided since their first exchange over the remchik.

It was as Attolia had said, one didn't want to make a misstep and start a war. Sounis wanted nothing to do with the Medes, but no sensible ruler offended another's ambassador on purpose. He just hoped his uncharitable opinion of Melheret didn't show.

"You don't like me, Your Majesty. I see my cause is lost."

Oh, gods, save me from having to protest my undying affection for the Mede, thought Sounis. "No, Ambassador, not at all," he said aloud. He might as well put his worries to good use. "I am unsure of my course, I will tell you. I—" He stopped short of saying he was still tracing designs in the plasterwork at night instead of sleeping. "Truly, I do not know what is for the best. Attolia counsels violence and I—I want to believe that I can bring my barons together peacefully, that I can convince them to honor me as their king without defeating them first. The cost to my countrymen in gold, in lives, will mean that even as I win, I will count it. It will be years before Sounis can recover what it has lost." To say it aloud was to be overwhelmed by it; waging a war to make peace seemed a sick sort of joke played by the gods.

"You are no butchering monster, Your Majesty," said the Mede. "Anyone can see that. If you will forgive me, let me say how I honor you. No, do not blush; you must accept your compliments."

Sounis's head was bowed but not to hide a blush. "I pray the gods will guide me on my path," he said, wishing that a convenient hole would open in the stone pavers under his feet and that he could drop through it, or better yet, drop Melheret.

"You are a man of good faith, and I know you will

not offend the gods," said Melheret. It was an obvious preamble to a larger point, but fast-approaching footsteps announced Ion, who swept up to where they were seated.

"Ambassador," he said, with diplomatic calm, "I must have forgotten your appointment with His Majesty; please forgive me, and let me ask you to arrange another. His Majesty is due to be on his way to his tailors now." He looked at the Mede with steely determination, and the Mede, unruffled, rose to his feet.

"Please forgive my forwardness in greeting you here, Your Majesty. I have had news from Sounis that I wished to impart, but now is not the time."

Ion watched him go with what looked like loathing. Then he bowed to Sounis. "Your appointment, Your Majesty?"

"Please."

Sounis followed his borrowed attendant back to his rooms, thinking over what Melheret had said in parting, that he had news from Sounis. It was bait, and Sounis would have to decide if he would take it. If he did, it would mean another meeting, arranged in a more official way, with the Mede. If he met with the Mede, he might then be expected to meet with all the ambassadors, the prospect of which gave him a headache. He was beginning to think he would never leave Attolia.

"Ion."

"Your Majesty?" said the attendant. He had delivered

Sounis to his own anteroom and had asked permission to withdraw. "Is there something else you require?"

"A word," said Sounis. He walked through his reception room, where his tailors waited, to his bedchamber without looking back to see if Ion followed.

"Close the door," he said.

When he heard it shut, he turned around.

"Your Majesty, I apologize," Ion said.

"Did you arrange the meeting with Melheret?"

"No."

Sounis waited.

"I did arrange the meeting with Zenia that the ambassador used to his advantage, and I will have to inform the king."

"And what will he do?"

"Send me away," said Ion. "This is one too many mistakes to forgive."

"You would prefer to stay?"

Ion shrugged at the irony of his situation. "I would."

"You could apologize," Sounis suggested. "He has a soft spot for idiots. He's always been very kind to me."

Ion shook his head. "I do not think he has any such soft spot for me, Your Majesty."

"Ion," Sounis said, coming to a decision even he found surprising, "tell him that if he releases you, I would like you to accompany me."

"Accompany you?"

"To Sounis, as my attendant," he said.

Ion's eyebrows rose. "You do me an honor I don't deserve, Your Majesty."

Sounis's insecurities nibbled at him. It was an honor Ion probably didn't want, either, but Ion unexpectedly smiled. "I would be gratified to serve Your Majesty," he said sincerely.

"You would rather serve Eugenides," said Sounis. "Only tell him so, and I will have to find someone else to keep an eye on all my new finery."

The dinner the next night was formal, all the court at tables, with Sounis and Eddis and the Attolias at the head table with the magus and Eddis's ambassador. All the other ambassadors were carefully placed beyond the range of polite conversation, to Sounis's relief. He had declined to meet again with the Mede. At last the talking was done, and the court dined in celebration of a treaty concluded between Sounis and Attolia.

Conversationally, Eugenides said, "What are you doing rescuing my attendants from their own folly?"

"Did you let him go?"

"I'm still thinking about it, shocked as I am to find you raiding my overelegant lapdogs for your own companions."

"I astonished myself," said Sounis. "I might perhaps have been prejudiced in my earlier judgment of them."

Eugenides popped a grape into his mouth and said seriously, "I will rethink my own judgments, then."

Sounis reached for a serving platter set in front of them both. When Eugenides cleared his throat sharply, Sounis pulled his hand back as if he expected to be bitten.

"Fetch the king of Sounis some lamb," Attolis said over his shoulder, and someone hurried away to do his bidding. Sounis noticed then that the food on the platter was all cut into bite-sized portions.

"I'm sorry," he said. "I didn't realize it was reserved for you."

The king was smiling out at the room. "It is," he said calmly.

"I seem to remember once sharing my oatmeal with you," Sounis remarked.

"I seem to remember *stealing* your oatmeal," said the former Thief of Eddis, "but it didn't have sand in it."

"Sand?" said Sounis, taken aback.

"Sand, and if my queen notices, she will have someone flayed."

Attolia was looking their way. Sounis hastily dropped his eyes to his plate. Gen was relaxed against the back of his chair, entirely at his ease. "There is still someone in the kitchen who adores the queen, dislikes Eddisians, and hates me," he said.

"She just hasn't met you, I am sure."

"She has, actually," said the king of Attolia.

Attolia's eyebrows were descending as she scrutinized the king. She looked from the platter to his face, and back again. She looked at Sounis. Eugenides sighed and reached for the lamb. To allay her suspicions, he was going to have to eat some of it.

"Let me fall on that blade for you," said Sounis, and served himself.

"You are a prince among men," said Eugenides.

"A king," Sounis corrected him with his mouth full.

In the morning the great plaza in front of Attolia's palace was emptied of booths and vendors and all their wares. No king departs without ceremony, and the stones were swept of straw and manure, and a dais built, before the morning mist had burned away.

There were prayers by the priests and priestesses of various temples to old gods and new ones. The king of Attolia was known for his dedication to his gods, but careful to make no move to offend any others. The high priestess of Hephestia, a massive woman swathed in red, came last to bless the men who were to be sent to Sounis to fight.

Eddis, sitting on the dais, on a borrowed chair that was far more elegant than the throne she used at home, admired the priestess. She was Attolian by birth and had risen to be high priestess of what was a minor temple in the city. Overnight she had become quite powerful, with a new temple rising on the acropolis above Attolia's palace. She had great wealth at her fingertips and access to the king's ear. She could have used that power to diminish other priests and priestesses, but she had chosen not to. When she called out the blessing on the soldiers before her, Eddis could hear the Goddess in the priestess's voice and wondered if others around her heard it as well. Eddis knew that Eugenides did and that it never failed to spark unease in him. Eddis was tired, and the Goddess's voice made her long for her mountains. She, too, had spent sleepless nights unmaking and remaking her plans.

When the invocation was complete, Sounis walked back to the dais to take his leave and accept a parting gift from Attolia.

As the horses and men waited, one of her women brought it forward: a small wooden casque with a bowed top and a plain brass latch. Sounis was as hesitant as anyone who receives a gift and is unsure whether to open it immediately or not. The queen's companion, versed in the moment, turned the case in her hands and lifted the lid. Inside the case was a dueling pistol, a king's weapon, wheel-locked, chased in gold. Eddis had seen it earlier that day. When Sounis lifted it out and tipped his head over the locking mechanism, she knew he was reading the letters inscribed there: *Onea realia.* "The queen made me."

Sounis thanked the queen prettily, years of training providing the appropriate words. As he went to replace the pistol in the box, he paused. There was a tab to lift the bottom of the box and clearly room to store something underneath. Keeping the gun in his hand, he reached with the other, but Gen forestalled him, holding the inset bottom of the box down with a single finger.

"You have heard my queen's advice. My gift is below. Would you wait to see it until you have decided what you will do with hers?"

Sounis nodded and returned the gun to its place. He took the box in his arms and hefted it, judging what he could from its weight, like a child with a present. It was heavy enough to be a substantial amount of gold. He handed the box to the magus, who handed it in turn to someone else, to be packed.

"Your destination?" Eugenides asked.

"Brimedius, to free my mother and my sisters." He and Eugenides had talked through his strategy in the tavern. It had been their one chance for a private exchange. "Then on to the pass to Melenze, to my father."

"Fare with the gods, and be blessed in your endeavors," said the king of Attolia.

Sounis bowed first, then embraced the king, and they kissed. Moving on to Attolia, with just a shade of deliberation, too slight to call a hesitation, he embraced and kissed her as well. Then he stepped before Eddis.

No ceremony was ceremonial enough without the appropriate clothing, and Sounis was wearing his best, his embroidered coat with the shining breastplate on top that Eugenides had commissioned for him. Eddis was just thinking of how much older he looked, with his finery and his scars and his appropriately solemn expression, when he met her eye. His stern gaze dropped. Sucking in his scarred lip, he cast her a sheepish smile.

The pain was as unexpected as a thunderclap in a clear sky. Eddis's chest tightened, as something closed around her heart. A deep breath might have calmed her, but she couldn't draw one. She wondered if she was ill, and she even thought briefly that she might have been poisoned. She felt Attolia reach out and take her hand. To the court it was unexceptional, hardly noticed, but to Eddis it was an anchor, and she held on to it as if to a lifeline. Sounis was looking at her with concern. Her responding smile was artificial.

"I will look forward to hearing of your future adventures," Eddis said. It was stiff, and he looked disappointed. She did not release Attolia's hand, subtly discouraging an embrace, so Sounis bowed instead. His polite expression returned. He bade her farewell and then went back down the steps to his men. The usual discordant shout of commands and the clatter of hooves and weapons and wheels against the plaza followed before the king and his retinue were finally departed. Throughout, the queen of Attolia never let go of Eddis's hand.

When Sounis was gone, and the rest of the royal guard was dismissed, Eddis left the plaza and went directly to the highest part of the palace, from which she could catch a glimpse, even if it was just dust rising above the road, of Sounis, as he drew farther and farther away. She would have gone to her room and locked herself in, but it would have been recognized as highly irregular. On the roof, she was not alone, but only her attendants were nearby, and it was not so unusual as to cause talk. It was as much privacy as she was likely to find without drawing attention to herself.

She heard the king of Attolia arrive. She didn't turn, and sensed rather than saw him draw near. From behind, his arms closed around her, and she was wrapped inside the long cloak he wore. When she grasped its edges, he used his hand to reach up and adjust the cloth of the capacious hood, creating a space no larger than the two of them.

"Did you send Attolia to me at the farewell?" Eddis asked.

"Not I," said Gen quietly. "The magus. I thought you knew that you loved him—the two of you have been like magnets drawing ever nearer to each other since you met—but the magus was concerned. He thought the grief of leave-taking might surprise you."

"I feel very stupid." She leaned back into his embrace. "'I will look forward to hearing of your future adventures.'" She shook her head in disgust and sniffed. "I should have had something better to say, something . . . more appropriate."

He couldn't disagree. Sounis had clearly hoped for some message of her affection to carry with him. "You could write him a letter," he said. "A fast horse will catch him before he reaches the pass."

"It's not a letter I want to send after him," she said. "It's fifteen hundred crossbowmen and a thousand pikes."

"You helped pick the numbers."

She sighed. "I was still sensible then. I am less so now."

"He wouldn't thank you for a company of nannies."

She looked out over the parapet. "Will he forgive us?"

"You aren't stealing his country."

"Neither am I helping him keep it."

"Helen," Gen said, "you sent me to Attolia."

She stiffened.

He held her tight. "We do what we must, but we are not defined by our circumstances. Sounis will not change."

"Did you warn him not to offend the gods?"

"There was no need," said Attolis, smiling. "He couldn't offend the gods with a pointed stick."

◆ CHAPTER SEVENTEEN ◆

WE left Attolia with horses underneath us and all the provisions we had missed on our previous journey. We had an escort fit for a king, and we moved no faster than the magus and I had traveled on foot. Your letter reached me before we got to the pass, and I read it over and over until I had it by heart.

Once in Sounis, we moved across country, avoiding the roads and towns. I had a tent that appeared like magic every night, with a bed in it, as well as a table and folding stools for our meetings.

It even had a writing desk so that I could have sent letters, but everything I wrote seemed silly under the circumstances. Eugenides had warned me in the tavern that letters would go astray and that once we left Attolia messengers could no longer be relied upon to be loyal or safe—just as I must assume that anything I said aloud in his palace would be conveyed directly to the Mede. The magus had said the same thing. Both of them had urged me to keep my plans to myself until we were inside Sounis. It reinforced a sense I had of being on my own every minute, in spite of being surrounded day and night by soldiers and advisors.

The food was never-ending. When I pointed out the attentions to my appetite, the magus had to remind me that I was Sounis. Across my little state there are merchants who dream of putting PURVEYOR TO THE KING over their shops. There are men whose lives will change if they can provide me with soap. I am a patron of the arts now. I can found my own university instead of just dreaming of sometime attending the one in Ferria. It gave me something to think about besides war.

As you know, we didn't get as far as Brimedius. We crossed through the main pass to Sounis and forded the Seperchia to avoid the fortified megaron there, then moved across the foothills heading inland. We had reached Atusi, where I meant to pick up the road to Brimedius, when we met the rebels. I had just brought my small army out of the hills and onto the road when my scouts came in to tell me that the rebels were both ahead of us and behind us.

I had prepared my Attolians and my Eddisians carefully. Every time I talked with the Attolian commander, I remembered what Eugenides had said: "He does not actually run on all fours and bay at the moon, but you will have to explain what you want from him very carefully." I know he did it to make me laugh, and it helped. I would have otherwise been too much intimidated by a man who reminded me so much of my father.

We were already assembled on the road. On our right, two ridges reached out from the foothills, and a shallow valley lay between them. To our left, olive trees came almost to the road. The road curved around the foothills, keeping the rebels ahead of us and behind us out of sight. It was an excellent place for a trap, and we had sprung it. My scouts warned me that the men behind us on the road were farther back but mounted and coming up fast.

Around the curve of the hill ahead of us, we had our first view of the men approaching from that direction. I sent my Eddisians forward and turned back with the Attolians and my mounted force, leaving our pack train with supplies in the middle.

It was my first battle. It was exhilarating and terrifying and sickening. The Eddisians and Attolians did just as they'd been instructed. The road sloped down slightly toward the Sounisians in front of us, and the Eddisians rushed down it to attack.

The force behind us was twice the size of ours, or more. When it hit the Attolian formations, the Attolians broke. They made an attempt to re-form but broke again and began to scatter. Their captain, at my signal, called the retreat. Some of the Attolians turned back toward the Eddisians to re-form with them, but fully half ran into the olive trees to seek cover there. The Eddisians had no one to cover their flanks; to save themselves from being surrounded, they were retreating into the shallow bay between the two hillsides. I was with my mounted men, trying to provide some cover to give the Attolians time to re-form. We weren't very effective, and I wasn't any use at all. Although Procivitus's instruction had helped my sword work, it was of little use to me on horseback. All I could do was wave my sword around to defend myself and try not to cut the ears off my own horse. I had to hope that my countrymen didn't really want to kill their own king. The magus and my personal guard never left my side until we turned to run ourselves, ahead of the Sounisians, toward the protection of our Eddisian pikemen.

The Attolians who had run to re-form with the Eddisians appeared disorganized. Though my horsemen had slowed the approach of the army behind us, the bulk of it was rounding the curve of the hill and would soon be charging across the small valley onto the Eddisians and the Attolians who had not yet reached cover inside the Eddisian formation.

Without needing a signal, the Eddisian captain whistled a retreat. The Eddisians went in better order than the Attolians had, but they went *fast*, heading toward the trees behind them, where the charge of rebel horses would do less damage. They would fight in smaller groups, withdrawing back uphill until they could regroup safely.

My mounted men were racing toward the trees at about the same time. The horses would have to be abandoned. I had been toward the front of my men when we were fighting. When we turned to retreat, I fell behind. My guard was still with me, but only barely, when I loosened my grip on my reins. In the blink of an eye, I fell off.

I landed badly, just exactly like a sack of rocks, and tumbled across the grass until I landed flat on my back with all the wind knocked out of me and without the breath to curse my breastplate, which I was certain had done me more damage than it had saved me from. When I could get my feet under me and straighten up, my cavalry was already far away. They had slowed and looked back in confusion, but I waved to them to ride on. I was not too far from the hillside that had hidden the rebel army on the road behind us, and once I got my feet moving, I scrambled up it. With my chest aching for air, my hands and feet felt as if they belonged to someone else. I kept falling on my face, but I eventually made it to the top, covered in grass stains and still not able to get a breath, to find the consequences of battle laid out before me.

The flat top of the hill was scattered with the bodies of dead men in the uniforms of Sounis and Eddis. The outposts of both armies had met here. As I stood staring, I thought, These are my dead. All of them. The battle hadn't been unanticipated or forced on me, as the raid in the villa had been. I had chosen it. These men, Eddisian and Sounisian alike, had died for my decisions.

When the magus stepped from the bushes toward the back part of the hill, I was more than horrified. I was perilously close to distraught.

"You aren't supposed to be here!" I shouted. "Get back!" When he ignored me, I was almost weeping. "If they catch you, they'll kill you." The magus just walked closer and grabbed me in his arms to hold me tight. When he pulled away and looked into my face, I knew that he would tell me that I was Sounis and that I needed to pull myself together.

"Your uncle," he said, "in all the years I saw him rule, never had a moment of self-doubt. Never a regret for a single life lost. Do you understand?"

I understood that I didn't want to be my uncle.

He patted me on the back and disappeared into the bushes, to work his way down the hill. Instead of continuing toward the Eddisians, he must have turned toward the trees as soon as I had fallen. He'd left his horse and worked his way back along the hillside toward me. I could only pray that the gods would lead him safely back to the rest of the troops. I turned around to face the people climbing up the open face of the hill. They had seen me fall. So long as I, too, didn't try to hide in the bushes, no one would look there for the magus. I drew my sword.

When the first men of Sounis reached the top of the hill, I shouted clearly, "I am the king of Sounis," on the slight chance that the silvered breastplate with the

Sounis colors in velvet underneath didn't identify me clearly enough. I raised my sword as they approached, but there was little I could do to stop them from surrounding me at a safe distance. We waited then for the baron of Brimedius to arrive. He came puffing up over the edge of the hill just ahead of the Mede I'd met in my father's tent, Akretenesh.

"What a surprise to see you here," I said to him, not surprised at all.

"Your Majesty," said the Mede as he bowed very low, "you are among friends here. It is a misunderstanding, a sad misunderstanding that has taken place." He looked at the dead men and shook his head. I wanted to throw my sword at him, but there wasn't much point. Instead I offered it to Brimedius, who politely handed it back, and we all went down the hill.

And so by late afternoon I was in Brimedius, almost exactly as I'd originally planned.

Our pack animals had been abandoned during the fighting, as had our horses. They were collected up by Brimedius's men, and I had my luggage with me when I arrived: my new clothes, my books and papers, my traveling writing desk, and the small case holding Attolia's gift. All of them were trundled up to a guest apartment.

Servants brought bathwater, while an attendant helped me out of the breastplate and clothes.

Unfortunately, he also helped himself to your letter, which I had tucked against my chest.

"Give that back," I said angrily. But by this time I was half undressed and in no good condition for browbeating anyone. He regretfully refused to return it to me, and I was helpless. We both knew it. There was no reason to blame the attendant, but I did. I quite frankly hated him. I hated them all passionately.

I sat in the hot water and sulked, ignoring the servants while they meticulously unpacked my luggage, taking out and keeping every parchment and paper that contained anything written, and the blank paper and writing supplies as well. Attolia's box was resting on a table in plain sight. I watched out of the corner of my eye as the attendant opened it, removed the gun and the bullets and bullet mold. I looked away as he lifted the divider to examine what was underneath. I tried not to hold my breath as he considered whatever was there, but didn't touch it, then replaced the pistol and lowered the lid.

So he knew what was in the box, but I didn't, though I could guess it wasn't parchment or paper, or he would have taken it. I had opened the box a number of times, even removed the pistol and slid my fingertips across the felt board divider, wondering fiercely what message the king of Attolia had sent me, but I had not looked to see it for myself. I hadn't yet decided what I would do with Attolia's gift or her advice. I wanted too much to believe that there had to be a better way to lead people than through intimidation. Gen had as much as said so when he urged me to look for alternatives.

Whatever was in the box, the servant had left it, with the gun and its bullet mold on top. What a strange world it is, where prisoners are left their weapons and the written word is a mortal danger.

I had an excellent dinner and wine in the company of Brimedius and Akretenesh, who were carefully assessing me. A sullen temper in no way impeded my appetite.

I am not Gen. I cannot tell a convincing lie. He and I had agreed that I was foolish to try when every thought that crosses my mind seems to appear on my face for all to see. Gen counseled that honesty would be my best policy, so I let Akretenesh see the truth: that I was wholly in his power and bitterly unhappy about it.

I did not conceal my scorn as Akretenesh explained the regrettable chain of events that had driven a wedge between me and my barons, all of it the fault of my uncle who was Sounis. As Melheret had, Akretenesh offered himself, and the Mede Empire, as a neutral negotiator. I said no, thank you.

When I asked about Hanaktos, Brimedius assured me that there had been a misunderstanding. The rebels knew that my father had supported an alliance with the Mede, and an end to the war with Attolia, and they would never have condoned an attack on him. He suggested that Hanaktos's breach of the laws of hospitality was an unhappy accident. "My King," he said sadly, "Hanaktos tells us that your father's men attacked first."

"Because Hanaktos meant to kill them all!" I said.

"Perhaps, My King, it was all a mistake?" Brimedius said.

I think my face must have made it clear what I thought of that. "And my abduction?" I asked pointedly.

Brimedius nodded apologetically. "For that we must beg your forgiveness. It was not our intent to precipitate so destructive a conflict, nor to inflict such a grievous insult on the person of Your Majesty. We hoped to make a king of you a little early, that is all."

"Well, that at least you have accomplished," I said.

Brimedius was sadly disappointed in me. I looked mulishly back, as truculent as I had ever been when faced with someone's disappointment.

"I would like to see my mother and my sisters," I said, but it seemed that was not to be permitted yet.

"Perhaps in the morning," Akretenesh said.

Brimedius diverted my protest, asking hastily if my attendant pleased me, and I said he was well trained, but that I wanted my papers back. The baron deferred to Akretenesh, who said no. I sulked.

At the end of the meal the Mede pulled out a folded

and much-handled piece of vellum. I sat up. It was your letter.

"You are a man of your word, Your Majesty?"

"Enough that I am offended you ask, Ambassador," I said angrily.

He unfolded the parchment. "I have read this several times." He smoothed it out on the table between us and looked up at me, watching my face. "It appears in every way to be a personal missive between you and . . . someone who cares for you."

"She is the queen of Eddis," I said stiffly, annoyed at his dismissive tone.

"I mean no offense," he told me. "On the contrary. It goes against my grain to withhold something personal. I would no more deny you this than I would deny you any of your property. You have seen, I hope, that we make no attempt to remove from you your possessions. Even your weapons. I am sure that in time our mistakes will be behind us. We will start fresh. This is your property, and I would like to return it to you, if only I could." He smiled disarmingly, and I gritted my teeth and wondered what he was going to demand of me in exchange for this piece of writing and wished he would get on with it. " . . . if I could have your word that there is no secret message here."

My surprise showed on my face. What possible message did he think could be secreted in a half-page love letter?

"Ah," he said, and was evidently satisfied because he slid the parchment across the table to me. I folded it and slid it inside my shirt.

He inclined his head graciously.

I tried to do the same.

So I began my second captivity. This time with good food, and a soft bed, and regular bathwater, and companions infinitely more despised. Brimedius soon disappeared back to his army, which was penning in whatever was left of my uncle's men near the pass into Melenze. Brimedius's wife had greeted me formally when I first arrived, but I never saw her again. I saw only the Mede and various servants and a few members of Brimedius's guard.

My attendant had a name. Of all ridiculous things, it was Ion.

"Is that a problem, Your Majesty?" he asked.

"No, not at all," I said. "What's your family name?"

"I am Ion Nomenus, Your Majesty."

"I will call you by the patronym, then, if you do not mind," I said.

"Anything that pleases you, Your Majesty." He was the model of good manners, then and for the rest of our time together. He brought me my food and would have helped me dress and undress if I had let him.

"I've grown more comfortable doing it myself," I told him, and so he contented himself with unpacking and refolding my fancy clothes.

"I had a number of books," I said, and he apologized that they would not be available to me. I observed that the written word in all its forms was forbidden, but he said no, he could bring me books from the megaron's collection, if I would like. I said that I would, and asked him to look for a copy of Mepiles's *Lamentations*. I thought it might give me some perspective.

· CHAPTER EIGHTEEN ·

AKRETENESH dined with me every day, chatted about this and that, presented himself to me as a reasonable man, a potential ally, a resource. Every day I asked about my mother and sisters. After the first few days he didn't even offer excuses, just smiled sadly and turned away. If I lost my temper and swore at him, I got nothing. If I was polite, he gave me a tidbit about their health or their activities of the day before: They had gone into the garden, or they had walked by the riverside, Ina had said this or that. Unspoken was the understanding that my behavior affected their freedom as well as my own. On the contrary, I was assured over and over again that I was no prisoner but an honored guest.

The first time I was told this I stood up and said briskly I was leaving, and my family with me. Akretenesh just looked disappointed. "You would never, I am sure, very sure, Your Majesty, be so rude to your host," he said. He used that phrase often, *I am sure, very sure*, always followed by something I desired but would not be allowed. I grew to hate it as much as I hated him.

◆ ◆ ◆

After some weeks of this, I was well practiced in controlling my frustration. I never thought I would have any reason to be grateful to my Ferrian tutor, Malatesta, but as it turned out, he had been good practice for dealing with the Mede. I did not swear or shout. I nodded politely when spoken to and let the most outrageous comments pass by. Of course we were as children to the more mature race of the Mede. Of course they knew better than we did how to regulate ourselves.

I kept myself busier than I had been out on the island of Letnos. I woke in the morning and occupied myself with martial arts. I had a practice sword and any number of helpful partners waiting on me in the training yard. I rode regularly and tried to improve my sword work on horseback. Akretenesh seemed to look with approval on these activities. I practiced firing Attolia's gun, and he didn't object. On the contrary, Brimedius's armory was most helpful about providing lead and powder. The lead was pulled back out of targets to be reused, but my consumption of powder was not inconsequential. If I could have cost Brimedius ten times as much to maintain, I would have.

In the afternoon I read whatever Nomenus brought me from Brimedius's library. Mepiles's *Lamentations* did help me put my own discomforts in context, and I read a little from it every day. I paced in my room, talking to myself, and rehearsing for future speeches. I worried daily about the fate of the magus and the men in my army. Akretenesh of course gave me no news. I didn't know even if the magus had lived or died, though I thought the Mede would probably have told me if my friend and advisor was dead. I worried about him, and wondered if he had safely reached my father.

I was free to move about as I pleased in the gardens and could ride out on one of Brimedius's horses so long as I had someone from his guard with me. In the megaron I could roam through the public rooms and in the corridors on the way to my apartments. I walked those corridors, usually with Nomenus at my side, listening for any hint of my mother and sisters. Eurydice could be heard, if she chose to exert herself, across several fields and a small river. I never heard a sound and never caught even a hint of their whereabouts.

I spent my afternoons walking in gardens surrounding the megaron in search of some sign they might have left, a footprint in the flower beds, a plant stripped of its blossoms, twigs in a pattern, an arrangement of stones. I found nothing. I had faith that Ina was a cunning prisoner, but there was no sign that she had even once outwitted Akretenesh's desire that she and Eurydice and my mother be kept from me.

I attempted to think charitable thoughts about Nomenus, who had taken on the role of my personal attendant, and the other people in the megaron, the servants and Brimedius's guardsmen. I couldn't blame them for my captivity. It was my own doing, after all, that had brought me to Brimedius. I tried to thank them honestly for their services. They were wary at first, but if they held me in contempt, they concealed it well. If the captain of the guard was a little stiff with me when we sparred in the mornings, he was never anything but polite.

I know that it may be wishful thinking or arrogance on my part to think so, but over time they seemed genuinely well disposed to me. Nomenus even scoured up a few more books of poetry for me to read from Lady Brimedius's private collection, which was considerate of him. He never spoke to me of anything but my personal needs, making it clear that the business of kings was not his business. It was a fine line between sympathy and pity that he walked, and I was gradually won over by his kindnesses.

Remembering Gen's suggestion that it is better if you believe what you want other people to believe, I tried to think charitable thoughts about Akretenesh as well. Except for the very essence of the matter—my captivity and his refusal to let me see my sisters and my mother—he was very accommodating. I still didn't like him. His narrow, inflexible mind, his unshakable faith that the Mede way was the best way, and his unwitting condescension in offering it to me made my hackles rise, even without the added offense of his blatant intention to appropriate my country. Also, I hated the scent of his hair oil, which is a stupid thing to care about, and I am not surprised that it makes you laugh.

Fortunately, I did not have to pretend that I liked him. He was content once he could see that I was willing to submit to him because I had no other choice.

One day after weeks of uninterrupted quiet and sick frustration, there was a visitor to Brimedius's megaron. Nomenus was arranging my meal on a tray when I asked him outright who had arrived.

"It's Baron Hanaktos," he said pleasantly, as if it were nothing that a man who'd tried to kill me was nearby. "The Mede ambassador has asked for an appointment this evening before dinner if that will suit Your Majesty."

This is how they maintained the polite fiction that I was not a prisoner. It was "Your Majesty, this," and "Your Majesty, that," and "if it would suit Your Majesty." Listening to Akretenesh say the words made me want to bite something, but Nomenus spoke them with a gentle amusement that made it bearable, as if it were an irony shared between us.

That evening Akretenesh brought me another letter.

"Your friend has sent greetings," he said. "Were you expecting them?"

I had no idea whom he meant. My first thought was of Hyacinth, and I had no interest in any news from him. Seeing my confusion, he held up the letter, and I recognized the seals.

"Her Majesty the queen of Eddis?" I said rigidly, and Akretenesh promptly reconsidered his wording.

"Her Majesty, yes," he said more respectfully.

I understood better how the queen of Attolia could have led her own ambassador by the nose. The Medes seem to be very conventional thinkers, so certain of themselves that they never even entertain anyone else's opinions. I do believe that Akretenesh saw no differences between a woman who was a queen and one who was a seamstress, though he would recognize all the differences in the world between a prince and a farmer.

I said that yes, the letter was unexpected, and no, I had made no plans for communications in case I was separated from the magus and the troops. No, I didn't think it likely that there was a secret message, but of course I couldn't say for certain. Akretenesh again laid the parchment out on the table between us and smoothed it with his hand while he considered. Finally, with a little sigh, he folded it again.

"I am sorry," he said. "It's too risky."

I looked away while I fantasized about throwing myself across the top of the spindly table and seizing Akretenesh by the throat to choke the life out of him, surrounded by the sound of crashing crockery.

After a deep breath, I said, "I understand."

"I am relieved Your Majesty comprehends the difficulties of my position," said Akretenesh.

"You have my sympathy, Ambassador. What

are your thoughts of Her Majesty?" I asked.

"I regret I have never had the pleasure of meeting the queen of Eddis."

"But your brother ambassador in Attolia has, and I know you have communicated." He'd certainly made it clear that Melheret had conveyed the news that I was heading for Brimedius. Akretenesh pretended to have heard only the most flattering things about my intelligence and maturity from the same source.

"Indeed," said Akretenesh, "I have heard much of Her Majesty. She is by all accounts most admirable, demonstrating that character in a woman is far more important than the superficial beauty or excessive pretensions to intelligence of her counterpart in Attolia."

I stared at him for a moment, thinking that the historian Talis once said that to be underestimated by an enemy is the greatest advantage a man can have. Presumably it is true for women as well. One part of me couldn't let the comment pass, while another part of me knew that I must, and I stood paralyzed as they warred their way to a mutually agreed-upon truth.

"The queen of Eddis is as beautiful as the day and as brilliant as the sun in the sky," I said.

He was a fool if he didn't believe me, but I wouldn't tell him so. He chuckled and quoted Praximeles about beauty being in the heart and not in the eye.

"You could retell some of what she said in her letter," I said.

Akretenesh considered, now that he'd had his chance to condescend. "I could. She writes about the fulfillment of a dream: to marry you in the Great Temple of Sounis and to wake in a marriage bed . . . which she describes in some detail"—he flipped the page over and read it closely—"'It will have the finest Eddisian linen and a carving of the silhouette of the Sacred Mountain on the footboard.'" He looked up from the page to see my face as I flushed deeper and deeper red. His voice grew more cloying still. "She sends her love from beneath the ripening apricots of the tree where she sits and says the dream is complete but for your presence. Is this a lover's missive," he asked, "or might some information be encoded there?" He watched me closely, his eyes narrow.

I said through my gritted teeth, "Perhaps it is just what women do."

Sighing, he refolded the parchment. "That may be it. My wife would write just such a description." He became brisk. "I am sorry I cannot allow you to return the message, but your queen is too much under the influence of her ambitious former Thief. He has stolen Attolia's throne and has tried to steal yours. She is very foolish if she does not realize how vulnerable she is, but fortunate that she may have you to protect her from her folly, eh?"

He was still watching me, looking for some sign that there might be a message in the text, but I am an idiot, and all that showed on my face, I am sure, was that I wanted to kill him.

We were interrupted then by Baron Hanaktos, who was immediately unhappy to see the letter from Eddis in the Mede's hand.

"I didn't bring that here so that you could deliver it," he said gruffly.

"Oh, why *did* you bring it?" I asked harshly, and the baron flushed. I almost smiled at his discomfort. No doubt I looked like a clod, putting on pretensions to cover my impotence, but the baron bowed and apologized. He insisted that his only concern was for treachery on the part of Attolia. I said that I understood completely. He said that he hoped that the sad rupture in our relationship would heal, and I pretended that I hadn't been attacked in my own home, listened as my servants were killed, and served as a slave on his estates. In short, I acted as if my family were just then being held as hostage for my good behavior.

We all mouthed our parts in the play; then we went in to dinner.

If the baron and I were bad actors, there was an inexplicable tension between Akretenesh and the baron as well. I wondered if the baron was beginning to change his estimation of his allies. He was unhappy about something, and all through the dinner there was a conversation I couldn't follow in obscure references and dark looks.

Hanaktos only stayed for the one night. He left again in the morning, and an exchange I overheard from an open hallway above the pronaos made me think the issue, whatever it was, was still unresolved. Akretenesh and Hanaktos were standing in the open doorway of the megaron. Their voices carried clearly.

"You will not put me aside," said Hanaktos.

"I assure you that nothing has changed," said Akretenesh.

He might have said more, but Nomenus was with me. I could not ask him to quiet his footsteps so that I might eavesdrop. Akretenesh and Hanaktos heard him and fell silent.

When he was gone, Akretenesh came inside to compliment me on my company manners. I suspected that the visit had been his own personal test of his control over me and that I had passed. I excused myself and spent the morning practicing with Attolia's handgun.

That afternoon I had nothing new to read and no patience for rereading. Idly I picked over a plate of food. I paced. I hummed the chorus's opening song from Prolemeleus's *City of Reason* and stood looking out the window for a long time. As I considered the landscape, it finally occurred to me that it would be an odd apricot tree that would be producing fruit in Eddis so far out of season.

I was lucky to be alone as I subsequently recalled the time when Eugenides, the magus, and I were escaping Attolia. Eugenides had been growing more and more distant as the blood leaked through his bandages, staining the shirt I had loaned him. I had been desperate to hold his attention, afraid he would fade away altogether.

I remembered asking him if he could be anywhere at that moment where it would be and he'd predictably said in his own bed. He had described with longing the soft linens and the carved image of the Sacred Mountain on the footboard with such loving detail that it came to mind easily. The magus had wished to see the king of Sounis marry the queen of Eddis, and I, not unlike Gen, had longed to be home, under a ripening apricot tree, with my sisters.

If I hadn't been such an idiot, and so angry at Akretenesh, he would have known, I am sure, that he had erred in teasing me with the letter. I would have perceived the message suggested by the text, and my face would have given me away.

There was no sign of my mother and sisters in Brimedius. I had circumnavigated the megaron for what felt like a thousand times, searching for a sign of their presence, and had seen nothing. I had begun to wonder if they had been moved elsewhere. Akretenesh insisted that he saw them each day, even bringing me verbal messages that did seem like Ina, but if he had lost his hostages, he would hardly want me to know.

I all but hooted with delight.

Was it wishful thinking? I had to ask myself. It might

have been only that, but I had watched Akretenesh underestimate the queens of Attolia and Eddis, and I wouldn't do the same to Ina. And whether my mother and sisters were safe in Eddis or not, there was nothing more I could do in Brimedius. I chose to believe that I had come to rescue my mother and sisters, and they had already rescued themselves.

I waited four long days before suggesting to Akretenesh that if it was true that the Medes would make me king, I would be pleased to see some sign of it. He accepted my capitulation with typical arrogance, and within the week, we were riding toward Elisa to the Barons' Meet, where I would face my barons and they would vote whether I was going to be king or not.

CHAPTER NINETEEN

IN Sounis only the barons hold the power to confirm a candidate as king. Of course their meetings have happened in all sorts of places, including on a battlefield surrounded by corpses in the case of Sounis Peliteus, but the official, dedicated, and sacred space is Elisa, on the coast, not far from the capital city.

The barons meet under truce. This is supposed to have something to do with the blessing of the gods and such, but I think it's more likely to be a matter of practicality. If every time they came together to name a king, the barons brought their armies, there wouldn't be a place big enough to hold the horses, much less all the men. When a group of Mede soldiers materialized around us as we traveled, I piously mentioned to Akretenesh the very sacred nature of the truce and the risk of angering the gods.

I wasn't surprised that he had brought a small army to Sounis. It was just what I expected of him, but I didn't want them tramping through the sacred precinct of Elisa. He assured me that we would leave his soldiers in Tas-Elisa, the nearby port town that served the sacred site. That, too, was just what I expected of him. On the one hand, he wanted to do nothing that would compromise my legitimacy as king, and on the other, the road from the port was one of only two serviceable roads to Elisa. I wondered how he would close off the other.

Once Akretenesh was confident that I understood that my only hope of becoming king was through his intervention, he had sent a message to Baron Brimedius, who in turn sent word to one and all to come to the sacred meeting. Akretenesh could have installed me by force, but he wanted no messy disagreements about legality to arise later. He wanted me legitimated by the council of the barons, so that all authority would rest in me, and I would rest securely in the palm of his hand.

He seemed confident of success. To be confirmed, I needed a golden majority, two-thirds of those present, plus one more baron. Akretenesh controlled the rebel votes, though we continued to maintain the pretense that he was a neutral mediator. As the magus and my father had lost ground in the spring campaign, their allies had parted company with them, but that still left more than a third of the barons not directly under Akretenesh's sway. My father's loyalists could still disrupt the vote, but the ambassador didn't seem worried.

He had to believe that my father would support me, no matter how clear it was that I was to be a puppet of the Mede. He probably had good reason. Given my father's opinion of me, he might prefer the arrangement.

On the road Akretenesh brought up the subject of

a regent. I was very young, and I had been in seclusion on Letnos for some time, he said; my barons did not know me well and would be more comfortable if a reliable man were to serve as my guide. I was not surprised. Arrangements have always been made before the meets to secure votes. A new king will promise a minister's position to a baron or offer a smaller office to the baron's nephew or son. It's done all the time. Akretenesh had been informing me delicately of who my ministers would be, and I was listening for the name Hanaktos. It hadn't come up yet. When he raised the issue of a regent, I thought I knew why.

"Baron Comeneus, Your Majesty, would be a fine man for the office."

I was surprised. Akretenesh thought I was reacting to the idea of a regent and was prepared to soothe my ruffled feathers. When soothing, Akretenesh was at his most infuriating. It was better to ignore him, and I did, concentrating my thoughts on Hanaktos. Had I overestimated his importance to the Medes? Was Comeneus truly the leader of this rebellion, and Hanaktos only a follower? It was Hanaktos's man who had carried out my abduction, it was done at his orders, and I was taken to Hanaktos afterward. How could he *not* be one of the rebellion's leaders? But why wasn't he in line for some repayment, a minister's position, if not prime minister? Perhaps Akretenesh *had* set him aside.

Akretenesh went on assuring me that I would be a

fine and powerful king someday, and I went on ignoring him as I turned this idea over and over in my head.

There are five roads into the sacred city of Elisa, which sits high in the hills above the sea. Three come from inland and two from the coast. Of the coast roads, only one is of any use. It runs between the port of Tas-Elisa and the sacred site. The other coast road ends in Oneia, which is just a scatter of houses on an exposed cliff top with a narrow slice of stony beach at its foot.

Of the inland routes, the widest is the King's Road, which leads to the city of Sounis. It comes into the sacred site from the opposite direction of the Tas-Elisa Road, so if one wants to go by land from Tas-Elisa to the city of Sounis, one must first climb all the way up to the valley in the hills and then go down along the King's Road from there.

The other two routes come over the hills from behind Elisa and are mere tracks. They might be as wide as a wagon, but you couldn't move one on them. No doubt, on the inland side of the hills where they were wider, they were lined with the camps of armies that had been left there by the barons as they came to the meet.

Tas-Elisa is a small town with a reasonable harbor and several far more serviceable roads out to the hinterlands. It was half a day's ride from there up to Elisa. As good as his word, Akretenesh billeted his men outside the town. He would have his men ready to hand if the truce was broken, and he also neatly blocked anyone else who might intend to bring an army through that way.

There was only one other route sufficiently wide enough to move an army quickly into Elisa.

"And the King's Road?" I asked.

"Baron Hanaktos will leave his men there," said Akretenesh.

We arrived at Elisa as the sun set. The great theater sits in a natural curve of the hills, and the best view of it from a distance is on the coast road. No one knows when Elisa's slopes were first terraced and lined with marble seats, but the temple keeps lists of the plays performed here during the spring and fall festivals, and they go back hundreds of years, all the way back to when the plays were performed in the archaic language on the open orchestral ground in front of the seats.

There is a stage now, built over rooms for storage space and costume changes, but the actors still come down to the open space in front of the seats. Each play has some special speech set there to take advantage of the miracle of Elisa's design. Standing in the right place, an actor can speak his lines in a whisper and be heard all the way to the back rows of seats.

If I had my say, all the plays would be performed in the old way, and there would be no stage. The building across the open side of the amphitheater spoils the view across the valley and over the lower hills between Elisa and the sea. I admit, though, that I am as delighted as anyone else when an actor in the role of a god is lowered onto the stage and even more so when he disappears through a trapdoor and then emerges from the doorway below to continue his lines. Those sorts of effects cannot happen with only the open ground to perform on.

Scattered at the base of the amphitheater in no particular order are the rest of the buildings: dormitories, villas, temples, and a stadium all hidden among the trees. Below them is the town. During festivals, the overflow of the crowds lived in tents, but there would not be so many for the barons' council. I was certainly not headed for a tent. We rode directly to the king's compound, where we were met by the steward and servants who were waiting to pay their respects.

I was sick with trepidation—and this at the necessity of meeting the servants, never mind my barons. But these weren't the lackeys at Brimedius; they were people who knew me as the heir of Sounis. I had come here every year for as long as I could remember to see the plays. I could measure my chance of success in their reaction when I arrived. When I climbed down from my horse, I wasn't sure my knees would hold me. I would rather be beaten again at Hanaktos's whipping post than relive that introduction.

The steward was very polite. He welcomed me in exactly the words I had heard him use to my uncle, while

I listened for the contempt I was afraid I would hear in his voice. When he was finished, he and all the servants bowed together. Then he introduced the senior members of the staff. I knew many of them and said gracious things and tried to memorize the names I did not know. I was looking to see some sign that they despised me, and not seeing it, I was convincing myself that I was blind. I was honestly grateful when Akretenesh suggested that I was fatigued and might wish to have a bath while my rooms were readied.

I escaped to the baths with just Nomenus, who had come with us from Brimedius to attend me. I'd washed in my rooms in Brimedius and hadn't had a real bath since I'd left Attolia. I hid in the steam room until I was too light-headed to care anymore what the Elisians were going to make of me. After the plunge, Nomenus was waiting with a robe.

"Your Majesty," he said as he wrapped me in it, "I believe you are most welcome here."

I twisted to look him in the face, but he dropped his eyes.

"I did not mean to offend Your Majesty."

"No, you didn't," I said, grateful for the reassurance.

When I reached my rooms, everything was carefully arranged, all my finery in the wardrobes and my luggage cases cleared away. Sitting on a table by the window was the box from Attolia. I ran my hand across the bowed top, and then flipped open the latch and lifted the lid, to see if the gun was still inside. It lay untouched within its velvet-covered bolster. One gun, against Akretenesh and all my rebellious barons. Akretenesh knew how insignificant it was. How insignificant I was. I wondered if my sisters had been in Brimedius after all, watching me from a window as I rode away. I wondered where the magus was. There had been no sign of him, and I had had no word from my father.

I thanked the three or four servants in the rooms with me for their work. They smiled, maybe not just in politeness, and I sent them on their way. I sent Nomenus away as well and sat on a stool in front of the table, staring at the gun for a long time.

In the morning I met with the first of my barons. It was their right to speak to me before the vote, and they wouldn't give it up. There was a protocol—Xorcheus first, as his was the oldest created barony, and then, after him, all the other barons in the order of their creations. A baron could choose to bring another baron, lower in seniority, with him. The more senior barons usually make some money selling off the privilege, but Xorcheus came alone. I think he would have skipped the entire process if he could have. He had a small property of almost no significance, and I got the impression that he wished we all would just go away and leave him to it.

He grunted a greeting when he was ushered into the

room and didn't know whether he would bow or not. I imagined asking for a full obeisance face down on the floor, and just the vision I produced in my own head helped me relax a little in my chair and wave him to sit before he made a decision we both would have to live with.

We were in a long, narrow room on the ground floor. I had asked to have the chairs moved as far away as possible from the shuttered window, but I had no way of knowing who was out on the terrace, listening for any word he might catch. Akretenesh had chosen the room. It had murals painted in panels between the timbers that supported the upper floors. Winter, Spring, Summer, and Fall, four beautiful women carrying baskets of fruit or flowers, or, in the case of Winter, bundles of spindling branches. All of them with their backs to me, which I didn't take for a particularly encouraging omen.

Akretenesh, as "mediator," was with us. He would be in every meeting as I tried to convince my barons not just to elect me king but to make me king without a regent. He didn't say anything. He knew that the rebels weren't likely to cooperate. The whole object of their rebellion had been to seize the king's authority for themselves. That they had started an all-out civil war by accident didn't mean that they would give up their prizes.

The loyalists wouldn't be much more easily convinced. My barons knew where I had been, that I had been abducted and had hidden in Hanaktos's fields, and that I had gone to Attolia to negotiate a surrender. The Medes looked better and better to them all the time.

So I talked myself hoarse. First to Xorcheus and then to the rest of my barons, one at a time or in small groups. I went over, again and again, my arrangements with Attolia, the loss of the islands but the end of the war. I had practiced my arguments on the magus as we rode from Attolia and polished them in the tent at night. I had gone over them again while I was a prisoner in Brimedius. I was determined to convince the barons to end their revolt without bloodshed. So I explained the advantages of peace and trade. I swore up and down that the Attolians would have no hand in our governance, only a promise of our loyalty and our support if they were ever attacked.

And my conversations all seemed to go awry. Was it true that I would swear an oath of allegiance to Attolia? I said no, that I would swear to Attolis, but that made little difference to them. They didn't like the Thief of Eddis any better as an overlord. There was nothing impossible in what I was saying. My arguments were good, but my barons would have to trust me, and they wouldn't. They looked from me to the Mede and back again. Then they said polite things and excused themselves.

Akretenesh watched, amused.

There was no point in trying to tell the barons the things that the magus had taught me, the way the Medes had dealt with their "allies" in the past. They weren't interested in history lessons. I knew that my uncle who was Sounis had set his barons against one another in order to keep them weak. I knew that he had used his army to threaten anyone who dared disagree with him. They hadn't liked him, they had lived their lives wondering when he would turn on them, but that was what they expected a king to be. I wasn't nearly intimidating enough.

I told them how things work in Eddis and tried to show them that there is a rule of law that is better than backbiting and self-interest as a means to run a state. My idealistic words made Xorcheus uncomfortable. They made the rest of the barons contemptuous.

At the end of one day, when I had worked my way through almost half the barons and was tripping over my tongue, so tired was I of talking, Nomenus came to the door of the audience room.

"I thought that was the last for now, Nomenus," I said.

"It's your father, Your Majesty. He has arrived from the north, and he asks an audience."

I stood up and went to greet my father at the door. He wrapped me in a hug as fierce as the one he'd given me as I slid from the back of his horse outside Hanaktos's megaron. I swallowed. So much depended on him. I had left him under attack by Hanaktos and gone to surrender to Attolia, and I had no idea what he thought of me.

"Won't you come sit down?" I said, and we crossed the room together.

"Ambassador," my father said, and reached out to take Akretenesh's hand. "Won't you join us?" So the three of us settled into chairs facing one another.

"This business of surrendering to Attolia. I am not at ease," my father said.

I shrugged. "You have heard all the arguments already from the magus."

My father nodded and rolled his eyes. "That man bent my ear mercilessly. He never stopped for an instant." He looked at Akretenesh. "Your empire has a history of absorbing its allies the way a tide overcomes a tide pool."

Akretenesh smiled comfortably, and I felt like a child again, watching from the corners while the adults talked. I couldn't tell from my father's brief comment when he had last seen the magus. I could only hope that the magus had made his way safely to meet my father after the battle near Brimedius. I didn't dare ask.

Akretenesh was speaking. "I know how things can change their appearance when seen from a distance. Our allies have become part of our empire by their own choice because it was to their advantage. But Sounis does not lie on our borders, the way they did, and cannot be integrated so easily into our system of provinces. Your case is quite different, I assure you."

My father nodded and looked around the room. "At any rate," he said, "I can see that all goes well here." To me he said, "You need have no worries. You will be king one way or another." Then he patted me on the knee and stood up, saying that he had to see to his men.

That evening I stood at the window looking at the amphitheater in the moonlight. Nomenus was tidying the room behind me and laying out my nightclothes. The night was cool. The armies waiting for their barons' return, on the inland side of the hills, would be baking in the heat, but Elisa, high in the hills, caught the sea breeze. I listened to the creak of the night insects and watched the leaves flutter against the white marble of the amphitheater that seemed to glow in the reflected light, and I wondered what my father thought of me.

I had no chance to speak to him again except in impersonal conversation at dinner. I had no privacy outside my own rooms. Akretenesh accompanied me at all times or handed me off to Brimedius or another obsequious rebel baron. It was Akretenesh who was with me when I saw a familiar figure ahead in a passageway, a figure just in the act of dodging down a flight of stairs.

"Basrus!" I shouted at the top of my lungs, and to my everlasting surprise, Hanaktos's slaver stopped in his tracks.

Not so Akretenesh, who slid hastily to stand between the two of us, one hand not quite touching my chest, as if to stop me from an assault. It was unnecessary. I was unexpectedly pleased to see the familiar, ugly face.

"Your Majesty has made an error," Akretenesh said in warning. "This is, ah—" He paused, apparently at a loss for a good lie. "This is the rat catcher," he said firmly. To my delight, he still couldn't come up with a name.

"Bruto," said Basrus, with a straight face.

"Yes, that's it. Your Majesty, Bruto." Akretenesh, being a Mede, didn't recognize the name from the nursery rhyme of Bruto and the rats. It didn't help that Basrus was winking at me over his shoulder.

"We have a vermin problem, and Bruto has been clearing the compound," Akretenesh said, perhaps revealing more than he meant. I wondered if the rats were of a human kind and if the quarry was in the compound itself or farther afield.

"I wish you success in your endeavors on my behalf, Ba–Bruto," I said. There was little point in contesting the Mede's story. If anyone standing there in the passage with me knew who Basrus was, he knew that I knew as well, and would understand the irony in my emphasis on "my behalf."

"It is an honor to work for Your Majesty." Basrus bowed. He straightened and looked me in the eye. "If I may say so, I was delighted to hear of the safe arrival of your mother and sisters in Brimedius." He bowed again.

"Thank you, Basrus," I said.

"Bruto," he said.

"Yes, of course."

Akretenesh was starting to give both of us the evil eye. He dismissed Basrus sharply, and the slaver turned back to the stairs. I went on to my rooms.

There were more meetings. Each day I thought with envy of Polystrictes. I would have preferred his goats to my barons. Every one of them seemed to come to me with questions, and I had to lay every concern to rest before I had any hope that they would listen to what I had to say. I wanted to hold my head in my hands and scream.

Instead I explained over and over that no, we wouldn't change our oligarchy, we had always had barons elevated above patronoi and patronoi above the okloi. My father himself was one of the four dukes created by my grandfather in imitation of the courts on the Continent. I would hardly disempower him. I only meant that we would have a rule of law for everyone, king, baron, patronoi, and okloi. That I would not constantly set the barons against one another, as my uncle had, and that no man needed to fear that he must be a favorite with the king to be safe from his neighbors.

But rumor was a hydra that regrew as often as I chopped it down. I came to rely on Nomenus, who would come with my breakfast every morning and tell me what fresh crop of misdirection had grown up in the night. He passed on to me the stories that he heard passing from one servant to the next, and I used the information to brace my arguments with the next baron in the order of precedence. I was sure Akretenesh was feeding the confusion, but there was nothing I could do about it other than try to convince my barons that they could believe in me. I continued to meet with as many as I could every day, in spite of Nomenus's asking me if I would like to have rest in the afternoons. I was battle hardened after all the meetings in Attolia.

The night before I was to meet with Baron Comeneus, Nomenus came to my rooms with a late meal. He had an amphora in his hand and another servant to bring in a tray with bread and cheese. He was usually able to manage this on his own, and I looked at the extra man curiously. Hesitantly, Nomenus introduced him as a friend from Tas-Elisa. He emphasized *friend* significantly. My hopes rising like birds on the wing, I thought at first that the magus had sent him. I asked if he brought news, but he knew nothing of the magus nor of the Eddisians and Attolians. "They say the goat-feet went back to the mountains and the Attolians with them," he said.

I sighed, not knowing if this was good news or bad, and even though I had grown to trust Nomenus more than was warranted, I was still too wary to ask more.

"What of Comeneus?" I said. "Does he really lead these barons?" I still couldn't imagine Comeneus in charge of anything larger than a hunting party.

"The other barons all yield to him," Nomenus said. "They say he will be regent for you."

"Does anyone mention Hanaktos? His army is blocking the King's Road. Does anyone say what he will get out of his part in this?"

Nomenus and the other man shook their heads. "We've heard nothing of him," the man said. "We only hear of Comeneus."

"We will tell you if we learn anything more, My King," Nomenus said, and I was touched that he addressed me as his King and not just as Your Majesty.

In the morning I didn't so much meet with Comeneus as sit to be lectured by him. Relative to Xorcheus, his was a newly created barony, only a few generations old, so he was very near to the last of the barons. I had wondered why he hadn't ridden in on an earlier baron's back, but when he came into the room, I understood much better. He wanted me all to himself. What he lacked in precedence, he made up in bluster. He was just as I remembered him, a large man with a thick jaw, a heavy mat of hair, and narrow-set eyes. He looked down his nose at me and declined to bow. He sat without being invited and as much as dared me to comment on it. He looked over my shoulder at Akretenesh and back at me with some satisfaction.

"Thank you for meeting with me, Baron."

"Glad to," he said gruffly. "No point in beating about the bush. Your uncle commanded people, made 'em hop. That's what we want in a king, but you can't do that yet, can you? A yearling needs to grow a little more before he carries any weight. A young hawk needs to be seasoned. You must give an olive tree years before it bears fruit."

Muse of poetry, come to his aid, I thought. Could the man produce one more metaphor of husbandry? He seemed to be trying.

"Green wood," I suggested, but even he sensed that there was something unfortunate about a metaphor for a king in which you dry out your royalty before you set fire to it.

"You see my point, Your Majesty." He went on, poking his finger at me with every point he made, to explain that my harebrained scheme of surrendering to Attolia was the result of my unseasoned youth. Like my uncle, I hadn't listened to wiser heads. He'd let his temper get the better of him. He'd been mercurial and unreliable. He'd been selfish and hadn't had the best interests of Sounis at heart, and that was the real problem. That was why the barons had oh-so-reluctantly risen against him.

I sneaked glances at Akretenesh, trying to see how Hanaktos fitted into his plans, because I could not believe that Comeneus was a partner in his schemes.

A pawn, perhaps. Akretenesh's bland expression of approval never altered, and I wished I had his diplomatic skills. It was all I could do to keep myself from grabbing Comeneus's finger and biting it.

Finally I interrupted him to say that I was grateful for his instruction, and even if he were not to be my regent, I would certainly consider his advice in the future with the attention it deserved. Before he could say anything else, I added that he had served Sounis as he had thought best, and he would certainly be rewarded for it. He nodded vigorously, like a big ox. He appeared to expect a very substantial reward, but he wasn't looking at me. He was looking at the Mede ambassador.

After I had listened to Comeneus tell me the mistakes of my uncle, I quit for the day and returned to my rooms. The servants stripped off my sweaty clothes and brought me a cup of iced wine. When the others were gone, I quizzed Nomenus for all he knew. Was there any more news from Tas-Elisa? Were Hanaktos's men still on the road to the capital? Were they moving on Elisa? Nomenus said that he'd heard nothing of the kind.

The day of the meet I dressed in my most elaborate clothes, thinking of Gen. The coat he had had made for me with the ridiculous pockets and the embroidery on top of embroidery on the outside so that I could look like a king and act like one was as stiff as a board. I felt like a box with legs. The night before, I had finally opened the lower compartment of Attolia's pistol case, dreading what I might discover. Whatever alternative Eugenides had urged me to find, I had not, and I had waited to look until it was too late to change course. When I saw what lay under Attolia's gun, I put my head down on the table and cried.

Dressed in my best, I went to the meet. I couldn't slouch without putting obvious dents in the lines of my elegant coat, so I kept my shoulders well back and bobbed my head at my court like a demented hen. The barons and their supporters had been gathering since dawn.

Each baron was entitled to bring two men, usually choosing an heir and one other. The amphitheater was full, from the prestigious seats in the first rows all the way up to the benches across the top, where people had to lean to see past the branches of the bushes that grew on the slopes behind them and hung down to block their view.

I climbed up onto the stage and waited patiently through the long protocol of the ceremony, sitting in one of a row of chairs with Akretenesh and members of my late uncle's council. The chairs, significantly, were all the same size.

It was late in the morning, and I was soaked in sweat by the time Baron Xorcheus proposed a regency. I stood up and stepped to the front of the stage. Xorcheus hesitated, unsure of what I was doing, and that gave me time to walk down the stair to the open ground in front of my barons. By the time I reached the center, the murmuring had faded away.

I can't really remember what I said. It was idealistic and it was naive. I reminded them that we shared one peninsula with Eddis and Attolia, that we shared a language, and that the gods of our fathers were the same. I said it was stupid to think that we could ever be anything but subjects to the Mede, that my barons needed to see beyond their own self-interests to the interests of all Sounis and to the interests of Eddis and Attolia as well. United, we would all benefit. I said exactly what I had wanted to say all along, because I knew that nothing I said was going to make any difference anyway.

Xorcheus called for the vote, and one by one my barons answered my idealism. They stood and called out "regency" or "king," and I waited in the center of the amphitheater for their judgment. A regent for even a short time would cement Akretenesh's power and make me no more than a puppet king for the rest of my reign. Once he had installed his own allies in every position in court, once he had complete control of the army, I would have lost forever.

There were a few "kings", but one after another, the votes for a regent came in. I looked each baron in the eye, and they were defiant, contemptuous, regretful, and in rare cases ashamed of themselves, but they voted for Comeneus and the Mede. That was the meet. When all the deal making was done, you had to cast your vote aloud for everyone to hear.

When the vote came around to my father, I held my breath. He stood and looked down at me for so long, I thought the sun had stopped in the sky. When he said "king," he said it so firmly that the people nearby him winced. I swallowed a lump in my throat and looked to the next man.

I watched Baron Comeneus as the voting drew near him. The barons voted in the same order of precedence in which they had come to meet with me. By the time Comeneus voted it was already clear what the outcome would be, and he called "regent" with radiating self-importance. He never looked anywhere except at me, but at his right hand sat his heir, a much-younger brother. He never looked at me at all.

When the vote was over, the amphitheater was silent. I heard Akretenesh speak just behind me. He must have come down the steps without my realizing it.

"Did you think they would make you king?" he said, contemptuously. His voice was quiet, but he'd forgotten, or perhaps never knew about, the acoustics. His every word was audible even to the men in the highest seats and I watched them, as a single organism, recoil.

"No," I said, turning. "Not on the first vote."

I put my left hand into the open front of my coat

to the pockets sewn inside. Narrow and three times as deep as they were wide, they were almost useless; anything you put into them would slip to the bottom and be out of reach, anything except the long-barreled handgun that Attolia had given me. It fit perfectly. I lifted it out of the pocket, directed it almost without looking, fixed my eyes on Akretenesh, and shot Hanaktos dead.

If Akretenesh's voice had been audible to the back row, the report of the gun was deafening.

In the shocked, silent aftermath, I said, "We'll give them a second chance."

With my right hand, I reached to the other pocket. I had known as soon as I lifted the false bottom in the gun case and looked underneath what it meant. I had tried without ceasing to find some alternative to Attolia's ruthless advice, and I had failed. Gen's gift reassured me that I had not failed for lack of trying. He had seen no other solution himself.

I lifted out the matching gun and read its archaic inscription. *Realisa onum.* Not "The queen made me," but "I make the king."

Looking at Akretenesh's startled face down the long barrel of the handgun, I smiled until I felt the scar tissue tighten. That one expression, I'd never showed him. My face gave away my humiliation, my rage, my surprise, and my embarrassment, but I had never let him see what I looked like when I smiled: my uncle.

His diplomatic mask dissolved, and he backed away.

In Attolia, I had been in front of a mirror at last, and I had understood what made Oreus back in Hanaktos ask me if my expression was a happy one or not. The smile rumpled the scar tissue under my skin, and dragged my face askew, giving me the leer of a man who'd never had a moment of self-doubt, who'd never regretted a life lost. I'd worried that I wouldn't have the nerve to carry this off, but in the moment, it was easy. Seeing Akretenesh recoil, I laughed out loud.

I'd fired on Hanaktos with my left hand. I had known exactly where he was, and I'd had all morning to prepare my shot. My aim was more reliable with my right, and Akretenesh was much closer than Hanaktos had been.

I had wanted to find a better way than shooting an unarmed man. I had wanted my barons to choose me as king because they believed in me and because they believed in my ideals as I did. But that wasn't the choice I had before me, and I had already decided that I would make them follow me any way I could. I would not stand by and let them be lost to the Mede or to Melenze or to an endless civil war where they would never be free of bloodshed until the whole country was stripped to the bare bones. If I couldn't be Eddis, I would be Attolia. If they needed to see my uncle in me, then I would show him to them. And I would take Attolia's advice, because if I identified my enemy and destroyed him, Sounis would be safe.

My enemy wasn't Comeneus, though I was fairly certain he didn't know it. His brother did. As one baron after another had voted for a regent, Comeneus had watched me, but his brother had looked to Hanaktos, and Hanaktos had looked to the Mede.

Staring at me over the barrel of my gun, Akretenesh said, "Did you not just days ago lecture *me* about the sacred truce?"

With my finger still through the trigger guard of the spent pistol, I lifted my left palm upward to the sky to see if lightning struck me down.

When none did, I smiled again. "We will have to assume that the gods are on my side."

"I am an ambassador," Akretenesh warned me, anger bringing his confidence back. "You cannot shoot."

"I don't mean to," I reassured him, still smiling. I adopted his soothing tones. "Indeed, you are the only man I won't shoot. But if I aimed at anyone else, it might give others a dangerously mistaken sense of their own safety." I raised my voice a trifle, though it wasn't really necessary. "We will have another vote, Xorcheus."

They elected me Sounis. It was unanimous.

When the voting was done, I told Akretenesh to collect his men and get out of my country. "You can get back on a boat at Tas-Elisa," I said.

He smiled his superior smile, his composure much

restored during the slow process of casting votes. "How will you make me?"

"I don't have to," I said. "Your emperor isn't prepared for war with the Continent, or he would be attacking already. You are trying to sneak a foothold here in Sounis to steal my country by sleight of hand. The Continental Powers dither, but they won't stand for an unprovoked assault, and your emperor is not yet ready for one. The Continent would come to my aid before he was ready for war and spoil all his plans."

"You think so? You bank on that?" Akretenesh asked. He'd been backing away and almost reached the double doors that led under the stage.

"I do."

"Well," said the ambassador, "we will see, then, won't we?" He threw open the doors, revealing soldiers armed with crossbows.

He turned back to me, shouting, "Ki—"

I shot him, too.

Had he been aware, Akretenesh would have been disappointed to see his assassins spitted with quarrels fired from behind me, before they themselves could get off a single shot. It seemed there was no end of people breaking sacred truces at Elisa that day.

I whirled around, but the arbalests must have been hidden in the bushes on the slopes above the amphitheater. I saw no one.

Someone shouted from the terraced seats, "Long live

the Lion of Sounis," and the amphitheater roared with approval. There was a great deal of backslapping and shouting, as if it were just what my barons had planned on all along.

I wasn't cheering. I was considering the ambassador. Dead ambassadors are a very bad business, and I approached his body with some trepidation.

Thank the gods, though I do aim better with my right than my left, the new gun threw to one side. I'd never practiced with it, and I'd only winged Akretenesh. His eyes were already open. I leaned down to look at him closely. I didn't think I'd even hit the bone in his upper arm, but there was no way to be sure. There was a crowd forming around me, my father and his men and other barons drawing close.

"The magus?" I asked urgently.

"Is here, as you wished," said my father, and I sighed in relief.

"Get Akretenesh to his rooms and fetch a doctor for him," I told my father.

I turned to give orders to clear out the bodies, but Akretenesh's thready voice called me back.

"Your Majesty," he said.

"Yes?" I answered, ever polite.

Akretenesh looked remarkably smug for someone being carried away with a bullet hole in him. "I rather thought that I could persuade your barons to accept a replacement more to my liking. How unfortunate that won't work, just yet. What will you do about my men, who will no doubt be marching up the port road very soon?"

"I knew you would hear that I was coming to Brimedius. I knew you would attack me on the way, and I arranged to have the Attolians and Eddisians scatter and appear to retreat," I said, rather smug myself. "They made their way here, in small groups, to hide in the hills long before anyone was watching for them. My magus went to explain this to my father and came down with him from the Melenze pass."

I'd stayed in Brimedius, hoping to give them time to take cover in the hills. Then I had hurried through the meetings in Elisa as fast as I decently could. There is only so long an army can stay hidden and only so long it can live on nuts and dried meat and still fight when it is called upon. It is not a ruse that would have worked anywhere but in the sacred precinct where the woods are uninhabited.

"The magus, with the Attolians and the Eddisians, is above the road from Tas-Elisa. They will turn back your thousand soldiers easily."

"Aaah," said Akretenesh, part enlightenment and part pain, "but there aren't a thousand. They are closer to ten thousand in number."

My polite expression froze solid. "Ten thousand?"

"Yes, they came in by ship in the last few days."

No wonder the bastard looked so smug. I'd just

assaulted an inviolate ambassador and started a war with a piddling company of bow and pikemen against his army of ten thousand justifiably enraged Medes.

"Why—" Akretenesh gasped a little and started again. "Why don't you join me in my rooms a little later, and we will discuss this unfortunate turn of affairs?"

Malicious son of a bitch, I thought, over my dead body am I discussing anything with you.

"Yes," I said, "I'll come right up whenever you're ready."

"Ten thousand!" I shouted at the walls, back in the room with the wooden shutters, now open, so that anyone could hear me, on the porch or probably across the compound. "That *arrogant* bastard landed *ten thousand men* at Tas-Elisa. In my port! Mine!" When I was a child and playmates snatched my toys out of my hands, I tended to smile weakly and give in. Years later I was acting the way I should have as a child. Probably not the most mature behavior for a king, but I was still cursing as I swung around to find a delegation of barons in the doorway behind me. My father, Baron Comeneus, and Baron Xorcheus among them.

They thought it was how a king behaved.

I ran my fingers through my hair and tried to pursue a more reasonable line of thought, but more reasonable thoughts made me angry again. Armies of ten thousand men don't just spring from the ground at the tip of a wine cup. It takes time to move them from wherever they came from and time to unload them from ships. There's space to consider, and logistics. The land around the port had to be wall-to-wall men. Someone had to have made a plan to feed them, and supplies had to have been coming in for weeks. Some of them, no doubt, had been hidden within the preparations for the meet by Hanaktos, but he hadn't done it on his own. There were more people sitting in the meet, and some of them maybe in the room with me, who had known that the Mede was bringing an army. And many, many more of them must have known once Tas-Elisa filled to the brim with soldiers.

Not me. I didn't have a clue.

Which means that my careful collection of "information" from Nomenus over the previous week had been a farce.

"Who knows anything about the ten thousand men at the port?" No one volunteered any information. There was a flicker of apprehension in Baron Xorcheus, but that wasn't enough. I knew he'd called for a regent, and I knew he was overanxious. I didn't know for certain why.

I remembered Polystrictes and his goats. I wasn't sure if I had a wolf or a dog, but I knew how to tell the difference. A dog does what you tell it to.

"Basrus!" I shouted, and the barons and their men looked at me confused.

"I want Hanaktos's slaver. Find him and bring him."

I waved the rest of the people away and paced the room until the slaver appeared at the door looking like a man who isn't sure if he's under arrest.

"Majesty, I—"

"Later. Who knows about the army at Tas-Elisa?"

Basrus's eyeballs rolled to one side, and before he said a word, Baron Xorcheus decided all hope of concealment was lost.

"Hanaktos warned me to have all my people well away from the port three days past. He said what the eyes don't see the heart doesn't grieve over. That's all I know myself. Baron Statidoros knows more."

I looked at Basrus, and he disappeared.

Baron Comeneus was staring at Xorcheus in outrage, reinforcing my conviction in the amphitheater. He *hadn't* known about the army. It was Hanaktos who had been in charge.

Comeneus turned to me. I thought he was going to call for Xorcheus's head, but I was wrong. "Your Majesty, that man," he said, pointing out the door after Basrus, "is an okloi! You cannot mean to send him to compel a baron!"

As if it mattered, here at what might well be the swirling drain of Sounis's history, whether or not Basrus was a landowner and entitled to a vote on legal issues.

"You cannot mean to suggest that you would consider his word—"

"Shut up," I told him, and he stared at me open-mouthed. I stared back; not the boy he'd condescended to, not my uncle's inept heir, I, the king of Sounis. "I may or may not survive as king, but if I am a puppet of the Medes, at least I will know it. Go ask your brother what he knows of Hanaktos's plans, and then come back and tell me what he said."

I waved my hand to dismiss them all; I needed to be alone to think. They didn't move. *Get out!* I shouted, and that had more effect.

Only my father stood his ground. He cleared his throat. "The truce is broken. You need guards."

He was right. Weapons were going to come out from any of a hundred secret hiding places, and it would shortly be every baron for himself.

I could trust my father and only a few others completely. I told my father, "Our men will be our guards here. You will arrange it?" He nodded. "Tell whoever you can that I am not wiping any slates clean. I will hold people responsible for their actions, now and in the future, but there will be, for every transgression, a remedy in the next few days. Tell the council that. Make sure they know that the future of the patronoi depends on their service to me."

Then I sent him away to arrange for more guards and to quell my barons' destructive tendency toward short-sightedness and panic.

❖ ❖ ❖

I paced until Basrus delivered Baron Statidoros, who spilled every bean as fast he could spit words out of his mouth.

What I learned of the Mede army: they were infantry. No horse. They were in ten companies of a thousand with a general and his lieutenants. I didn't recognize all the names, but one of them had a name very similar to my ambassador's and might well have been a relative. I could count on him to be personally, as well as professionally, unhappy with me.

Though he was trying to bluster his way through the moment, Baron Statidoros was frightened, and he had good reason. He didn't have anything I needed, and we both knew it. His patronid was not located somewhere strategic. He didn't control many men, and he didn't have a fortune I could "borrow" to help secure my throne.

He was a loyalist, he insisted. If only he'd known that I was alive, that I was returning, etc. His protests might have been convincing if he hadn't made it clear earlier in the week that he was Comeneus's man. I didn't believe for a minute that he'd thought I was dead.

Baron Xorcheus had sent poor Statidoros as a sacrifice. Both Statidoros and I knew that as well. His job was to give me just enough information to strike at a few of the lower members of Hanaktos's conspiracy but not to betray its leaders. He would take responsibility for the transgressions of others and be condemned for it. Whether he was a volunteer who had a reward coming or a victim caught between me and a threat of death from his own side if he failed, I didn't know, and I didn't really care. As this became more clear to him, he became more frightened and unfortunately less coherent.

I had a fast-expiring period of grace, while my erstwhile ambassador was having lead shot dug out of his shoulder. My barons would be growing more anxious, and more stupid, with each passing moment, and a message was no doubt already on its way to the port, Tas-Elisa. The magus would stop any traveler on the road, and the woods would be watched as well, but the hills that had hidden my army for weeks would conceal, just as reliably, any number of Mede emissaries. The message would go like water running downhill to the general in charge of ten thousand Medes: The king of Sounis had fired on his ambassador and seized the reins of government.

I knew whom I couldn't trust, but outside of my father and a few others, I didn't know whom I could. I had to start trusting some people, and I had to choose which. I had to decide what to do about the army that was on its way, and I didn't have the information I needed and didn't know how I could get it. Basrus could do me only so much good. He could tell me whom he'd seen work with Hanaktos, but not which of them might still be useful to me now.

And then my worst nightmare arrived, weeping and

wailing in the doorway. Berrone. I had no idea where she had come from. And her mother was with her, gods defend me. I hadn't known that either of them was in Elisa, and I was going to kill Nomenus, I thought, kill him.

Berrone was content to stand in the doorway with her hair a wild mess and her face streaming tears, but her mother, bowed over obsequiously behind her, must have given her a pretty savage poke, because Berrone suddenly flung herself at my feet, crying, "Oh, my father, my dear father, how could you murder him and betray me, who rescued you from, from, from—"

From your father, I thought, but I didn't say anything. I looked down at her, and my conscience hit me from behind. The words weren't hers, but the tears were, and they were real tears. Whatever Hanaktos had been to me, he'd been her father, and I'd killed him.

"Berrone," I said helplessly.

"What will become of us now, Great King?" said her mother. "What will become of my poor daughter, betrayed by—"

I didn't even hear the rest, and my sympathy snuffed out like a candle dropped in a well.

"Get out, all of you," I said to the rest of the room. "Berrone, get up. You can sit on the couch."

Baron Statidoros, looking as if a god had descended from the ceiling to rescue him, scuttled through the door without another word. Everyone else bowed and exited as well, except for Berrone's mother, who was busy trying to accuse me of indecent intentions.

"My daughter," she was saying, "a chaste beauty, whom you have violently stripped of her father's protection—"

I stepped around Berrone, who was still on the floor, and advanced toward her mother, and I think my intentions were perfectly clear because she backed up hastily.

"Great King!" she cheeped. "Mercy! Mercy on a poor widow and her only daughter," she cried as she backed through the doorway.

I returned to Berrone and lifted her up, guiding her by the arm to a nearby couch, where I sat beside her.

"Berrone, I am sorry," I said.

"Everyone's been so angry at me," she sobbed. "They've yelled at me and been so mean. They sent Sylvie away. And now Mother says that it's my fault that my father is dead and you have to marry me. Will you?"

"Will I *what*?"

"Please?" Berrone asked pathetically. "Mother says you have to or she'll never stop being angry at me, and we'll live on the street and I won't have any pretty dresses and all my kittens will be drowned. Please?" She wept.

I almost wept myself.

"Berrone, it isn't your fault that your father is dead. That's his fault, and my fault, but not yours."

"It is my fault," said Berrone, sniffing. "My mother said everything is my fault. She found out that I paid for you in the market and that you were at the megaron all the time they were looking for you, and then they found out I let you go, and my f-f-father said I spoiled all their plans, because he was supposed to be the one to rescue you. I don't see why it mattered if I rescued you instead, even if I didn't know it was you, and I didn't, you know," she said earnestly. "I had no idea that was you. But Mother was angry and said I wouldn't be able to marry you after all and be queen like they'd promised."

"Like they had what?" I raised my voice without meaning to.

Berrone wailed.

I patted her on the back, as a number of things became clear. Of course Hanaktos wanted me to marry his daughter. What a perfect plan. First encourage a revolt against my uncle, then abduct me, and then rescue me, and then foist his conveniently beautiful daughter into my arms because, surely, any grateful young man would be eager to marry the bird-witted Berrone. What a nightmare. I could now guess at the source of recent tensions between Akretenesh and Hanaktos. The Mede would have been happier to bring Eddis under the imperial thumb as well, but Hanaktos had wanted his daughter on the throne.

It was a subtle and beautiful plan. If I had been even moderately cooperative, they needn't even have forced a regent on me. I wouldn't have lived a year after my heir was born. A sudden illness or a hunting accident, and Hanaktos would have had the long regency he dreamed of and a grandchild to inherit the throne. The Mede would have had a dependable ally, because he would have known the truth and could have threatened Hanaktos with it at will. Comeneus had also escaped an early death, I thought, and his brother was going to be disappointed.

"Mother says that now that you have killed my father, you will have to marry me after all. Will you?"

"Gods, no, Berrone."

"Oh."

I sighed. "It will be all right, Berrone. I promise. I'll make sure you have pretty dresses, and we'll get Sylvie back."

"No," said Berrone firmly.

I was puzzled. "No?"

"That's what men say to girls they don't want to marry, and I know because Sylvie told me—" She was getting upset again.

"Men will tell you that they'll find Sylvie?" I asked quickly, and she was distracted.

"Noo," she said slowly. "Sylvie said they'll promise me pretty dresses."

"Well, I won't promise you pretty dresses. But I will get you Sylvie back. Tell me again, who said you were going to be queen?"

"My mother, she—" I stopped her before she repeated the entire scene again.

"That's all I needed to know, Berrone. Thank you."

I handed Berrone out the door at the same time that I waved to Hanaktos's widow.

"A word, Lady Hanaktia."

I summoned my victims to the largest room and had them wait for me. One by one, I called them away, but these weren't the strained and circuitous interviews I'd sat through before. As each baron entered the room, he saw Basrus sitting to one side of me and Hanaktia on the other, as terrifying as any sphinx from a fireside story. By the time I received word that Akretenesh wanted to see me, I was well on my way to knowing what to do with my barons, and they were well on their way toward full cooperation.

All in all, it was not a profitable discussion with the Mede ambassador. He refused to tell me anything that I didn't already know about his plans. I suggested that he might like to be sent down to the port by litter to see his own doctors, because I wanted him out of the way. He declined. He told me he would prefer to wait until his army came to him.

"It might not," I said.

"We'll see, won't we?" he answered.

"In the morning we will run for Oneia," I said to my private council, hastily selected.

They had wanted me—my father most strenuously—to take what horse we had and to try to cross through

Hanaktos's army on the capital road. If they could get me safely away, either by convincing Hanaktos's cousin, who commanded the men, to let me pass, or by fighting our way through, I could ride for the city of Sounis to try to hold it against the Medes. Unfortunately, I would leave most of my barons behind to change sides yet again. Those who didn't change sides would bear the brunt of the Medes' revenge, as would the Attolians and the Eddisians I would be abandoning. I refused.

I waited for someone to say the obvious. We didn't have enough men to stand against ten thousand Medes. We'd be cut to pieces when we reached the dead end that was Oneia. No one said a word.

"The magus, with his remaining men, will slow the Medes. They won't reach Elisa until noontime, and we will have time to arrange the men on the Oneia Road. Then, when we reach Oneia and turn to fight on the open ground, most of the Medes will still be stuck on the roadway. If we fight well, they will still be there when our armies make it across the hills behind Elisa and come down on them from the rear."

It was a plan that might see most of them dead by nightfall of the next day, and they nodded agreeably and went to inform their men. They didn't ask, and I couldn't say, why I thought we should make our stand at Oneia. I had made my decision, and they had made theirs.

+ + +

It was well into the night before I was finished with plans and staggered up to my rooms to find Nomenus waiting for me.

He was sitting on a stool not far from the fireplace. His hands were clasped together on one knee, and he was miles away in his thoughts, not even realizing at first that I had arrived. When he saw me in the doorway, he stood. He looked me in the face briefly before lowering his eyes.

"Your Majesty," he said softly.

"I thought you would be long gone," I said.

He shook his head.

"Nowhere to go?" I asked. "There are ten thousand Mede soldiers in Tas-Elisa to welcome you."

He nodded. "I know."

"Brimedius won't take you in?"

"I am not his man," Nomenus replied. I knew whose man he was.

"I killed Hanaktos," I said.

"Yes."

I walked closer to him. He was less calm than he appeared. "You're shaking."

He shrugged again, the barest shift of a shoulder. "I would kill me if I were you," he said.

I didn't know what else to do with him. I certainly wasn't going to let him walk away free and clear after he'd served me with lies and deceit.

"Your Majesty, they have cells here," he said, "in the

outbuildings. I might yet serve you if you didn't—if I wasn't—" Finally he said flatly, "Things might not go as you hope."

"If Akretenesh wins?" I had to laugh. "If I am installed as his puppet, you are saying that I could call you back to lie to me?" I made no effort to hide my amazement.

"I could serve you. As well as—"

"As well as they'd let you?"

He gave up a shaky sigh and dropped to his knees. He bowed his head, and then he just waited.

I'd had an entire day of whining, self-serving patronoi denying their every transgression and vomiting up excuse after excuse. This was a man who at least didn't try to pretend to stainless virtue. It was probably calculated, and if so, it was well done. He knew me better, after all, than the barons did and knew what was most likely to sway me. I found I had no desire to see him die.

I called in the guards from beside my door and sent him off with them to be locked up somewhere.

"See that he's fed," I called after them, "and taken out occasionally for air." At my words Nomenus struggled briefly in their arms. As he looked back at me over his shoulder, I saw the fear in his face. He didn't say anything, though, just stared at me as they led him away.

If Akretenesh did defeat me, and if he didn't kill me outright, I would have Ion Nomenus to attend me in my puppet show. At least I'd know he was a liar; I wouldn't have to wonder.

In the dark hours of the morning, I exercised the privilege of a king: I slept. I never even heard the noise as the Eddisians and the Attolians I had asked the magus to send me arrived. I had more than five hundred men among the barons and their retinues. I'd been correct about the weapons that had been concealed. Every baron and his men were armed, but they weren't an army, and altogether we were fewer than two thousand against ten.

When the sky was growing light, my father knocked on my door. I washed my face and dressed, missing Nomenus already, and then went down the stairs to find something to eat before the day began.

By the time the sun was up, we were far down the narrow road to Oneia. The first spot I had in mind to stand and fight was more than two-thirds of the way to the sea. The road followed a watercourse, and the hills for most of the way were too steep to climb without care and attention, but the narrow valley began to open out as it neared the coast. The hillsides beside the road were both less high and less steep. I knew, as I hoped that the Medes did not, that just behind the rise of those hills there was a level spot. Then, out of sight from the road below, the hillside rose much higher. I put my Attolians just behind the top of the lower hill and sent my barons and the Eddisians to find cover on the upper slope.

When the Medes came, their weapons glinting in

the sun that had burned off the sea mist, the Attolians brought their crossbows to bear, firing down with accuracy too deadly to ignore.

The army was traveling only ten abreast and cheek by jowl on the narrow roadbed. At a shouted command, a block moved forward and reordered itself as it came, shaping into a phalanx of twenty by twenty and moving up the hill at top speed. The Attolians' fire slowed them not at all.

The Attolians on the hill formed into their own blocks and charged down. That did slow the first of the Medes, but as more phalanxes came up, they pressed forward. I was on the upper hill, screened by takima bushes, but I could see very well. The noise was overwhelming. I didn't remember noise like this at the battle near Brimedius. The hammering sounds of weapons ran together and were so loud that very soon, instead of hearing it, I felt I could hear nothing at all.

The Attolians couldn't hold the hillside. Step by step they were forced back. Suddenly, they broke ranks and retreated. The Medes followed, lured out of their phalanxes, their mouths open in inaudible shouting.

They topped the hill, and their expressions changed. Too late they looked for their side men, but their side men were out of reach. On my command, the Eddisians charged from above. Their momentum carried them through the disordered enemy and across the brow of the lower hill. The weakened Mede phalanxes disintegrated, like trees losing leaves in a high wind. The Eddisians continued on down the hill toward the army below, still in its tight marching formation.

All the ten thousand men of the Mede fighting force were trapped behind their own front line. Those in the frontline troops, with the enemy bearing down on them, recoiled. The front line pushed back into its own pikemen, who couldn't stop the men behind them, who were pushing forward.

I should be humble, but I'm not. I was delighted. Everything was working just as I'd hoped. I stood on the hillside and cheered. The men around me shouted with me. We watched the confusion traveling back up the line of the Mede army like the contractions of an earthworm, while the Eddisians continued to hack at the front line. Then we scrambled and slid down the hill to the road and hurried on toward Oneia.

We could have stayed and replaced the Eddisians in the battle line as they fought to the last, but we would have been putting ourselves in the same position as the Medes: most of our men in back with just a few at the head of the line to fight. With both armies limited by the narrow roadway, the Medes would soon prevail.

Instead we hurried away. Once the road was clear, the Eddisians would turn and follow us at a run. The curves of the road were all that would protect them from the Mede fire until they reached the open ground around Oneia, where we would be waiting to give them cover.

We would have the advantage of space to spread out and fight. The Medes would still be in the roadway, and as they issued from it a few at a time, we would take them. Sooner or later the great pressure of men would overwhelm us. That would be the time for each man to kill as many as he could before he died.

I ran, with my father just behind me. I slowed, but he didn't move up, and I realized he was shielding me. My armor plate would stop an arrow or a bullet at that range, but not a crossbow quarrel. There weren't any crossbow quarrels, however, or bullets, and all it did was slow me down. I was staggering by the time I heard the shouting ahead of us, and the clanging of metal against metal. My father suddenly passed me and then slowed and looked backward, clearly undecided which enemy to face.

Gasping, I tugged on his shoulder and tried to catch enough breath to reassure him. The men around us slowed, but I waved them forward and staggered on. It wasn't shouting, it was cheering, I was almost certain. We came around the last curve in the road, and we saw them: rank after rank of men in the blue and gold of Attolia waiting for us, banging their weapons and yelling.

"Attolis," I gasped to my father. "He sent more men."

CHAPTER TWENTY

EARLIER in the day, the magus had slowed the Medes on the coast road as they tried to fight their way from the port to Elisa, so that nearly a third of their column was still in the Elisa Valley and not yet on the road down to Oneia when the armies of my loyalist barons came over the hills from the hinterlands. The loyalists had been traveling all night by torchlight and went directly to battle without a rest.

Down in Oneia, the head of the Mede army was crushed with the help of the fresh Attolian troops. The Attolians had arrived only the day before and during the previous night, transferring in small boatloads to the tiny beach below Oneia. If the weather had not been calm, they couldn't have done it and would have been sitting offshore as we died.

As it happened, the Medes were forced by the pressure of men coming down behind them along the roadway and out into the open to face a coordinated attack where their greater numbers never benefited them. It was madness for their general to commit all his forces on such a road, and I can only think that he fatally underestimated me. Perhaps he, too, had been listening to the Mede ambassador in Attolia.

When the Medes finally organized their retreat, we followed them up toward Elisa. I'd sent men around to reach our ambush site from behind to cover the hillside with their fire, so that the Medes could not treat us as we had treated them.

I learned afterward that in the Elisa Valley the Medes had tried to break away and drive for the capital road, only to find that pass blocked by Hanaktos's army. Hanaktia is a woman of iron and had taken me at my word when I said that there would be a remedy for all transgressions. She had left the safety of Elisa and ridden herself to her late husband's soldiers to rally them to fight against the Medes.

I am afraid that the side effect of all this will be a burnishing of our reputation for two-faced deal making. It is unflattering, but the Medes will think twice before making any bargains with future rebels if they believe we are all unreliable allies.

Unable to clear a path of retreat toward the capital, the Medes were forced to fight their way back across the valley and down the road to the port at Tas-Elisa. They were harried at every step and arrived in complete darkness. Thanks to the magus's work with the townspeople, before the Medes even arrived, the soldiers found themselves locked out of the walled town.

The Mede ships in the harbor had cannons to provide covering fire. Under that and the small-arms fire from the town walls, the few thousand Medes who were left scrambled into shoreboats and were hauled to their ships. My army settled into the tents that had been provided for the Medes, ate their provisions, and enjoyed their wine, while the townspeople sensibly stayed inside their closed walls and refused to let anyone in, including me. Being turned away was a surprise, but I was too relieved by the entire course of the day to care. I rode up to Elisa in the dark, with the sounds of victory slowly fading into the song of nightbirds and insects, and fell into my own kingly bed at dawn.

The bodies were gathered over the next few days, stripped, and then burned. The weapons were collected in a makeshift armory in Tas-Elisa. I meant to restore the truce at Elisa as quickly as possible, so I stored no weapons there. I will pay a whopping fine to the treasury to assuage the outrage of the priests. Though I have escaped any lightning strikes of the gods, I regret bringing war to the place of festivals, and Elisa must have its truce if Sounis is to elect any kings in the future.

We acquired twelve cannons as well, which was an unlooked-for windfall. Evidently the Medes had off-loaded them from their ships to be used at some point in the future. We found them the morning after the battle as the proctors attempted to bring some order to the chaos that was several thousand soldiers sleeping off a drunk. Akretenesh told me I must return the cannons, and I laughed in his face.

Akretenesh was not a happy man. I did try to take a conciliatory approach, but he would have none of it, and my politeness was long at an end when he told me he wanted to take the cannons with him. I packed him into a litter and had him carried down to the port, where with great relief I saw him laid in a boat and pushed off to the Mede transport ship. He made some unpleasant threats, but I doubt he will have an opportunity to carry them out. He will face his emperor over the loss of an army when he reaches home. I do not expect to see him again and am glad of it.

There were more meetings, confirming my impression that talking is the most important thing a king does. I had promised Hanaktia that her children would not lose Hanaktos if she fulfilled her bargain with me. I kept my word but settled one-third of the holdings on Berrone as a dowry and made my mother's brother her guardian. That it didn't please her mother was no concern of mine. My uncle will take care of Berrone's best interests. I don't trust her mother or brothers to do so.

I went to see Nomenus the day I left. There were six cells in an outbuilding. The building was high in the middle with low eaves, and the doorways of the cells faced each other across a central breezeway. Frankly, it was more pig house than prison. The door to Nomenus's cell was little higher than my waist and made of woven metal strips. Nomenus lay curled against it. He was asleep, which was not astonishing. He had no blanket, and I assumed it was too cold in the stone building to sleep at night.

As I squatted beside the webwork of iron, he stirred and sat up. "You are triumphant," he said. "I heard from the guards."

"I am," I said.

"I'm glad," he said grudgingly, tucking his fingers under his arms. "Not wholly glad, you understand . . . but glad."

I peered past him into the darkness.

He said, "It is not so cramped farther back. I sit here because it is warmer."

I had come to see him because I thought that out of sight and out of mind might be a dangerous attitude to take. I wanted to have a very clear idea in my head of where I had put him.

"Unlock this," I said to the guard with me.

Nomenus backed away from the door once it was open, and I got on my knees and crawled inside. The prison cell did open out; its roof was higher than in the cramped passageway by the door, and the floor in the rest of the cell had been dug out, so it was lower and Nomenus could stand upright. I sat in the tunnel that was the entryway and dangled my legs over the lip into the cell. The dirt having been dug away, what was left was a collection of boulders and the lumpy bedrock.

There was no flat space outside of the entryway where I sat.

I waved to Nomenus, and he settled uncomfortably on a rock. He had a huge bruise on his forehead that did not please me. He touched it gingerly and said, "It was no unkindness by your guards," as if reading my mind. "I first came here in the dark, if you remember."

"I see." I couldn't think of what else I wanted to say. I watched him watching me. Finally I asked, "What are you thinking?"

He swallowed. "Useless excuses that I am trying to keep unsaid."

I waited.

After a moment he tossed up his hands, and to my intense discomfort, he started to cry. "You are king," he said, his voice breaking. "What I did doesn't matter very much now, does it? And what else could I do but be loyal to my lord? Is it my business whom my lord is loyal to?"

"Do you believe that?"

"No." He pushed himself farther back and drew his legs up to be wrapped in the curl of his arms. He rubbed his face against his arms. "I wanted to be on the winning side, and I thought I was."

He was either a flawed but fundamentally decent man or a very convincing actor, or possibly, he was both.

"Please," he said, with obvious reluctance. "I hadn't meant to ask, but, is it . . . forever?" His tears had made streaks through the dirt on his face.

I said, "No. It isn't forever, but it's going to be some time."

He nodded.

"When I have other things dealt with, I will deal with you," I promised him.

Later, as I climbed onto my horse's back and rode for the capital, his last words were still in my ears. His cell had already been locked behind me, and he hadn't been talking to me. He was praying to the gods, I think, when he whispered, "Don't forget me. Please, don't forget me."

I stayed only two days in the capital. I was welcomed by a cheering citizenry, who threw flowers at my head. It was disconcerting to think I could have put almost any young man in my retinue on a white horse and they would have thrown flowers at him instead. It was not me they cared about, only what I meant to them: a cessation of hostilities, a chance for prosperity, food on the table.

I left the city of Sounis almost immediately because I had backed Brimedius into a corner, and he had admitted both that he had held my mother and sisters and that they had subsequently disappeared. He admitted that he had no idea where they were. Clearly, he expected to be held responsible for their deaths. I did not relieve him of his fears, and wouldn't until I had seen my mother and sisters with my own eyes.

I was anxious to get to Eddis. In this, my father was my greatest ally, putting his foot down when the magus suggested I should travel with all my Eddisians and Attolians at a snail's pace. I took a guard and a change of clothes and left the rest to travel at the speed of armies and gastropods. We changed horses frequently and arrived in Eddis almost as quickly as any royal messenger. I didn't question for a minute that it was my desire for haste that moved us, not until we arrived in the great court of the Eddisian palace.

My father dropped from his horse almost before the animal had stopped moving and strode, oblivious, through six layers of a ceremonial reception, to take my mother in his arms. I stared, remembering his words after we'd escaped Hanaktos. As I watched him lift her off the ground, watched her wrap her arms around him and lay her head on his shoulder, it was apparent that I had misunderstood what he meant when he said that only I was "important."

Our parents' behavior seemed to be no surprise to either Ina or Eurydice, who left them to each other and ran toward me. To my relief, the Eddisians in the court didn't seem to mind the disruption of the ceremony they'd planned, and I was able to seize Ina and Eurydice in my own arms and all of us could babble our questions and answers at one another while the Eddisians looked tolerantly on. The majordomo efficiently dispatched my guard to quarters and swept us all inside to rooms where we could be private and I could ask about the one person I had looked for but not seen, the queen of Eddis.

Ina told me, "She has taken her court to Attolia and waits to see you there."

"Her Majesty has kindly given us this time together," said my mother, "knowing that we have much to catch up on."

Indeed, we did. Settling on the couches, we shared our adventures. Ina and Eurydice told me how Ina had led them out of Brimedius, while my mother sat between me and my father, looking comfortably at each of us in turn and speaking very little. She did not appear particularly brave or daring, hardly even strong-minded. She seemed as quiet as ever, but I didn't doubt that she had done just as Eurydice said and run a sharpened stick down the throat of one of Brimedius's hounds. Even with the evidence of their happy outcome, I am left with nightmares at the dangers they faced and know I have many debts to repay to people and to gods for their safe arrival in Eddis.

It was the next day that my mother sought a word in private, looking for me in the small chamber attached to the palace library where Gen used to have his bedroom. Pausing at the threshold, she framed a question. "I thought you would be in a hurry to be on your way to Attolia?"

"I am in a hurry," I said. "But that's no reason you

should be made uncomfortable. It will be much more pleasant for you if we go back to the main pass and await the soldiers returning to Attolia and then travel with them."

"It will be slower, though, won't it?" she asked, as she settled lightly on the arm of a chair opposite me.

I looked studiously at the book in my hand.

My mother waited.

I finally gave up and closed the book. "I broke the truce at Elisa and I shot an unarmed man. I shot the ambassador. I cost the lives of her soldiers and Attolia's as well as my own, and my hands are *covered* in blood. What if Eddis thinks there was a better way? What if she is glad she has not already agreed to marry me, and what if she wants nothing to do with me now?"

My mother said very reasonably, "You can't hide from someone in her own palace. If you don't go to Attolia, she will come here."

I hunched my shoulders and went back to looking at my book.

My mother stood, saying peacefully, "I will tell your father that you will go tomorrow by way of the Old Aracthus Road. The rest of us will travel with your borrowed military."

She looked back before she pulled the door closed. "Your questions—you know I am not the one to answer them."

She was as right as ever, and so I have come to the queen of Eddis, to ask her for answers.

· CHAPTER TWENTY-ONE ·

SOUNIS folded his hands and waited. He had arrived
at the palace late the night before and had risen
early in the morning, expecting to find no one but the two
honorary royal guardsmen and his own personal guard in
his anteroom. Instead he found Ion, the attendant of the
king of Attolia, waiting by a bench against the wall.

"You're still here, then?" asked Sounis, in surprise and
pleasure.

"Yes, Your Majesty. My king thought that you might
wish to dress with particular care this morning. There
will be an official reception in a few hours." Ion was
smiling. They both knew that Attolis hadn't been referring just to the ceremony planned for the day.

Sounis looked down at the clothes he'd put on. He
hadn't given them a thought, but Eugenides was probably right. He opened the door wider and turned back
toward his bedchamber.

Ion had brought scissors, and after he shaved him, he
trimmed Sounis's hair and added a light coating of oil.
He opened a small jar and took a pinch of gold powder
and shook it to cling to the oil.

"Ion," said Sounis, dismayed.

"It's for luck," said Ion. He packed his case and went to Sounis's wardrobe.

"My clothes are still in cases in my reception room, except for what I am wearing."

But Ion was already pulling a suit from tissue paper. "His Majesty—"

"I hazard to guess," said Sounis. "The tailors still had my measurements?"

"Indeed," said Ion, and helped him out of his clothes and into a linen shirt so fine that it was easy to see the shape of his arms right through it. It was covered by a sleeveless tunic in dark blue.

"Boots, too?" said Sounis.

"He likes to think of everything."

"Yes, yes, he does."

"An opal earring, Your Majesty? Or would you prefer onyx?"

When Sounis was finally presentable to Attolian standards, Ion opened the door to the reception room and bowed. Xanthe, the oldest of Eddis's attendants, was standing just outside. She turned away and said to someone not in view, "Your Majesty, the king of Sounis."

Eddis was waiting for him on a carved seat by the window. She stood. Her dress was of linen as fine as his own. It had an overdress decorated in knotted cord and a waist of satin covered in tiny beads in the same pattern as the knots.

Sounis swallowed. "I did not realize," he said. "I would have come to your rooms to speak to you."

Eddis smiled. "I intrude?"

"No," said Sounis, trying to breathe. "Of course not."

Ion had excused himself to the anteroom, but the door was open, and Xanthe as well as the queen's other attendants came in and left from time to time. Eddis's attention never wavered. When Sounis finished, she said, "Your mother was right, I think."

"She usually is," said Sounis.

"Did you think I would change my mind?"

"I failed to persuade my barons, and I fell back on violence and murder."

"You made your choice," said Eddis.

"I did. I hope you understand why I cannot back away from it."

"Even if I condemn you for it, as you condemned Nomenus?"

"Even then," said Sounis.

"Sophos," said Eddis sadly, "I sent my Thief to Attolia, and when she had maimed him, and knowing the risk, I sent him back. I have started a war of my own, sent my cousins to die, taken food from the mouths of widows and children to feed my army." She took his hand. "We are not philosophers; we are sovereigns. The rules that govern our behavior are not the rules for other men, and our honor, I think, is a different thing entirely, difficult for anyone but the historians and the gods to judge. There is no reason I can see that I would not be honored to join Eddis to you. But it is complicated by many things that I must tell you about first."

"Of course," said Sounis, his grin too boyish to be reminiscent of his uncle. "More talking!"

"Yes, and some of it important. I would ask—"

But Sounis was too pleased to register any nuance. He only knew that he was happy. He interrupted her. "I thought, when I first met you, that you would marry Gen."

"I would sooner have strangled him," said Eddis.

"I didn't see that," said Sounis. "I still don't, honestly. He has saved Attolia."

"Gen and I are too close to marry. If he has saved Attolia, then she has saved him as well, and I've told her as much. But—"

"Your Majesties." Ion bowed in the doorway. "Please forgive me. The king and queen of Attolia ask that you join them."

Eddis sighed and let the matter go, thinking there would be time enough to reveal her plans to Sounis after he had sworn his loyalty to the king of Attolia. She and Sounis rose and walked to the anteroom, where they were greeted by the beaming attendants and Sounis's magus, who stood with a broad smile splitting his face. Eddis felt the blood rising in her own face as the magus bowed.

"Our felicitations, Your Majesties," he said.

"We thank you," Eddis said to the magus, and kissed him on both cheeks.

"We certainly do," said Sounis, and kissed him as well, before being kissed in turn by Xanthe. Then, in response to Ion's polite prodding, the room was emptied out into the passageway.

Eddis and Sounis parted on the way to Attolia's throne room. Eddis was to enter by the main doors and wait with the rest of the court. The magus and Sounis continued on to a retiring room where the king and queen of Attolia waited.

Eschewing ceremony, Eugenides said, "You *shot* the ambassador?"

"You gave me the gun," protested Sounis.

"I didn't mean for you to shoot an ambassador with it!" Eugenides told him.

"Oh, how our carefully laid plans go astray," murmured the magus.

"You shut up!" said Gen, laughing.

The doors to the throne room opened, and there was no time to say more. Those awaiting the sovereigns observed their smiles and smiled in turn.

Attolia took no part in the ceremony, not even ascending her throne, but standing instead to one side of the dais while the complicated oath was read out by the high priestess of Hephestia.

Sounis swore his personal loyalty and his obedience to Attolis. He swore his state to Attolis's service in the event of war, external or internal. He pledged his men to Attolis's armies and his treasury to Attolis's support. He swore on behalf of himself and his heirs loyalty to any heir of Attolis, binding the two nations together permanently. Attolis, in his turn, promised to protect and defend Sounis and his state, to preserve Sounis's autonomy in all matters internal to the state, to make no interference in Sounis's authority except as it affected the needs of Attolia.

Sounis bowed over the king of Attolia's hands, kissed the backs of them both, and held the real one to his forehead. Attolis pulled him close to kiss him on the brow, and the court clapped in congratulations.

Stepping back, Sounis said, "Congratulate me, My King. I am to be married."

Eugenides smiled. Attolia looked sharply at Eddis, who shook her head. The room quieted.

"She is your subject?" asked Eugenides.

"Indeed not," said Sounis, insensible to the significance of the question.

"Well, then," said Attolia, drawing his attention as she stepped onto the dais. She seated herself and laid her hand over Eugenides's, forestalling him. "It would not be a matter wholly internal to Sounis. You would have to bring it to your king for approval."

His expression changing, Eugenides looked from his

wife to Eddis, and then back to Sounis, who stood confused and uncertain before him.

His easy manner yielded. "Indeed," said Eugenides quietly, "I would not see your loyalty divided between myself and your wife. There is an easy answer, though, if she is also sworn to me."

"No," said Sounis, swallowing misery whole. "She is not."

"Then perhaps you should broach the subject with her before we speak again."

"Indeed," Sounis managed to say in the bleak silence.

He bowed, and the ceremony was wrapped like a package and hastily sealed by the priestess of Hephestia. The sovereigns retired without meeting one another's eyes, and the rooms were cleared. The court withdrew to change out of its sumptuary and into less precious clothes. With the magus's hand under his arm, Sounis stumbled back to his own apartments to find the queen of Eddis and her attendants waiting there.

Eddis was in the reception room. She sent her attendants back to the anteroom. The magus excused himself, pulling the door closed behind him, and Eddis and Sounis were alone.

Sounis approached her where she sat on a low seat and took her hand before he dropped to one knee to offer his apologies. "I misspoke. I am sorry. I swear I did not know that he meant to do this, or I would not have engaged you in a promise to be immediately broken."

"It need not be broken," said Eddis. He held himself as if he were in pain, and she cursed herself for hurting him, but she had not considered that the ceremony would slip from its careful scripting.

Sounis shook his head as if trying to clear it. "I cannot argue with his interpretation of my oath, though I would not have sworn it had I seen this outcome. You think he will change his mind?"

Eddis shook her head then and said gently, "No. I mean something else, Sophos. I was not unaware of Gen's requirement when I accepted your proposal."

He stared at her for a moment before jumping to his feet. "No!" he said, staring down at her. "You cannot yield your sovereignty of Eddis to marry me. You cannot believe that I would allow that?"

"Sophos . . ."

"It would be monstrous!"

"You do not understand," she warned him.

"I understand enough!" he answered. "I understand that he will make himself a great king over Sounis, Attolia, and Eddis. I understand that I cannot allow it. How can you not see that?"

Eddis stood very slowly and took a deep breath. "I do see," she said. As he watched helplessly, she pulled her skirt free from where it had caught on the upholstery, and she crossed to the door. She tapped its latch and someone on the far side opened it. It closed behind her without a sound.

Sounis stood at the window, looking across the city toward the port, and as he watched the shadows of clouds move across the water in the distance, he felt a chill on the back of his neck. It was self-doubt, the black beetle that had pursued him all his life, pinching at him, poisoning his every success, whispering in his ear about his flaws and his failures and his unworthiness. He hadn't felt it in months, but the pinprick of its claws was instantly familiar. They informed him with their tiny tattoo that he had almost certainly done something immensely, irrevocably, and unforgivably stupid.

He turned away from the view and lunged across the room to throw open the door to the anteroom.

"The queen of Eddis," he said as he headed for the outer door of the apartment, past the startled magus. "Which way, which way back to her rooms?"

The royal guard stared at him.

"Which way?" Sounis shouted.

The guard pointed. Sounis rushed through the outer door of the apartment and disappeared down the hall.

The Attolian palace, like any building hundreds of years old, put rabbit warrens to shame with its corridors and intersections. At the first of these, Sounis stopped and listened. He heard footsteps and headed indecently fast in the direction that they came from, praying he wouldn't run, unreflecting, into the Mede ambassador to Attolia and his retinue. At each corner he had to stop and listen again, but he was gaining quickly. He almost lost them when he passed a stairwell but then remembered that once earlier he had climbed stairs between his apartment and Eddis's. At the top of the stairs, he saw, down a hallway, female figures rounding a corner and hurried after them.

With his quarry almost in sight, he might have slowed and composed himself, but he didn't spare it a thought. He rounded the corner and nearly spitted himself on the business end of an Eddisian pike. Throwing up his arms, he stopped on the tips of his toes with the point of the weapon an inch or two from his chest. He thought of the breastplate that he'd been made to wear for weeks. He lowered himself very slowly and kept his hands out from his sides. Behind him he could hear his own guard stamping up the corridor to catch up to him.

The queen of Eddis was surrounded by her attendants, all of them armed, which was enough to take anyone aback, never mind her Eddisian guards arrayed in front and behind, watching for attack from either direction.

Eddis said quietly, "No need for alarm," and the weapons disappeared like morning fog. Eddis turned and moved off, followed by her attendants and her guard, leaving Sounis behind. Gingerly, he followed, stepping between two of her guards and catching up. Eddis's attendants grudgingly made room so that he could walk beside her. He tipped his head forward, to watch her profile.

"I have a gift," he said, speaking quickly, not sure how much time he had. "I always used to think it was a curse, but now I am not sure, because maybe it's like the goats from the god, and one just has to know what name to call it." He had to take short steps, but quick ones, to match her pace. "My gift is that I always know when I've made an ass of myself."

Eddis's eyes glanced briefly in his direction and away again. She did not slow. As she turned a corner, Sounis thought it was marvelous that she knew so surely where she was going.

"Whenever I went to my uncle's megaron, whenever I met with my tutor, tripped over something that wasn't there, said something inane, I knew it. I used to watch other people making idiots of themselves, and they never seemed to know it, but I always have. All my life I've wished that if I was going to be an ass, I could just be an oblivious one." Eddis still hadn't looked at him again. "I was stupid. I'm sorry. It was wrong of me to think that I could allow or disallow anything you choose to do. You are Eddis."

She slowed finally and turned to give him a smile. He experienced a brief moment of relief before he realized that it was artificial. She walked on.

Sounis stood as everyone else brushed past him and watched her move farther and farther away. Long years of experience told him to turn and go back to his own apartments, but more recent events kept his feet rooted to the floor.

"We all make mistakes," he said loudly. Eddis surged on without looking back, but he knew he had caught her ear. "You sent him to Attolia, didn't you?" He called after her, deliberately cruel. "He told you it was dangerous, and you sent him anyway. Was it worth it?"

Eddis walked even faster, furious. Sounis pushed past her guards, who flinched but didn't stop him, and seized her by the arm. She swung around so sharply he stepped back, but he didn't let go. "I do not care," he said, "how much of an ass I am right now. Because every night that I dreamed in Hanaktos, I dreamed of you. Every night. When I dreamed about my library, you were there, reading a book, looking from the windows, never speaking, but always there. And I knew that everything was just the way it should be, do you understand?" He said, "I'm sorry. I should have had more faith in you. I understand why you are angry with me: because I disappointed you, and also we don't all throw things when we are angry, I understand that now, too. But we all make mistakes, Helen," he said again, "all of us. And I think, I really think you will regret it if this one time you could forgive me, and you don't.

"Please," he added.

Eddis stared at him for a long time, knowing that

forgiving someone because you have to is not forgiving him at all.

"Come with me," she said at last. She led him through Attolia's palace to a double set of carved doors. At her signal, the guards pulled them open, and she passed through. Inside the room, she turned and waited. Sounis stood paralyzed on the threshold.

CHAPTER TWENTY-TWO

T HE room was Attolia's library.

"You have not seen it before," said Eddis.

"No," whispered Sounis.

"I did not think you had, or you would have recognized it. Gen made sure no meetings were held here."

It was a long room lined with books. High windows let in light all day, but none that would reach to damage the delicate contents of the shelves. The glass-paneled doors on the opposite side of the room faced north, not toward a view of snowcapped mountains but toward a perfectly ordinary view of the city of Attolia. The ceiling above was coffered and white; the cases along the walls were carved with familiar figures. Sounis recognized a lion and then a rabbit. He looked for the fox and found it. He moved to touch its pointed ears with a hesitant finger.

"Who made this place?" he said in a choked voice.

Eddis hesitated. "The architect was Iktenos, Gen's great-great-grandfather and the Thief of Eddis, though that is not well known in Attolia, even now."

"He dreamed of my library."

"It would seem so."

Slowly, Sounis turned away from the carving of the fox. He reached for a tabletop and ran his hands over it, clutching the edge until his knuckles turned white.

He wanted to know that it was solid. Eddis knew that all the world would seem to him insubstantial, as if it might tear away and reveal something else infinitely larger and more terrifying.

"I broke the truce at Elisa," he said, wild-eyed.

"Pay your fine," she said reassuringly. "Had you offended them you would know by now."

"My tutor?"

"Moira, I think. She is nearest to mortals."

"They are real?"

Eddis said nothing.

"Do they appear only in dreams? Or do they have physical properties? Can you touch them? Can they—" He looked up. "Can they bring bolts of lightning?"

Eddis shrugged.

"Tell me!" cried Sounis.

"Answer your own questions!" Eddis shouted back, and he blinked.

"You don't know?"

Eddis shook her head.

Sounis sat.

"Write it down," Eddis said. "It will grow less clear. First, it will begin to seem that it really was just a dream and a mere coincidence that this library is so familiar. Then it will be a memory you have of a dream you can't quite remember, and then even that will be gone."

Sounis considered the authority in her voice. "What have you dreamed?" he asked.

"I dreamed of you," Eddis said, her eyes bright. "In the library, talking to your tutor." She wrapped her arms around herself and turned away as he rose from his chair. "And I dream of the Sacred Mountain exploding and see people clutch their throats and fall to the ground and fire fall out of the air and everything begin to burn. A river of fire washes down the slopes of the mountain, and the reservoir explodes in a huge cloud of steam, but the fire doesn't stop until it has devoured the city of Eddis entirely."

Horrified, Sounis didn't know what to do, or say. Then he remembered his father in the forecourt of Eddis's megaron in the mountains, and he put a hand on Eddis's shoulder. He did not take her in his arms so much as he offered them to her, and when she moved into this embrace, he held her tightly.

"I need to empty the city of Eddis," she said, laying her head on his chest. "I need to give every man and woman and child a reason to think that life would be better for them away from the mountain, down in the lowlands, out on the islands. Anywhere but Eddis."

"You need to marry me," he said.

"Yes," said Eddis.

"And I am a pig, like my uncle."

Eddis laughed. Her head fit just under his chin, and

Sounis could feel the chuckle in his chest. "No, you are not, or I would not love you as I do."

"I loved you the first time I saw you."

Eddis laughed again. "You were four," she said, without lifting her head.

Startled, Sounis said, "I was?"

"My father who was Eddis paid a visit to the court of Sounis. My brothers and I accompanied him."

"I don't remember, " said Sounis. "Unless, perhaps, I do," he added, wincing, as hazy recollections grew clearer.

Eddis confirmed the worst of them. "My brothers made you cry."

Sounis tilted his head back and closed his eyes. "Are you certain that you want to be my wife?"

"Absolutely," said Eddis, quietly. "Eternally certain."

Holding her tight, Sounis looked around the library. "Does Gen know?" he wondered aloud, and he felt Eddis pull away slightly. He looked into her face. "What does he dream?" he asked, afraid to hear the answer.

"They aren't dreams to him, Sophos," said Eddis, feeling his arms tighten again around her at the implication. "I believe that the veil for him is always thin, and that he walks through the world gingerly."

"Can *he* answer my questions, then?"

Eddis was amused by his persistence, but shook her head. "In my experience, the more you know of the gods, the more you know what you cannot understand."

"There is a great deal I don't know," he said, seriously. "And not just about the gods."

Looking into his unsmiling face, Eddis knew it was as close as he would ever come to an accusation. He had been saved by the men Eugenides sent, though he did not yet know the ferocity with which the king of Attolia had stripped those men from other posts, the capital he had expended, the secrets that had been revealed in order to send help to Sounis. But Sophos had to know that she and Eugenides had let him ride away with an Attolian army at his back, believing he needed it. With more faith in himself, and his father's army, he could have retaken his throne without Attolia's aid. He might not have followed that bloodier and more costly path, but Eddis and Attolis hadn't offered him the choice.

"Yes," Eddis admitted, praying that he would not ask for an apology she could not give.

"But you will tell me everything now?"

"Now and forever," Eddis promised.

CHAPTER TWENTY-THREE

T HE king of Attolia reclined in a chair in a loggia high up in the palace. His feet were braced on
a footstool, and he had a robe around his shoulders. The
sun was setting somewhere out of sight, but its light
still filled the corner of the stone porch where he sat.
His eyes were closed, and he didn't open them before
he spoke.

"Have you convinced him?" he asked.

"Gen," said Sounis.

Eugenides started violently and knocked the wine
cup on the arm of his chair. He made a halfhearted
effort to catch it but only added a spin that flung the
wine farther. The cup broke on the ceramic tiles.

"Gods damn it," he said.

"You can say that?" Sounis asked, approaching the
back of his chair.

Attolis considered the younger king of Sounis over
his shoulder. "There has been no objection so far. I
take care not to link anyone specific to the word *damn*,
though."

Sounis said, "I broke the truce at Elisa."

"Pay your fine," said Eugenides dismissively, "and

assume they are on your side. That's what I do." He resettled the robe around his shoulders.

"Eddis said that, too." Sounis looked at the robe. "Are you all right?" he asked.

"I'm fine," Attolis responded, a little shortly. "I am drinking my wine hot, with foul herbs in it, as a favor to my palace physician, who wants to show the queen of Eddis's physician just who's in charge here. Sit." He waved his hand at a nearby chair. Sounis pulled it over and placed it just out of the sunlight, which was too bright to suit him.

"So that wasn't an accident?" He looked at the mess an attendant was hastily wiping up.

"The initial reaction was," Eugenides said evasively. He could have saved the wine if he'd wanted to. "You surprised me."

"I thought nothing surprised you."

"And I thought you were the queen of Eddis." He looked malevolently over his shoulder at his attendants waiting by the door to the porch.

Sounis defended them. "She was here." After she had been announced, but before Hilarion could introduce Sounis, Eddis had raised her hand to silence the attendant and wordlessly withdrawn. Sounis wondered if she thought Gen might have refused to see him if he'd been announced on his own. If he would have retreated again to remote formality.

"Being a mere mortal," said Eugenides, "I am

surprised as often as any man. *Has* she convinced you?"

"Yes." Sounis had spent most of the day in the library with Eddis. They had been interrupted only once, when Xanthe knocked to admit a group of servants with food and drink.

"Why didn't you tell me to take Attolia's advice from the beginning?"

"I thought you should figure it out. What you learn for yourself, you will know forever," said Eugenides.

"Pol used to say that," said Sounis, surprised.

"I learned it from him. I just wish to my god that I had his patience for the process," said Eugenides, looking with dislike at the new cup of wine his attendants brought him, but taking it all the same.

Thinking of the guardsman he had admired, who had died during their pursuit of Hamiathes's Gift, Sounis looked out over the stone balustrade of the loggia at the buildings of Attolia below him. There were no clouds visible, and the sky was filled with the liquid light of late afternoon that poured down over the city. He could see people in the streets beyond the outer wall of the palace, standing talking to each other or walking from the wider avenues into the narrow alleys out of his sight. A man with a horse was trying to coax it to pull a wagon over a shallow step in the roadway. If Sounis leaned forward, the sun hit him in the eyes, but he could still make out the bend in the roadway where he had perched on a marker with a peashooter to capture the king of Attolia's attention. He found that he didn't want to talk about the gods.

"Won't Eddis's people resent her decision?" he asked.

"They won't be angry at you," Eugenides told him. "They will be angry at me. They love Eddis too much to desert her, and she has in many ways prepared them for this."

Sounis lifted his feet onto the footstool. "How angry will they be with you?" he asked.

"Very," said Eugenides. "I'm trying not to think about it," he added as he shifted his feet to make room for Sounis's. "I am glad you got the message about the troops at Oneia."

When Sophos didn't respond, Gen put his cup down and straightened.

"I sent that information in every manner I could think of, including by pigeon. If you didn't get it, why did you take your army down a narrow road to a dead end?"

Sounis shrugged. "There was no point in running for the capital. The Medes would have followed and laid siege. You might have eventually lifted it, but you couldn't have saved me from being the king who ran away. I would never have been Sounis, just your puppet on the throne."

"What if I hadn't sent reinforcements to Oneia?"

"But you did."

"You should credit Irene," said Eugenides. "I had the

men and the transport, but she told me where to deliver them."

"Where did you get the boats?" Sounis asked.

"Stripped them off the Neutral Islanders, with the permission of their headmen."

Sounis stared. "Were you behind the negotiations on Lerna and Hannipus?" he asked.

"I have no idea what you are talking about," answered Eugenides with a straight face.

Sounis glanced at the attendants and let the subject drop. "We would have died without the additional men," he admitted matter-of-factly. "But we would have taken the entire Mede army with us. Poets would have written about us, and songs would have been sung about us—"

"For all the good that would have done your dead bodies," Eugenides cynically interrupted.

"Well, I wasn't looking forward to it," said Sounis caustically. "But over our dead bodies the Medes would never have been accepted by the people of Sounis. Much more likely that they would have allied with Attolia." He looked at Eugenides, who was still eyeing him in surprise. "I didn't *expect* to die," he said. "I knew you would send help."

"Why?"

It was Sounis's turn to be surprised. He said, "You told me you needed me to be Sounis. I am. I needed my king to send me help. You did. There had to be reinforcements at Oneia, so they were there." To him it was obvious.

Eugenides swallowed. "I see."

They both returned to looking out over the city. Sounis's thoughts turned to Eddis. He had given up his sovereignty to Attolis for reasons anyone could understand. He wasn't sure that anyone would ever know how Eugenides had become king over Eddis. If he couldn't bring himself to speak of the gods aloud to Eugenides, who would he ever tell? Who else would ever know of Eddis's dreams of fire and death from the Sacred Mountain?

"She would have married your uncle," Eugenides said, as if sensing his thoughts and turning them in a new direction.

"I am glad she will not," said Sounis.

"Me, too." Eugenides smiled.

"The Medes will find us united against them," said Sounis.

"I should hope so," said Eugenides. "You shot the ambassador."

"You gave me the gun."

They both laughed.